I0594660

Wake of the Sadico

Jo Sparkes

PORTLAND, OREGON

Wake of the Sadico

Initial Content Editing by Janet Tapper
Editing by The Pro Book Editor
Cover Design by Matt Davies

ISBN: 978-0-9853318-9-4

1. Main category—[Fiction]
2. Other category—[Thriller]

Second Edition

To Dad & Jake

If we have been pleased with life, we should not be
displeased with death, since it comes from the
hand of the same master.

–MICHELANGELO

Contents

The Summoning

They'd fooled her.

Melanie fumed as she rubbed suntan lotion into her shoulder. Caribbean vacation, they'd said. She ought to be sipping frozen margaritas from odd-shaped glasses, lying on a beach, and watching muscled hunks slam volleyballs at each other. There ought to be luxurious resorts, gourmet dining, dancing under the stars. Instead, here she lay, alone in her ridiculously expensive bikini, on the bow of a dilapidated boat. An oceangoing sailboat should be elegant, not cramped and old and shabby. Never mind the Jacuzzi she'd hoped for, there wasn't even a bathtub. No hot water at all unless you boiled it yourself on the tiny stove that swiveled with the motion of the boat. Even ice was precious because they had to cart it with them, and the huge bags stored in the cooler only lasted a few days.

Being this close to the equator, you needed ice. And she couldn't even play with her new smart phone. There was no reception and no Wi-Fi.

She, Melanie Mason, deserved better than this. Tall and blonde, she had the kind of figure few men could resist, and they usually took better care of her.

Enrolling in the dive certification course had been an impulse. She'd been suckered by a British accent and liked the image of herself wearing bikinis on the edge of the diving pool. To think she'd actually turned down a charity ball invitation for this.

Gazing across the sun-damaged deck, she spied her pink dive mask beneath Jill's prized Best Diver in Class T-shirt. She grabbed her magazine and hurled it at the pair. Her aim was too good—mask and shirt tumbled over the tiny rail and splashed into the water.

Shit.

Melanie scooted to the edge to see the pink plastic and T-shirt bobbing in the sea, well out of reach. Glancing around, she saw no net or pole to fish the stuff out of the water. No tool to rescue the items.

And no one to witness their loss.

Without her mask she couldn't dive, which wasn't so bad. She didn't actually like diving. And if Jill lost her prize shirt...well, boo-hoo.

Shifting back to her towel, Melanie shrugged off a nagging guilt. The others sure were taking their time. She could hear them below, shouting excitedly over the clanging compressor filling their air tanks. No concerns about abandoning her while they dove on a stupid reef. Wall thought she had a headache, for Christ's sake. Shouldn't he be more concerned?

Jill's laugh drifted through an open porthole, adding to her annoyance. Best in Class Jill. Served her right if she got eaten by sharks. Served them all right. Insensitive pricks.

A spike of doubt fluttered her stomach. It was bad luck to wish like that.

"I don't care!" she hissed. "They deserve it!"

The words wound through her skull, echoing on the breeze. Except the breeze used a male voice.

The hair bristled on the back of her neck.

For an instant, the air stilled as if the world held its breath. She really ought to take that back.

Melanie deliberately stretched out on her stomach, nestled her head in her arms, and shut her eyes. "They deserve it."

A puff of air ruffled her discarded magazine. Wood creaked as the sea lapped at the hull. A shadow flickered across her face.

Peeping through her lashes, she caught sight of the dive mask and T-shirt slowly rotating on the water's surface. Her eyelids drooped.

As the murmuring breeze faded, another sound teased her. Sort of like...marching feet. On the edge of sleep, Melanie ignored it.

The wind stirred again, and in its wake tramped the men. Louder. Stronger. Her forehead wrinkled in denial, but still they came.

One eye slit open enough to see sunlight glistening off the teak. Through her lashes, moving across her field of vision, she saw rows of men clad in gleaming metal. One man strode through sunlight and obscurity, through dream mist to solid deck. His boots stopped at her nose.

Hazily, she peered up at a dark face, a black beard, and blue eyes. Pale, watery blue.

His mouth curved in a smirk that made her hair stand on end as he reached a hand toward her. "Come, Isabelle."

Fear shot through her stomach, and she scrambled backward until her spine smacked against the sailboat mast. Gasping, Melanie blinked.

She was alone on the deck.

Slowly, very slowly, she recovered her breath. She lay back on the towel, feeling foolish. At least no one had witnessed her panicking over some stupid dream.

But she didn't close her eyes again.

Melanie never saw the mask in the water, spinning at cyclone speed.

Bait

"I DON'T WANT TO dive with Wall!"

Startled, Wall forgot to duck and thumped his head against the door jamb. Mike sniggered behind him, probably at Jill's outburst from the galley rather than his own clumsiness. Though as the Americans say, he wouldn't bet on it.

"Lower your voice," he heard Jon admonish her. "He's good with novices. You'll learn from him."

"But you're better. Let me dive with you."

"Next time, mermaid."

Shouldering the two dive tanks, Wall dipped low this time to maneuver safely out of the compressor room. The old boat's tiny doorways forced his six-foot-six frame to duck and slide through like some sort of circus freak.

Recovering his balance, he strode noisily around the corner.

Jill and Jon faced off in the galley, both short, both slight. Jon beamed; the girl scowled and crossed her arms.

Did she know he'd overheard and didn't care? Or had his noisy approach fooled her?

The pair looked like the cousins they were, apart from skin color. The girl's mother had been white, or so Melanie whispered as if it were some sort of secret. Jill was lightly tan to Jon's deep brown, though she echoed his long dark hair, thick eyelashes, and delicate features. He was a small man; she was petite. From Wall's perspective, they seemed veritable children.

Wall nodded a belated greeting and ambled toward the ladder, halting when Jill skittered out of his way. Her cheeks flared red, eyes lowering like an awkward teenager's. Melanie liked to joke about the girl's frantic need for ample personal space.

"Need any help?" Jon asked.

"Nah," said a voice behind him. Mike trotted past, bearing all the remaining dive tanks on his shoulders. Swinging them down by the base of the ladder, he winked at Jill. "Me and Jill got it." He then climbed up and out to the sunshine.

Though five inches shorter, Mike never failed to make Wall feel insignificant. Possibly because of his muscle mass—the man was an amateur body builder—though more likely because he sauntered through the world upright and proud, while Wall habitually slouched to make himself less prominent.

Years ago, his grandfather had called him 'that great, crumbling wall,' and the name had stuck ever since. His christened name, Trevor, had vanished along with his toy Womble and comic books.

"Hand 'em up, Jill." Mike's massive arms reached down from the top deck, muscles gleaming with sweat.

She actually bent to comply.

Wall touched her arm, and she hopped back as if scorched. Suppressing a smile, he hoisted a tank up to the waiting hands. The weight made him grunt, and Mike's lips twitched.

Jill folded her arms protectively across her chest. "We're buddying."

"I heard." Her cheeks burned red as he lifted the next tank. Christ, he hadn't meant to embarrass her. "Looking forward to this reef."

She didn't smile. "I'm...sorry. Just thought I'd be diving with Jon. First time out, I mean."

"I understand."

With a last unhappy glance, she climbed the ladder until the muscle man plucked her out with the same ease as he had the tanks.

Wall sighed. His first warm water dive was not quite shaping up as he'd hoped.

∞

Snatched out of the hold, Jill was dropped onto the sunny deck. Mike's high-handed tactics annoyed her, but then he knew that. Since the first day they'd met, when she was all of eight years old, he'd teased her like a kid sister. Apparently, her relationship to Jon precluded his normal Lothario act, which suited her just fine.

Now, with her feet planted on teak, which gently rocked with the current, she finally found her sense of humor. She wouldn't be diving with Jon, but she'd still be diving.

Warm water diving in the Caribbean, that mystical place she'd dreamt about since the age of seven. The age when she'd first watched Jon and his bigger-than-life family leave for vacation in this exotic paradise, abandoning her to her father, whose idea of vacation was sneaking her into the campus swimming pool during summer break.

Her dad was Chris Sadicor, brother to the famous Ray Sadicor. Just like Ray, he was a retired athlete. Unlike Ray, her father had never made enough money to 'sit on his ass all day.' He coached football at an NCAA Division III school, much removed from the hectic competition of Division I. Still, it was an all-consuming religion for him.

After her mother had left, Jill had rarely seen her father. Jon swore it was the loss of her mom—and not the sight of his daughter—that the man couldn't face.

Jon was the only male in her life she admired. Though seven years separated their ages, her cousin had always championed her, helping equally with a geometry test or a bully on the playground. He'd once bestowed an old Phillies baseball cap on her head as she cried over her scraped knee. She wore it day and night till the thing fell apart.

When he first started diving, she'd begged to go. Her father had denied permission, and later, her college and career had eclipsed such yearnings. But Jon never forgot.

On her twenty-fifth birthday, he gave her a spot in his dive certification class, with the Caribbean trip to follow. His dive shop, the Crusty Porthole, boasted the top-rated training in Delaware.

Standing here now, sun on her face and sea sparkling below, Jill deeply appreciated his gift.

A fluttering on the bow drew her eye.

It was Melanie jerking upright from her nap, mouth gaping in surprise. Honestly, the woman seemed to expect the ocean to jump up and grab her, or a swooping gull to snatch her sunglasses.

She didn't look like she had a headache.

For an instant, Jill's anger flared. If the blonde would quit reading magazines and dive, Jill could buddy with Jon.

Wall, the Brit, knelt beside Melanie, speaking softly. She tugged his hand to her lips and caressed his thigh. Awfully touchy-feely for someone so ill.

Jon popped out of the cabin and winked at her. She grinned back. No point in being pissy when she was about to fulfill a dream. And poor Melanie would miss out, after all.

Moments later, Jill found it harder to remain enthusiastic. The makeshift metal platform creaked beneath her as she buckled her gear, then Wall suddenly spun her about. He was doing the buddy drill—each dive buddy ensuring the other's gear was properly assembled—but he loomed so close, his shadow blocked the sun as his hands roamed her air lines. She hated to be crowded.

Fortunately, Jon caught her eye before she spoke. This was, after all, a safety routine. And as Mike had wickedly pointed out, the Brit stood for all things safety.

When Wall tapped her tank twice, Jill turned to find the bottom half of his tank in her face. The top part, with its valves and hoses to be inspected, stood high out of reach. Geez, he was tall.

The temptation to tap his rig and pretend she had finished died a quick death. The consequences of an error could be catastrophic. Besides, when assisting in class, he'd been known to deliberately miss a connection just to see if the student caught it.

"Kneel," she said.

Exasperatingly, the Brit merely glanced over his shoulder.

"Kneel down," she told him. "I can't see your gear."

Swift comprehension and fleeting amusement crossed his face. Before she got properly riled, he steadied himself on the stern ladder and knelt. Something about his needing the ladder made her smile.

Then her hands roamed the hoses from tank to regulator to the buoyancy control device. The B.C. gave a diver the ability to rise or sink in the water by inflating or deflating a sophisticated life jacket. Without it, as Jill had discovered in the quarry dive, she was too heavy to swim fifty feet up to the surface.

Mike, in full gear, fell backward off the platform, splashing into the ocean.

Realizing she was lagging, Jill swiftly finished her buddy check. Rather than touch him, she edged her way around to his front. "You're good."

He stuck his wrist out, showing his dive computer displayed a full tank of air. "Click this button here," he said, "to sequence through bottom time, air in tank. Even the water temperature."

After the briefest hesitation, she nodded. Truth was, she envied Wall's wrist computer. Jon refused to give her one, insisting the added complexity of paging through screens wasn't good for novices. She had to suffer with the more awkward console display dangling from her equipment.

The Brit grabbed the ladder again to haul himself upright—and Jill suddenly noticed the stern. "Whoa—Jon!"

Her cousin turned, one fin extending over the sea.

She pointed to the boat's painted name—*SADICOR*—with the R scratched and faded. "The '*Sadico*'? Uncle Ray would be pissed."

Jon frowned. "I'll see if we've got any paint later."

Bobbing in the sea, Mike spit in his mask and ran a finger around the inside. "Shake a leg, Sadicor!"

Determined not to be last—not to appear a novice—Jill leapt off the platform.

Her splash drowned out Mike's next words. Through the water running down her faceplate, she saw him lift something from the sea. Melanie's dive mask and some soggy material.

Her T-shirt.

"You ladies," Mike set them on the platform, "need to be more careful."

So now they lumped her in with the chickenshit blonde. Great.

∞

Her mask slipped below the waterline, and Jill's world changed.

Caribbean sunshine coyly followed her down, bathing the water and the diver beside her in glowing detail. She could actually see the snorkel tucked against his temple.

Better not get distracted, she realized. Clasping her console up to her dive mask, Jill cautiously dumped air from her B.C. Dump too quickly, and she'd drop too fast, maybe burst an eardrum. Dump too slow, and she'd lag behind.

Wall stayed beside her, nodding when she made eye contact. She almost basked in his approval until she realized what she was doing.

Breaking off eye contact, Jill glanced down, gawking at the watery world around her until free flowing bubbles obliterated the sight below.

Diving in Delaware, quarry or ocean, was like swimming in murky soup. Visibility averaged fifteen feet, with everything a colorless gray. Now slowly rising up to greet her was an undulating mass of color.

Jon's 'small' reef looked large, with a gap almost dead center making it in fact two reefs—twin masses of vivid orange and blue, writhing red and yellow. She couldn't begin to distinguish the fish from the coral.

The depth gauge flashed fifty-three feet as her fins set down in sand.

Coral swelled before her in rounded lumps and purple pipe tubes stitched together by strands of seaweed. The reef loomed well above her head, though surely Jon had said it was only four feet high.

More colors appeared as she stepped closer. Neon ribbons of fish darted in and out, moving so rapidly that they seemed not to swim so much as vanish from one spot and appear in another.

Enthralled, it took a moment to realize she was the only one standing on the bottom. Her companions hung suspended in the water, Wall floating beside her.

Jon and Mike drifted higher, pointing at the reef ends, gesticulating at each other. Plucking his ridiculously huge knife from his sheath, Mike zoomed over to tap the coral with the handle.

The hollow thunk seemed to vibrate in her ears.

Kicking her fins, Jill swam up to see. She caught a glimpse of a green scaly head and needle teeth before sinking back to the sand.

Damn.

Clawing back behind her shoulder, she snagged her console and squeezed a puff of air into her B.C.

Nothing.

More air, and finally her body lifted, rising like an astronaut in space. She glimpsed Mike actually stroking a moray—and the eel rubbing against his glove like an affectionate puppy—before floating higher toward the surface.

Jill quickly dumped air before changing direction to fall back into the sand. She immediately swam upward—she'd figure out that floating thing later.

The eel looked friendly, except for the evil grimace of the mouth. It seemed to love Mike, and the big man certainly had no fear.

Jill tried to find the courage to touch it herself, but she hesitated placing fingers near those needle-teeth.

Wall seemed content to watch. Maybe mere spectating wasn't so chickenhearted.

Jon hovered at a distance, too far to pet it. In fact, he was too far to see. He took off, skimming along the top of the reef.

Shouldn't he stay closer? Or should Mike be with him?

She spoke the question into her regulator, but neither Mike nor Wall so much as looked up. Just like the quarry dive, when she'd talked underwater and no one even flinched.

Jon explained later that no one had realized she'd spoken, much less understood. Sound waves traveled differently—deceptively—underwater, tricking the ear into believing some were louder and closer, while others seemed oddly muted.

A puff of sand startled her. Jill had stopped kicking and sunk back to the ocean floor. Frustrated, she clawed behind her shoulder to snag her tethered console again. This would be so much easier if she had a nice wrist computer.

PING.

Mike shot off as if jet-propelled, making a beeline for the now-distant Jon.

Metal on metal, she realized. A diver's method to communicate underwater.

Jon must have found something.

The Brit dropped right in front of her. Startled, Jill jerked backward, tripping in her flippers. She floated down, ass first, into the sand.

Wall's face leaned in to peer into her mask, expecting her to panic, no doubt. Even more annoying, he himself never touched the sea floor. Instead, he hovered horizontal at whatever spot he chose without so much as glancing at a depth gauge.

When he gave her the thumbs-up, it was all she could do not to give him a different finger.

∞

Wall felt the girl's exasperation. Suppressing a chuckle, he pantomimed squeezing his air valve.

To Jill's credit, she tried it, though naturally putting too much in and soaring upward. He snagged her ankle to haul her back down. When she frowned, he reached to dump her air, and Jill jerked away again. Fortunately for her, he succeeded first.

Now she looked confused. He wished he could explain.

Using a B.C. to control water 'altitude' was a delicate art. Experienced divers employed subtle amounts to position themselves precisely. Novices used way too much, only stopping when they were hurtling in one direction or the other. Because beginners were overweighted to begin with, it took time and practice to learn how to float.

Grabbing her attention—and ignoring her glare—Wall used his hands to demonstrate a deep breath in as he rose a foot off the sand. The more minute adjustments were done with the breath, not the B.C. Breathing out, he lowered back to her level. When she made no movement, he repeated it.

Jill caught on. The girl sucked in all the air her lungs could hold while staying firmly planted in the sand. Definitely overweighted.

Wall moved to help her—slowly, so as not to startle her this time—and saw Jon and Mike hovering above the split in the reef. A ghost image flashed behind them, darting off just as Jill shoved her instrument console at his mask.

A red number blinked insistently on her screen—no wonder she was anxious.

Checking the readout, he chuckled. The damned thing was measuring water temperature. It wasn't telling of troubles but of the tropics. He calmly pointed to the 'TEMPERATURE' on the screen.

After a moment, she nodded.

Movement flickered where the ghost had vanished.

Wall turned to watch something approach the unsuspecting men, looming behind them. It moved slowly, a gray bulge and fins.

A shark.

Do something, his mind screamed. But his body refused. He realized he was holding his breath—something he never did underwater.

Jill erupted in frantic thrashing.

The shark veered off, disappearing from view.

She swam straight for the men before Wall could stop her.

∞

Jon looked up in astonishment as Jill flailed toward him.

He only stared as she clutched his arm, dragging him downward with her weight. Wall followed her, something in his very speed indicating a warning. It took Mike's nudge to turn him around to see.

A timid reef shark, barely five foot, shied off. Curious she might be, but she'd come no further. Just a baby—and an absolute beauty.

Remembering the lobster he'd caught earlier, Jon dug into his net bag, grabbed the crustacean and thrust it out.

She was tempted. Altering course, the baby circled back slowly. Coyly.

For an instant, he imagined feeding her as divers did in videos. How exactly did they hold the food? He wouldn't want to lose a finger.

It didn't come to that.

The reef shark neared and shied off. Something worried her, and when he checked, Jon saw an odd swirl in the water, sucking sand off the bottom. Like a sea-born dust devil.

In all his years, he'd never seen anything like it.

When he turned back, the shark had vanished.

∞

Jill couldn't tear her eyes away from the spot where the shark had disappeared.

She only became aware of the mass of bubbles free-flowing around her when the Brit reached past her mask to snag her dive console.

When he tilted it toward her, she saw the red gauge flashing—not from temperature but lack of oxygen. Her tank was running low. Surely they hadn't been down so long?

She watched as Wall calmly checked his own computer and grasped his air valve. When she only stared, he flashed his wrist at her—showing his own depleted tank—and jerked his thumb upward. Either telling her to surface or asking if she was okay. Probably both.

For all the world as relaxed as if they had all day.

Shaking herself, Jill fumbled at her B.C. and squished the valve hard, wondering if she had enough air to inflate.

She did. It took all her will not to rocket to the surface. Without Wall's steady presence, she'd never have succeeded.

The sea brightened, sunlight swelling. Peering down past her fins, she kept an eye out for sharks. When her head burst free of the water, Jill yanked out her regulator and gasped surface air as if her tank had run bone dry. It hadn't, of course.

Her buddy snatched off his mask, studying her.

"How..." she had to swallow and start again. "My air. I wasn't down there that long."

Wall spit out his regulator and grinned. "Fear tends to suck a tank dry."

"A shark!" Jill told him, hoping the rising emotion in her voice came off as excitement. "Jon tried to feed a shark!"

The man nodded, watching her with those chameleon eyes. Mike called them chameleon—hazel irises that changed color according to their surroundings.

"Jon," Wall coolly explained, "is a bloody ass." He waved her toward the boat.

His splashing crowded her, herding her on. She scrambled awkwardly up the thin aluminum ladder, still wearing her flippers.

"I was nervous," she muttered. In truth, she'd been terrified. "I wanted to put Mike's machete between it and me." Why the hell was she telling him this? Let him think she was warning the others, not scared out of her wits.

The blonde appeared above, leaning over the cockpit railing. She smiled and waved. The Brit smiled back.

"I didn't want to abandon you," Jill rambled on. "Just hoped you'd follow."

Her knees collapsed, and she sat hard on the platform, her tank pinging against the metal.

All my limbs are out of the water, she told herself. *Nothing can bite them now.*

It took time to remove her gear. Trembling fingers fumbled the buckles, and peeling the short wetsuit off slick skin proved no easier than the full wetsuit she wore in Delaware. When Jill felt Wall observing her, she deliberately turned away.

To confront the painted name *SADICO.*

Free of equipment, Wall stretched long and loud before reaching up to caress Melanie's face, hovering above them. "Feeling better?" he murmured.

The woman nodded. "You were down there so long."

"Sharks," Jill blurted out. Melanie started, and Jill realized she'd hoped for that reaction. "Just one," she added quickly. "Probably not that dangerous."

"And a fantastic coral reef." Wall grinned. "Exactly what we'd hoped to see down here. You'll love it."

The woman hesitated before nodding, and Wall touched her again. "Headache's really gone, Mel?"

"It's...better."

Jill had her own suspicions about the nature of the so-called headache. But then, she hadn't warmed to Melanie. Even her name was annoying, more appropriate for a novel—the kind with a heroine draped over a handsome male's arm. So different from the everyday, plain names bestowed on lesser women.

Names such as 'Jill.'

Turning away, Jill eyed the sparkling sea. "Shouldn't Jon and Mike be up by now?"

"They probably still have oxygen in their tanks," Wall replied.

She glared back.

"Because they're not beginners, Jill. They're much more relaxed, breathing easily."

"You were out of air."

"My anxiety level...had elevated." He grinned suddenly, mounting the stern ladder and swinging his gear up over the railing. "Not fond of sharks myself."

Jill breathed deeply, gasping it all out again in a single blast. Her trembling finally ceased.

The Brit stepped back down to snatch her rig, swinging it up to join his. All the while, the painted word 'SADICO' mocked her.

Wall pointed, and she looked down to see the salvaged pink mask and t-shirt huddling on the platform. Apparently, Melanie hadn't bothered to move either.

Grabbing both, Jill handed him the one before climbing up the stern and on to the cabin roof, where she gently laid out her shirt to dry in the sun.

"How did these wind up in the water?" she wondered aloud.

"Wind," said Melanie.

∞

Twenty minutes later, Jill perched on a cockpit seat to munch her chicken wing. Mike and Jon had yet to appear, and her temper alternated between anger and worry.

She'd thought they might be decompressing. A diver had to decompress when he stayed down too long, resulting in too much nitrogen in the blood.

Wall, however, scoffed at the notion. Apparently at a depth of fifty-three feet, they were more likely to run out of air before bottom time. Wall wasn't happy because they'd all agreed to stick together.

Actually, Jon had agreed. Mike had been less enthused, but then he'd been less enthused about the Brit, period. 'Limeys' in general—and this one in particular—were too concerned with rules for rules' sake.

So where were they?

The cold chicken helped settle her stomach. Her teeth found another bit of meat, and her shoulders relaxed. The breeze ruffled her hair and whispered in her ear. Not loud enough, however, to cover the sounds from inside the boat.

"There's no ice." Melanie's voice was petulant.

"Did you try the cooler?" Wall's tone soothed—or

ought to have soothed.

Jill heard the woman's snort. So much for romance.

A week ago, Melanie had been cooing over Wall, over his gallantly paying for her trip and his romantic foreign accent. All the women seemed to love foreign accents.

Jill never had. She actually found them unnerving.

When you got hung up on the different lilt—the odd phrasing—you couldn't really know what the speaker was truly thinking. Foreign men with foreign brow, she re-called the phrase from somewhere.

And when she did decipher his meaning, the guy was too tepid. Along with Mike, she'd protested Jon's inviting the man, declaring him 'hesitant and indecisive.'

"Unlike us Sadicors?" Jon had countered. "I should think you'd welcome the change."

Now, when Jon's head broke the surface, she flung her picked-over bone at him. "You're late."

Mike popped up, yanking his regulator from his mouth. "What are you, his mother?"

"Being late means we can't dive for...what? Five hours?"

"No more diving today," her cousin informed her. "We're heading to Antigua for supplies."

Jill gaped. "But we just got supplies in St. Kitts."

Mask and fins slapped on the platform before Mike vaulted out of the sea. "We need new supplies, mermaid. Plans have changed."

Jon sprang up the ladder, shaking his head like a wet dog after a successful romp. "Turns out, little mermaid, that's no reef below us."

He and Mike exchanged a grin.

"That's a shipwreck."

Regress

Wall swung out of the cabin into the sunshine, balancing with the roiling gait of the ship under sail.

God, he loved sailing.

There was something about harnessing wind and wave, using skill to travel instead of forcing your way with a motor. Sailing was finesse, adventure. Challenging the elements.

Jon stood at the helm, hand resting on the wheel, eyes scanning the waters ahead as spray bathed his face. Barechested, the man's crystal pendant swung when he leaned to see past the tall mast. A solid twenty-four-carat gold chain dangled a crystal worth five bucks.

Apparently, Jon believed in metaphysics. A Master Diver convinced his crystal warded off the bends.

Wall found himself smiling from the core of his being, drawing an echoing one from Jon.

"You honestly think that's a wreck?"

Jon nodded.

"I saw nothing down there."

"Sunken ships rarely lie in pristine condition," Jon leaned out with the boat, seemingly savoring the feel of the wind. "The shape gave it away. Squarish, perpendicular corners. Gotta be man-made."

Wall's face must have echoed his doubt.

Jon grinned before adding, "Mike and I chipped at the reef in two different spots...found wood beneath the coral. It's a boat all right."

"Wood?"

The small man nodded.

"Wouldn't have expected wood to survive long in warm water."

"Those reefs have been down there since I was a kid. Much smaller back then—one lump half the size of the other. Mostly buried in sand. Mike figures a storm must have shifted the bottom." Jon grinned, exultation in his eyes. "Anyway, my father would never have seen them. He's not a wreck diver."

So Jon wanted to impress his father. Wall could identify with that. "Still, if it's wood, it can't be too old?"

Jon shrugged. The light in his eyes did not diminish.

"Do you really think there's anything worth salvaging?"

Jon's smile grew with each bounce of the *Sadicor*. "It's an undiscovered wreck, over forty feet in length. Be a shame not to check it out."

CLANG.

Wall started.

Jon chuckled. "Relax. Mike's working on Matilda."

∞

In the galley, Jill plucked two beers from the cooler. The clock on the bulkhead—not the cat clock with the dangling tail, but an expensive brass thing—proclaimed the time to be nearly 4 p.m. She'd bought Jon the cat clock as a sailboat-warming gift, which he'd inexplicably hung in the dive shop instead.

Inexplicably, until she discovered cheap clocks don't work on boats. Something about all the bouncing around.

Jill sighed.

They were supposed to be setting up a barbecue on Jon's little island, followed by a night dive to see all the activity after dark. They were supposed to be exploring sea life and coral, not more stupid rocks that everyone swore were really wrecked ships.

Popping the bottle tops, she staggered—the boat was bouncing through waves—to the compressor room.

'Room' was a generous term. Closeted in the tiny space stood the compressor used to fill dive tanks. Large and metallic, it barely left enough area for the wall-mounted water trough, which cooled the tanks as air pumped inside. Mike had named the contraption Matilda, and he took great pride in keeping the thing running.

Squeezing between machine and trough, Jill emerged by the workbench shoehorned in the back. Mike perched on a tiny stool, plying a screwdriver to Matilda's inner workings. His back was to Jill, and with the roar of the machine, he couldn't have heard her. She snuck up and stuck the cold bottle against his back.

He merely held a hand out.

Sighing, she set the beer in his grasp.

"Thanks, mermaid."

Taking a long drink of her own beer, she leaned against the wall. "A shipwreck? Really?"

Mike kept working.

"You guys promised me long-snout seahorses and colorful dancing thingies. You know," she added at his raised eyebrow, and fluttered her fingers in a wavy pattern. "Spanish dancers! You two always seem to be wreck diving."

"Not like this." Mike flipped the machine off. "Those wrecks at home been picked over by every diver on the eastern seaboard. This is virgin, Jill...no one's touched this sweetheart. Anything that sank with her is still there for the taking." Tossing the screwdriver aside, he took a long, cool drink and grinned. "Might be a safe. Might even be jewelry. She's not exactly small. And who knows how old..."

They heard the door bang and a soft curse. Wall stuck his head around Matilda. "We're making great time, I'm told. Should reach Antigua in another hour."

Mike's eyes narrowed at the Brit. "Jon sent you to make sure I wasn't gonna fill the tanks."

Wall nodded.

"Tell that little rat bastard—sorry, Jill—tell that little rat bastard I'll fill them while he's loading supplies."

Jill didn't understand. "Why does he care?"

"I hate wasting time while we're moving, but Jon's afraid if we hit a whale or something, a tank could fall and break a valve."

Wall stepped closer, and Jill pressed back against the compressor. Feeling a metal edge scrape her back, she realized she was doing the personal space thing again, but for the life of her, she couldn't stop.

Jon said she needed a lot more personal space than most people. Maybe he had a point.

Her palm flattened on the cold metal, feeling the notches. Main Matilda, the compressor back at the Crusty Porthole in Delaware, also had notches, which had steadily increased to the current count of fifteen.

"Breaking a valve off a tank of compressed air could pose a problem," Wall said dryly.

She counted again. "There's four notches now! I know there were three before."

Mike blandly ignored her.

"It's wrecks, isn't it? You make a notch every time you guys find a wreck."

The muscle man kept his face innocent.

Disgusted, Jill caught the Brit suppressing a smile and realized he was in on the joke. Annoyed and a tad hurt, she shoved past Wall despite her personal space issues. Inadvertently bumping his lower anatomy, she practically ran out the door.

Truth was, Wall had a way of making her feel stupid in class. She'd committed her share of mistakes, but so had everyone else. Jon and Mike had loved her fearlessness, praised her prowess. Her cousin labeled her intrepid. Mike called her 'the mermaid.'

Wall had a way of making courage seem foolish. "It's not just your own life you risk," he'd once admonished. "You risk your buddy's as well."

So no, she hadn't been thrilled to hear he was coming. And then to learn that the blonde was also a guest, the woman who wore nail polish in shades to match her dazzling array of swimsuits. The slowest student in class, yet always the center of attention.

"You okay there?" she overheard Mike from inside the room.

She imagined Wall calmly nodding. At least she hoped he was nodding.

Apparently, he also thought her out of earshot. "The Canadian stewardess?" he asked.

"Oh, yeah." Mike chuckled.

The notches! She really was as naive as Jon claimed.

Wall always made her feel stupid.

∞

Wall felt a pang of guilt as he entered the stern cabin.

While it wasn't the height of luxury, it was the best on board. Being guests—Jill had insisted—warranted the top accommodation, meaning a door with a lock and a double bed shoehorned with a built-in dresser. Jill had chosen the tiny cabin in the bow of the boat, which was nothing more than a hollowed-out triangle fitted with a mattress and a curtain for privacy. Jon and Mike slept topside under the stars.

The door stuck, again. He had to use his body to move it.

Inside, Melanie lay on the mattress, flipping through one of the fashion magazines she'd bought at the airport.

Still clad in her bikini, provocatively posed, he realized she'd been waiting for him.

"Let's see what animal you are," she said, and poked at a glossy page. "Do you have more friends than enemies, or enemies than friends?"

"Pardon?"

"It's a quiz to discover what kind of animal you are. I'm a gray wolf."

Tugging his sopping shirt off over his head, Wall stuffed it into the laundry bag. "Friends. Doesn't everybody outside of prison?"

"True friends are rare. There are scads of enemies."

Snatching fresh clothing from the single drawer Melanie had allotted him, Wall glanced at her. "I would hope a true enemy is just as rare."

"You do overthink things, don't you?" she sighed. "That answer puts you in the herbivore quadrant. The ones that get eaten."

He grinned and sat beside her. "You look delicious. I should have come down earlier."

"You should have indeed," she murmured, stroking his arm. The tiff—or whatever it had been—was over.

Wall brushed his lips along her shoulder. "We're an hour outside Antigua—and Jon plans to stay the night, you know. We could catch a taxi and head into St. John's. Maybe lobster for dinner?"

"We...five?"

He flicked her cheek. "We...two. Gotta load supplies first, but that won't take all night."

She sprang up on her knees to adjust a falling strap, riveting his eyes to the soft skin peeking from the pink swimsuit. "Maybe dancing?" she prodded.

"Most certainly dancing. Mind—I'm more enthusiastic than skilled."

Melanie took his hand, lifting it to her mouth. "Enthusiasm is all that's required." Locking eyes with him, she nipped his finger.

He stepped away to lock the door.

∞

Lounging later on a cockpit bench, Wall sipped a beer as the *Sadicor* sliced through churning waves toward the Antigua shore. He'd offered to help, but Jon had already lowered the sails.

His mind churned at the thought of spending the night in St. John's, finding that resort he'd promised Melanie.

Jon thrust a boat hook at him as the dock loomed. "You ever penetrated a wreck?"

The words hung in the air as the dock approached.

"No."

In fact, he'd never been tempted. Open water diving had risks. Most, however, were countered by simply inflating the B.C. and rising to the surface. Diving with a ceiling—be it artificial like decompression diving, or the very real ceiling of a cave or shipwreck—meant simply hitting the air valve was useless. Instead, you relied on lines tied at the entrance and played out to create a trail back to safety, which meant more time needed to return and the danger of lines getting tangled, broken, or even lost. A wreck could be dark and confusing, riddled with unexpected obstacles and complex mazes. In the weightlessness of water, just knowing which way was up could be tricky.

Jon spun the wheel, aiming the sailboat toward the wharf. "After seventeen years diving, I'd say you're ready."

A handful of private vessels crowded the long dock, but a comfortable end spot remained. Was that luck, or a privileged berth reserved for the *Sadicor*?

"We'll get you a reel in town."

Wall drained his beer. "Do I need anything else?"

"Just a good dive light."

"What about..." His voice died as Melanie appeared, wearing a soft drapey top in danger of revealing too much in the breeze.

Both he and Jon watched in fascination.

Then Jon hopped onto the wharf, securing lines to cleats. "You might want good cutters," Jon said. "I've got a pair I can lend you."

Ruby lips pressed against Wall's forearm, distracting him. "Ahhh—I've got a knife," he answered.

"Lots of things to tangle on in a wreck. Best not to have to hack your way free."

∞

"Enough dive talk for now," Melanie murmured. "But if we go now, we can do a little shopping in St. John's."

Melanie winced, hearing the wheedling tone in her own voice. They'd barely set foot on dry land, and here she was complaining.

"Your boyfriend's here to work," Mike told her, with a smirk she itched to slap. "All able-bodied men need to load crates. Go spend your own money, princess."

She barely held her retort and her temper.

"We'll go in an hour." Wall stepped close to cup her cheek.

Out of the corner of her eye, she caught Jill's instinctive retreat. The brunette's personal space was both unusually large and sacrosanct.

It apparently included her cousin. Jon stood a full two feet away from the girl as he handed over a business card. "Nita at the Enclave," he told her. "Put it on my account."

Jill's nose wrinkled as she read it. "You run a tab with Lentil Stirrers?"

"The Center for Spiritual Studies," he corrected her. "You keep saying you want to fix your..." he stepped closer, lowering his voice.

Melanie strained to hear.

"The personal space issue. This is how you do it."

Jill shook her head.

"You can't fix an old problem without trying a new approach. Just *try*, Jill. Just this once, try it."

With a last long look, Jon and Mike headed off.

Wall didn't kiss Melanie—he avoided public displays of affection—but he squeezed her hand before following the others.

"Are you coming?" Jill spun on her heel and strode up the slope.

What else was there to do?

Palm raised to shield her eyes against the sun's glare, Melanie followed the girl through patches of grass. Piles of dirt speckled a road that looked more like an old country drive than a resort boulevard. More like West Virginia than the tropics, except for the ocean in the background.

Melanie had grown up in rural West Virginia. She hated it.

She was starting to hate the ocean.

Jill paused, waiting.

Melanie searched for something to say. "Who is Nita?"

"One of Mike's amours." She kicked at a pebble. "Supposed to be psychic," Jill added, scowling like a two-year-old, which somehow dispelled Melanie's own annoyance.

"Men," Melanie laughed. Her hand automatically lifted to touch Jill's arm, but fortunately, she caught herself in time. "They so love to tell us what to do."

Jill slanted her a look and suddenly grinned.

"At least we're away from all the testosterone." Melanie smiled. "Let's counter with a weapon of our own...something sexy and red." To her amusement, the brunette looked doubtful.

Jill really was an odd thing.

The incline was steep, and Melanie found herself panting by the time they crested it. Jill, on the other hand, seemed in better shape and a better mood.

"Tropical islands." The girl's dark eyes swept the landscape. "This is really something, isn't it?"

For a moment, Melanie believed Jill felt exactly as she did—hating this backwater jungle when she'd expected the Caribbean found in brochures. "It's just dirt," she said aloud. Then she caught the girl's face and saw she wasn't being sarcastic.

Jill was truly delighted to be there.

They had very little in common.

The street of shops turned out to be rows of tourist stalls, tables swamped in layers of T-shirts and hats, sea-shell key chains and cheap sunglasses mingled with homemade flip-flops and painted tiles. Everything practically steamed in the sticky heat while shopkeepers called out in the singsong lilt of the island.

Melanie sighed.

One of the few solid buildings offered shade from the afternoon sun. Gratefully, she followed Jill inside only to discover more of the same street offerings.

Jill strode past it all to a counter in the back.

A tiny, wrinkled man popped up, his grin revealing brown teeth. "Cigarettes?" His fingers clutched what surely looked like a marijuana joint.

"No, thanks." Jill looked to the shelves behind him. "Advil...or aspirin?"

Startled, Melanie realized the question was for her. "Ahh—no, thank you."

"But your headache?" The brown eyes pinned her and narrowed. "You don't have a headache, do you?"

"I really didn't want to dive."

∞

At least it was an honest statement, Jill thought. "At all?"

"Oh, I'll dive," Melanie shrugged. "Can't really avoid it, can I? But scuba doesn't hold the delight for me that it seems to hold for you."

"Then why come?"

Another slanted look—this one sparkling with amusement. "Wall, of course. When we first met, he'd just volunteered to assist with the dive class. Seemed a good way to pursue the relationship. And anyway, twenty men to only four women in the course. You had to like the odds."

Jill burst out laughing.

The man with the suspect cigarettes vanished, and they headed back out to the sunshine.

"So you haven't known him long."

"My office hired some computer geeks. He was the least geeky."

Jill hated the word 'geek.' It hit too close to home. "You can't be labeled a true nerd if you do outside sports."

Melanie shrugged. "I enjoyed class at first—playing in the pool surrounded by tons of bare-chested men. But diving in the quarry was no fun. Dark, cold. More isolated."

"If you need any help, or—you know, if there's anything I can do…"

Another slanted look from the green eyes. The amusement was no longer shared. "I'll let you know."

Chagrined, Jill moved farther away and looked for a distraction. Melanie had a way of making her feel immature. Spying a table of purses, she trotted over to fish through them. "I wonder if they have any of those fanny packs."

Melanie gave her a confused look.

"You know. The little pouches you wear around your waist." Jill assessed a black leather, rejecting it as too ornate.

"I know what a fanny pack is. Spinster gear." Melanie shook her head. "Look, you don't need more safari-woman stuff. What you need is a dress. A pretty one."

"On a sailboat? On a dive trip?"

"How else will we entice the boys into a little more fun? I checked. There are great places above sea level around Antigua."

"They think diving is fun." Jill rejected the notion. "Anyway, Jon and Mike don't alter course once set. 'Specially if a wreck's involved."

Melanie snatched up a vivid blue cloth with a subtle woven pattern. "Try asking in this."

It was awfully pretty. Jill touched the material—silky soft, light. "But it's just a square...with strings!"

"It's called a sarong."

Somehow, Jill had thought those things only existed in movies.

Melanie thrust it against her, and Jill recoiled automatically.

"Oh, for the love of...hold still and lift your arms."

Hesitant, Jill complied.

The woman draped the cloth around her and stepped back. "Pretty. You look more female, less tomboy. Put a flower in your hair, and you're an island girl."

Jill couldn't decide if she was making fun.

The blonde stepped behind her, sweeping her hair back, yanking it around. "Just see if that doesn't get some attention."

Suspicious, Jill glanced at her reflection in a nearby mirror. The woman gazing back looked...confident. Maybe even attractive. "But there's no point in prettying up for my cousin," Jill pointed out to herself as much as Melanie. "And certainly not Mike Burke."

"Mike Burke could be a lot of fun...his type always is. Anyway, this belongs in your wardrobe."

"But there's not much room in my suitcase."

"Just shut up and buy it."

Jill did.

The dress was tucked neatly in a bag, and they were halfway to the next store before Wall's girlfriend spoke again. "Your father is black? Your mother white?"

Jill hesitated before nodding. This, she knew from past experience, was a dangerous conversation. "I got teased a lot in school. Made for a difficult childhood."

There was no sympathy in the green eyes. "I remember reading about mixed race in New Orleans—Creole, maybe? High yellow."

"Don't forget 'mulatto,'" Jill ground out.

"It's supposed to produce beautiful women."

Jill stopped in her tracks.

At her expression, Melanie burst out laughing. "I'm not teasing you, sweetie. Look—let me do your hair and makeup tonight. You'll be stunning, you know. I'm a bit jealous."

"I thought we were all splitting up. Going our separate ways."

"Another night, then. We'll insist they take us out for an evening on the town. A real town," she added, surveying their surroundings with contempt.

"They won't do it." The idea repelled her, though Jill didn't know why. Maybe Jon was right. She had too many hang-ups.

"Sure they will." Melanie smiled. "You just need to know how to ask."

It was a ten-minute stroll to the end of the street.

Jill caught herself doing everything possible to delay it. Shifting through piles of the same wares again and again, asking ridiculous questions, encouraging Melanie to stroke the handmade jewelry.

And all the while, that gate beyond the shops loomed large.

Why she dreaded it, she wasn't sure, though it might have been easier if Melanie wasn't along to watch.

Now only one stall stood between them and the gate.

The gate, in the most Gothic sense, was an old metal arch held upright by a net of twisted vines. Six white tiles stood out against the dark green leaves, displaying hand-painted letters: Center for Spiritual Studies. The "C" was faded, turning the word into a command.

It reminded her of the faded 'R' on the boat.

"Spiritual Studies?" Melanie drawled.

"Jon's forte."

"How odd."

It did look odd, as if all the vegetation on this part of the island had been swept into this one peak, almost eclipsing the shadowed path beyond.

For a wild instant, Jill found herself on the balls of her feet, preparing to flee. We took too long, she imagined telling her cousin. There just wasn't time. Then Melanie passed her, strolling through the arch.

There was nothing to do but follow.

They walked between two wooden houses to find a cleared circle. Stepping within was literally emerging from shadow into light. Deliberate, Jill was sure.

Both buildings gleamed with fresh white paint and were trimmed in an ornate, colonial style. Both had red doors. But while one felt new and unblemished, the other reeked of age.

A welcoming cluster of tables and benches spread before them, displaying books and crystals, herbs and oils. Not in haphazard lumps as the wares on the street, but in proud, neat collections.

The benches held two elderly women in caftans and turbans, and a younger lady. A dazzlingly beautiful lady.

The lady stood. "May I help you?" she asked, and her lips suddenly twitched to a smile. "You're Jill."

Jill blinked.

"Jon spoke of you."

So you must be Nita, Jill longed to retort. Mike spoke of you. That's the sort of thing Melanie would say, taking control with just the right touch of sarcasm.

But even knowing the words, Jill was too polite to say them. Or lacked the backbone.

Nita's smile deepened, as if reading her mind. Reaching out a friendly hand, she invited Jill to clasp it yet respected her personal space. Jon had apparently told her more than just her name.

She hesitated, feeling herself on the brink. Nita merely waited.

Unable to do anything else, Jill took the hand.

∞

Melanie strolled along behind the pair until the Center woman glanced over her shoulder. "Sessions are private."

The brunette stopped short. "I thought she could get one too. Maybe go first."

"Not today."

Still gaping from Jill's comment, Melanie watched them mount the steps of the older house.

Too bad she'd miss this session of Jill's. Obviously, she feared it. It could well have proved the highlight of this silly shopping trip. Waiting wasn't an obligation, and she could leave if it took too long. But it might be fun to see Jill's face upon escaping the fortune-teller. Or whatever she was.

Melanie turned to the wares and old women. Might as well find something to read.

Rows of shiny covers flashed in the sun, temporarily blinding her. Closing her eyes squeezed out the bright light, and when she opened them again, she was able to focus.

Conversations with Seth, Views of Reincarnation from Every Religion, and *Past Lives, Past Pain.* Not a decent bodice ripper among them.

"This one is for you."

Melanie looked up to find a third old woman—this one a crone with straw hair and a hooked nose. The old biddy lacked only a wart to be straight out of the Hansel and Gretel fairy tale.

Her gnarled hand clutched a heavy tome with a ragged binding: *Repeating the Past.*

"I'm more a Clive Cussler type." Melanie pushed the book away.

"You're more a Scottish laird ravishing silly blondes." The crone chuckled, thumping the book against Melanie's chest. "But this is the one you're living."

She automatically clasped the book, and her spine prickled with ice.

One of the caftan-clad women rose from the bench, her voice loud and sharp. "How many women do you see?"

The crone cackled.

Caftan woman approached, her firm tread belying her age. Grasping Melanie's skull, she yanked it down to study her eyes. "How many women do you see?"

"Three!" Melanie cried, breaking free.

Clucking like a hen, the woman turned to scan the surrounding tables, and she snatched up something dark.

It was a black velvety cord, from which dangled a crystal pendant. A tiny, clear shaft of crystal wrapped in a silver vine, delicately wrought with three leaves. The top leaf was hollow with the cord strung through.

"Rubies are my thing," Melanie told her, feeling her pulse race. "My birthstone...July..." Releasing a deep breath, she added, "So much better than rough crystals."

"Avoid rubies. They are bad for you." The woman looped the cord over Melanie's head and pressed the crystal against her heart.

It was all Melanie could do not to leap backward in her best Jill imitation.

"This vibrates with pure energy," the caftan woman said. "This protects. Worn long enough, this purifies. Raises your own vibration."

Intending to fling it from her, Melanie snatched at the thing and went still. Heat radiated from it, nearly burning her hand.

"Your vibration needs raising, my dear. Now, how many women do you see?"

Startled, Melanie gaped. The smirking crone had vanished.

"Do not take that off," the elder told her.

∞

Jill followed Nita through a sort of front parlor, a waiting room devoid of any waiting people. Brochures lay on polished burl wood, and magazines and books were scattered about haphazardly on fading velvet upholstery.

Nita glided through it all, turning down a narrow hallway with many doors on either side, like something in a haunted-house film. She continued to the very end before disappearing through the last door.

Hesitating, Jill glanced over her shoulder, tempted to bolt. But eventually, Jon would hear the tale from Nita if he couldn't pry it out of her. And he'd get that pitying look on his face, that sympathetic, "Sorry you didn't have the guts" regard that always made her squirm.

He might even usher her back that night, while everyone else dined in St. John's. They'd all be curious, asking questions. And Jon would answer cryptically.

And she'd die of shame.

So, taking a deep breath, Jill marched past the many doors to the threshold where Nita waited.

Painted in vivid green, the tiny room invoked a Caribbean vibe at odds with her own mood. Plants in colorful pots crammed the corners, the bookcase, the windowsill. Bizarre pottery and ancient books filled the space, and an old lava lamp sat on a table nearby.

Nita struck a match, lighting a mound of incense inside a pottery frog. Then she turned, and Jill beheld the modern masseur's table, blanketed in a crisp white sheet and oddly hospital-like.

"A massage?" Jill asked warily.

"I won't invade your personal space." Nita smiled. "A regression requires no hands on. It will be of great benefit to you."

A past-life regression. Jon had been after her to do this for years. He'd exclaimed over the experiences, the results. But come to think of it, he'd never been specific about the details. "I don't care if I was Cleopatra in a previous life."

"You weren't."

"I don't believe in reincarnation at all."

"Then this will be nothing more than an amusing exercise." Nita stooped to toy with a small electronic device, producing soft, odd music. "You've nothing to fear."

Jon and his stupid airy-fairy nonsense. If she'd had any backbone, she'd walk straight back to the boat.

But the fresh sheet on the table, the sandalwood aroma, and even the gentle music reached out to intrigue and tempt her.

Jill climbed on the table.

"Close your eyes," Nita soothed.

Surrendering remaining doubt, she did.

The music grew louder. A window shade was lowered to dim the sunshine. "Just relax," Nita murmured.

Difficult, when all the worst scenes from horror movies danced in your head.

"You're standing in a meadow filled with sunshine," Nita commanded.

Hypnosis, Jill sighed. Jon often spoke of being hypnotized. Well, she didn't believe in that either.

The voice droned on, soothing and demanding. Pleading for Jill to feel the warmth on her face, soft grass at her feet. To follow a butterfly knowing she was perfectly safe.

It wasn't until she treaded spiraling steps down into the ground that her shoulders quivered in a sudden chill.

For the stairs circled up—not down. Stone steps in a castle turret. Which should have been romantic, echoing epic adventure and heroes. Instead, there was dirt and cold and spiderwebs. Spiderwebs with occupants silently awaiting their prey.

Although she'd never been in a castle in her life, this all felt hauntingly familiar. She didn't want to do it.

Panicking, Jill tried to back down, back out of this silly dream, but she was in much deeper than she'd realized. Ensnared.

Above her, a hand reached out from a shadowed void. A female hand, with a wedding band of silver twined with gold.

Her grandmother's ring.

The fear vanished, and Jill hurried up the last few steps to see her grandmother again.

She stood in what looked like a sixteenth-century bedroom. The windows were narrow slits, and the stone floor was icy against bare feet. Her grandmother wasn't there, but somehow, she wasn't quite alone.

Against the far wall was a bed, more square than its modern cousin. She knew the mattress was straw.

Ugh. How uncomfortable.

"Oh, no," a voice in her mind told her, "*it's very comfortable.*"

And suddenly, Jill remembered sinking down into it, the warmth rising up to envelope her body. Much better than what she slept on today.

This voice was herself—and not herself. It was an old, old her. A skinny girl living in this castle, this room. Jill felt her with a wave of delight.

Where's my bookcase? Jill asked the girl. *I always have a bookcase in my bedroom,* she thought, and marveled at the implication.

The startled girl asked, "*You mean books? To read? Only one person in the entire castle can read.*" And she trembled.

Instantly, the girl's memories flooded Jill—a tidal wave of horrible images. Of an awful man with greasy red hair, long and tangled with tiny bugs living in it. He'd locked her in this room, where he'd kept her for more than a year.

She hadn't seen another living person in all that time.

He came often to hurl her on the bed; he'd do as he would. Afterward, he'd sometimes stroke her shoulder. More often not. And though she tried to run from the knowledge, she knew that man was her sire, her father.

Jill found herself quaking with a mind-numbing fear. *Tell your mother,* she begged the girl. *Tell your mother.*

"*Do you mean she who bore me?*" And Jill had a vision of a bitter woman working the kitchens. A woman who felt only jealousy for this brat who'd attracted the lord of the castle. The man who'd burdened her with child in the first place but had never kept her away from toil.

Jill and the girl gazed out the narrow window, seeing the fluffy tops of trees below. Wondering for the thousandth time if she could survive a leap into them, letting the branches break the fall. The Jill of modern times knew such a fall would kill.

Jill also knew she'd jump anyway.

Boots tread the stairs beyond the door, and a scream welled in her throat.

"Move on," a female voice decreed.

∞

Jill suddenly rested cheek to grass by a still pool in a wooded clearing. Her horse, Lady Fair, grazed nearby.

This was her sanctuary. The place she ran to when her governess wished to practice French. Here she was coddled, beloved by a titled father, indulged beyond reason, as the servants said.

So why did she need a sanctuary?

Hazy recollections rose of a handsome man with curly black hair; a noble's second son and her suitor. More prominent men had asked for her hand, but her father had chosen the gentlest for her husband. One with wealth to care for her and a tender heart to appreciate her. A man who loved her.

And in her heart, she knew all these words for truth. She should be honored that her father had found him for her instead of seeking a more advantageous connection. She should be thrilled.

Dread was her true state. She felt a wordless panic at the approaching nuptials and the night to follow. She dreaded that which a man did to a woman, and in truth, it was an event this particular girl knew nothing about. There were no words to explain this terror and no one to understand.

This girl, too, died young. Falling off Lady Fair just days before the wedding.

Tears streamed down Jill's cheeks.

∞

"Jill." The voice was far off.

She didn't want to answer.

"Wake now, Jill. You're perfectly safe."

She flew from wherever, yanked back with an audible pop in her ears. Her cheeks were sodden, and she had to pry her eyelids open.

Black hair framed the face peering down.

Clawing her way to consciousness, Jill recognized Nita; she recognized the calming room in the old white house. Recognized the present.

"You were crying," Nita frowned. "The second life should have been healing, happy. Yet you cried."

"She was so scared," Jill whispered. Her mind roiled from the revelations of the castle...the sudden understanding.

When she was six years old, she wore shorts under her dresses, even after her mother yelled at her for it. She'd never liked hugging men—not even her father. She'd never liked being touched at all. All stemming from a faint, nameless fear.

Leaping to her feet, she stared around the room, stared at Nita. Emotions flooded her brain, but her mouth failed to find words.

"There was a life farther back—but you're not ready to see that yet. The life you first saw was the one you needed to see.

"But the life after that...the second life. It should have been happy." Jill controlled her panting, forcing herself to calm down.

"What did you see?" Nita asked.

"My grandmother," Jill whispered, "beckoned me."

The beauty nodded. "She thought you ought to know."

∞

It was a full hour before the brunette returned.

Melanie paced most of that time, wanting to flee but strangely hesitant to venture down the shadowed path alone. Her emotions ran high by the time Jill emerged from the red door.

"You took your time."

Jill nodded, distracted. Oblivious.

Nita followed her, snatching something off one of the tables. "Take this to Jon." She grinned, offering a red book.

Melanie squinted against the sun to read. *Revisits: Theory of Soul Returns to the Earth Plane.* Jesus, these people were criminally gullible.

Jill wrapped her fingers around the red cloth cover, accepting the thing without so much as a blink.

"Let's go." Melanie tugged on her arm.

For once, Jill didn't leap away from the touch.

"That pendant costs ten dollars." Nita held out her palm.

Happy to fling the thing at her, Melanie grabbed the crystal and hesitated. Her eye wandered from the two women in caftans to the empty spot where the crone had stood.

"How many women do you see?" she asked Jill.

The brunette shook herself, finally fighting off whatever fugue she was in. "Three."

Melanie rummaged through her purse to find the cash.

It wasn't until they walked back through the village that she realized Jill had included Nita in her count.

Forward

Clutching the book Nita had given her, Jill trudged silently down the hill. The blonde trudged beside her, for once holding her tongue.

Her father and uncle had always laughed at Jon's spiritual beliefs. He was crazy, they'd said, letting his fear of dying invent proof that he wouldn't. Reincarnation was a stupid idea. Her father couldn't be wrong. Uncle Paul was never wrong.

Except Jill knew to the core of her being that those other lives were real.

It was after five by the time they reached the *Sadicor*. The men back and supplies stowed, plans for the evening were set and underway. She could have used a little time alone, sorting through the experience of the afternoon.

Well, trying to sort through.

Melanie had slipped below deck when Jill handed Jon his book. He grinned appreciatively, stroking the worn cover as if it were an old friend.

"So you did go." He didn't press for more, and she doubted she could have spoken if he had.

"Early dinner?" he suggested. "There's an outdoor pub on the edge of St. John's."

Metallic banging thumped the deck below her feet. Mike must be working on Matilda. "If we can pull him away."

"He's eating later." Jon hopped onto the dock, reaching a hand to assist her up. "Someone has to remain on board."

Wall emerged, hair damp from a shower, tucking a clean shirt into pressed slacks. Jill felt worn and rumpled beside him.

"Let me at least change," she said.

"No time." Jon's palm inched closer, insistently. Good thing she still had her purse.

He led her along the wharf, toward a driver waving from a battered cab. Glancing behind, Jill saw Wall easing Melanie out onto deck—her shoulders bare in the red sarong and blonde hair swept up in a sophisticated twist.

A proper, romantic date, Jill realized. Just as Mike probably planned with Nita, once she and Jon returned to watch the boat. Hence Jon's hurry.

The pang she felt—and firmly suppressed—was envy.

∞

Harbor lights glittered on the water, competing with the crescent moon and companion stars in the sky. A distant ship's horn cried softly.

Couldn't have planned this better if I'd tried. Wall smiled to himself. They were seated at a cozy table for two by the glass wall. A perfect view for a perfect meal.

Melanie gazed at the former, her profile tilted toward him as she sipped her champagne. Her second glass, which was a good thing. They'd ordered a bottle, though he preferred a complex cabernet. She'd had a rough day, after all, and deserved a little pampering.

"You've been married before?" she asked.

He nodded. "Fresh out of college. We'd been together for almost three years. It was...expected."

Her eyes never shifted from the harbor; her lips never formed the next question.

He supplied it all the same. "After ten months, we realized we'd made a mistake. We just—were two completely different people. Different goals, different plans for the future. It was a very amiable split, actually. My father said indecently so."

"I've never been married," Melanie murmured. "Picked out a wedding dress twice, but never actually made it."

'Made it.' Rather an odd phrasing. "What happened?"

Her green eyes turned to him but seemed to see something else. "Just... things." She tossed down her drink in a single gesture.

She must have been brokenhearted, he thought. *Left at the altar, maybe caught a fiancé in bed with a close friend.*

Her fingers drummed the table.

He clasped them reassuringly. "Ready for that dance I promised?"

That brought her smile.

Wall left her at the bar while he found the elusive waiter to pay their bill. He returned to find her clasping a martini, perched on a barstool between two very attentive males.

∞

The taxi delivered them to the Barnacle's bright yellow stoop, a sight that made Jon smile. He loved Antiqua, particularly St. John's and Mama Lena's.

It was still early.

Few people had made their way to the festively painted tables adorned with plastic orchids and hot pink toucans. Watching his cousin's nose wrinkle, he grinned.

"Mama Lena's taste in decor runs to the whimsical."

Jill threw him a look.

"But her fungi is unsurpassed. It's a sort of cornmeal-okra dumpling."

She didn't look impressed.

She did, however, clear her plate. Licking the last drips from her tinny fork, she frowned. "Maybe I was just hungry."

He shoved his remaining callaloo toward her—a bright green, leafy soup dish.

She eyed it without enthusiasm. "I'm not hungry anymore."

Their outdoor table stood by a brick half-wall, separating them from a street lined with bright blue doors on pink houses. Jon loved the colors of Antigua, the bold hues slathered fearlessly about by a people unafraid to be noticed. People unafraid to be happy.

A little whimsy was good for the world.

He'd intended to wait, to ask her back on the *Sadicor*, but somehow the first salvo burst from his mouth. "I've always been drawn to the idea of reincarnation."

Her eyes narrowed.

"Science tells us of conservation of matter, conservation of energy. Only follows there's conservation of souls."

Jill sniffed in disdain.

"Dr. Mallory, here on the island, convinced me."

"How?" she demanded. "Did he swear you were Sir Francis Drake? Or I know...Nelson at Trafalgar."

There was genuine anger in her tone. What had Nita shown Jill to get her this upset?

Leaning across the table, he grasped her hand as she automatically started to pull away. "When I was little, mermaid, I...rebelled. Constantly, against all authority. And it only got worse as I got older. Dad threatened, punished. Even sent me to counseling."

She wasn't ready to release her anger. But she was listening.

"Once when I was ten, he made me do yard work," Jon continued. "I wanted to play with my friends, but Dad refused to let me go until the leaves were swept clear. I stuck a hard metal rake under his car tire."

Jill choked on her iced tea. "Uncle Ray's Porsche?"

He nodded. "Half the reason Dad's so stern is I flat-out defied him practically as soon as I could walk. I'd do anything Mom asked, but no man could order me around."

"Dad did say something once," Jill told him slowly. "When I kept pushing to spend the night at a friend's house. He said I was getting as annoying as you."

Jon's grin faded. "I did learn to hide it better...but the resentment itself remained. Until the day I met Dr. Mallory. He convinced me to get regressed."

Jill's brown eyes narrowed again, but he sensed he had her full attention now.

"Turns out I served a vicious master in a previous life. Really vicious. My choice that lifetime was to go along with it and serve his ways...or stand against him. I rebelled."

"Well...good."

"Don't you see? Jill, it explains everything to me. I rebelled because I was so determined to rebel—actually scared of NOT rebelling. I saw poor Dad through a haze of anger—anger at someone else from another lifetime."

The brown eyes widened.

Jon saw the startled recognition. "What did Nita show you?"

Her lips pressed firmly, and for a moment he was sure she wouldn't speak.

A tear welled in her eye.

And then she told him.

∞

The red hues of a dying sun sparkled everywhere as the taxi stopped by the *Sadicor*. Jill practically sprang out, feeling better than she had for a long time.

Jon proclaimed her regression successful, even miraculous. She wasn't ready to buy that yet. It was sharing experiences with her cousin that had brought this feeling of relief. They'd genuinely bonded over dinner.

Just the fact that he hadn't laughed at her or patted her on the head like she was still five years old proved he'd accepted her as an adult. She'd finally heard about his own regression, a tale she doubted even Mike knew. And he, too, had been led to a second life, where he had an odd vision of himself as a young girl, dancing about an angry young man who couldn't see. That man stalked around a large manor house, and the young girl had been exasperated at his anger. She'd also been delighted that her bare feet could no longer feel the chilled floor. Apparently, the girl had just died and wished the young man would just get over it. She'd been happy to be dead.

And when Jon, in his regression, had asked this dead girl if the man was a brother or a lover, she'd told him it didn't really matter. At a higher level, love is the same.

Now Mike hailed them with a beer bottle, leaping off the *Sadicor* before Jon stepped aboard. He was dressed for a night out—Mike's idea of dressing up being his red "Sadicor & Burke" T-shirt.

"The Barnacle still serving Mama Lena's best?" Mike asked as he swung Jill onto the teak deck.

Jon nodded. "And she's made a sort of fresh berry cobbler tonight."

The muscle man sent a grin over Jill's head. "Perfect timing."

Jill turned as Nita appeared and hugged Mike's arm to her.

"How do you feel?" she asked Jill.

"Okay. Fine." Wary of Mike, Jill answered awkwardly.

The big guy, however, had no trouble putting two and two together. He took a step into her space—a gesture he loved to do—fists on his hips. "Not you, too?"

Jill's normal reaction was an immediate hop backward, often colliding with a wall or a bystander. Now she held her ground, though her cheeks burned. She had, after all, snickered with him over some of Jon's more outrageous foibles.

Nita yanked him toward the taxi. "Don't knock something you're afraid to try."

He snorted, casting Jill a last look before draping his arm around the beauty.

Jon scooped her up in a surprise hug. "Well done."

"What?"

"That was the first time you didn't react when Mike invaded your personal space!"

She shrugged, though the back of her neck prickled. "I just knew it was coming."

Jon smiled warmly. "Maybe."

∞

Feeling her pull stiffly away, Mike knew he'd annoyed Nita.

Why women—and Jon, of all people—believed in that lentil-stirrer nonsense he couldn't figure. Living over and over as squirrels and butterflies seemed pretty stupid—and anyway, what fucking difference would it make?

No. Dead was dead, and people would be much better off just accepting it. That prevented you from wasting time doing foolish things.

"Live like there's no tomorrow," he'd told Nita. "Saves you from wasting time."

Watching her skirts twitch with her walk—not in the smooth, 'watch me walk' glide but an all-out angry march, he knew he needed to fix this. Or spend the night alone.

He clamped a hand on her arm to stop her.

Halted, she faced away from him, shoulders square and head straight. Hair dangled down her back in a fancy braid.

"Sorry, baby," he said, and kissed her where the shoulder jutted out from the delicate neck.

When she didn't react, he drew a circle with his tongue. He felt the air escape her lungs in a long hiss, the shoulders suddenly pliable. Her head tilted ever so slightly, and he knew he'd won.

The taxi driver peered out the window.

"How hungry are you?" Mike murmured against her skin.

"We can eat later." She sighed softly.

Mike waved the cab off.

He thought he'd averted the crisis, but as frequently is the case with women, he'd only delayed it. Females had this capacity to store each perceived slight, tucking them away only to hurl them in your face when you least expected it.

What he loved about Nita was her lack of inhibition. An island girl trait. It made for a spectacular evening.

Later, lying among the scattered bedding, they dozed in a particularly well-earned afterglow, her face pillowed on his abdomen. He cuddled her close and weighed the wisdom of mentioning dinner. His wristwatch, propped strategically against her bed table lamp, showed 10:17 p.m.

Her muscles tensed, so he tried to head it off.

"My lioness," he murmured into her hair. When she didn't whisper, "My warrior," he knew he was in trouble.

∞

Nita caught his surreptitious check of the time.

It needled her as nothing else had. Not his refusal to consider her ideas, not his outright laughter at her work. Not even his implication that the Center's purpose was to bilk money from fools.

The room glowed in candlelight, the aroma of lavender oil flavoring the atmosphere. Crystal pendants hung in each window, one of them refracting the moonlight such that only she could see it.

She was tired of being the only one to see things.

"Let me regress you." She rose up to watch his face. "Find out your past adventures."

His eyes rolled, blinked, and then looked blandly at her. Considering his best move to get his dinner, she realized. Humor her or sweep her off to town.

Her annoyance doubled. She felt used, even though she didn't believe in such things. *Others do not use you—you allow them to use you. Well, not this time.* Nita sat up, rolling on top to straddle him. "What are you afraid of?"

That he couldn't well refuse. He knew it, too, seeing right through her words. One of the things she loved about Mike—he played the male rogue to perfection, but he never took himself too seriously. He knew he played the role.

Just as he knew now that she had played him. He would do it, she saw in his eyes, not because she'd trapped him, but because he'd decided to allow her to do so.

How did he always make her want to punch him and ravish him simultaneously?

"Get your crystals," he growled.

Nita would have preferred to do it in her room in the old house, with her table, her incense, her soothing taped music. She didn't dare press him, however.

Despite his cocked eyebrow, she placed crystals at his crown and feet, lit her expensive sandalwood incense, and even tucked a pillow under his knees. He presented a picture of a relaxed man.

On impulse, she sat herself at his head, moving the crystal to lie on his third eye chakra and slipping her hands beneath his shoulders.

His one eye opened, pivoting to her. "Do you do this for all your clientele?"

"Relax," she murmured, massaging the muscles beneath her fingers.

On instinct, she sang to herself, softly and without words. Minutes passed without any affect, but eventually she felt his tension seep away.

"In your mind, Michael, form the image of a meadow. The grass underfoot, the trees nearby. The sun on your face."

Her palms felt no reaction, so she continued.

"Stride, Michael. Stride through the grass, feeling the sun. Feel your legs pumping rhythmically, easily. You love the physical. You enjoy movement."

His eyebrows twitched, and she smiled in triumph.

"Ahead of you, yawning in the grass, is a staircase down into the earth."

His body felt relaxed, at ease. For a moment, she thought he'd succumbed.

"The stairs loom larger as you approach. You can see now they disappear in the dark. A warm, safe darkness, like the womb of your mother. You're curious... You want to see what's down there."

"Not without a flashlight." He chuckled. Grinning, he winked at her. "And a picnic lunch. If I'm going to play Indiana Jones, I need sustenance."

Rising from the bed, he stretched in a very masculine maneuver and reached a hand down to her. "Come, sweetie. Fix your traveler his dinner."

Exasperated, she finally took his hand.

Naked, they strode to the kitchen.

"Say it," he commanded as she spread mayonnaise on bread.

"My warrior," Nita sighed.

He always won. And no matter how outrageously he did so, she could only laugh and shake her head. Ever since the day she'd met him, he'd somehow commanded her heart.

When she closed her eyes and tried to look into the future, she saw them together. Married, no less, and living in this house. He and Jon had somehow sold the business, and he had enough money to play for a while.

It was a strange future, but full of comfort. Happiness.

"Mmm—I like that," he said. It took her a moment to realize he spoke of her words, not the future she saw. "Warriors are fighters, fierce and true. We always win," he said as he bit into his sandwich.

"Warriors always die young," she shot back.

∞

It took Melanie all night to undo the damage.

Not to Wall, of course.

All that required, when he found her in the bar between those two lawyers, was to rise eagerly to her feet, bestow a dazzling smile, and take his arm. Giving him the role of the victor in a male dispute.

Not that he acted victorious, of course. But the two who had bought her the drink had been disappointed.

Massaging him in the fancy hotel room later, as he lay face down on the expensive satin bed cover, kneaded away any lingering doubt. They made love over champagne and strawberries.

And in the afterglow conversation—why didn't Wall just fall sleep like every other man?—he spoke of diving and buying a few specialty food items early tomorrow as a gift to the others. No mention of the lawyers.

The true damage had been to herself.

Wall's face when he saw her with those men reminded her of Craig, her first fiancé. His look of startled hurt, swiftly covered up. In Craig's case, it had festered beneath the surface, rising again when least expected. Brian, her second fiancé, had simply walked out then and there.

A self-destruct gene ran through her family tree.

Her mother frequently demonstrated it; her father too, or so the stories said. Whenever Melanie had a man in her life, a relationship headed someplace, it blew up in her face.

She blew it up.

Those men tonight had certainly smiled at her, but it was she who approached them, edging her way between the two to order a drink. Knowing they would pay for it— delighting when they dueled over whose credit card to use. It had been a kick to manipulate them into buying her a drink.

Brian had accused her of deliberately embarrassing him, but that wasn't true. She'd had no thought of Brian at all. Her mind sat quietly in the background, watching as her base nature took charge.

Now it had happened again, and Wall wasn't even her fiancé. Just the poor sap who'd paid for this vacation.

The next morning, the Brit smiled softly as he helped her aboard the *Sadicor*. His face showed no doubts, no re-criminations. She might have gotten away with it this time.

For Chrissakes, she was less than two months away from her thirtieth birthday. The big three zero. She couldn't afford to keep ruining her life.

Good thing they were going to be at sea for a while.

∞

Jon leaned his face into the wind. He loved the feel of his *Sadicor* under sail.

Mike had just taken the helm, so he ought to go below to grab some breakfast. Maybe check in with Wall—find out how the prospect of wreck-diving affected his British caution.

Still he stayed.

"We forgot the paint," he said aloud.

Mike shrugged. He didn't know what Jon was talking about.

"Paint...to fix the boat name. You know? Redo the 'R' on *Sadicor*."

Mike shrugged again to indicate he didn't care. Mike was a direct communicator, as his dad used to say. His dad had meant it disparagingly, but Jon always appreciated that about his partner. The big man never hid his true meaning in misleading words.

Like, say, his dad.

The sailboat leapt over a rough patch, momentarily airborne before slapping down enthusiastically. Eager to race on, eager to return. As eager as he was.

A shipwreck. Undiscovered and unknown. Oddly split in half, as if some giant had sawed it straight down the middle. Wall was probably right. It had to be a modern day vessel. No gold doubloons or antique jewels, but that didn't mean it was worthless. Could be a safe onboard. Might even hold enough to startle his father.

The famous Ray Sadicor might actually be impressed with his son for a change.

Ray had played twelve years in the NFL, nine of them as cornerback, three more as safety. He'd made more money in his first signing bonus than most people would see in their lifetime. And he'd expected Jon to outdo him.

Jon had tried.

He tried in high school, getting brutalized as a running back, then as a receiver. Undaunted, Ray pushed him into playing quarterback, explaining Jon's intelligence would make him legendary. At least that's how the colleges saw it, and most were happy to take a chance on Ray Sadicor's son.

But if Jon had the smarts, he lacked the skills. Or perhaps, as one coach gently suggested, he simply lacked the drive. Jon quit the team in his sophomore year, and he quit school altogether the next.

Since then, nothing he did interested his father. Ray cut off his allowance, telling him a man made his own way, and firmly closed the front door.

Mike, Jon's best friend since fifth grade, had a dream of owning a dive shop. They got a loan from a bank—even after explaining to the bank manager that Jon's father was not cosigning—to open the Crusty Porthole. And while Ray never lifted a finger, Mike's grandmother and Jon's Uncle Chris had made a few calls to nudge a few friends. Once they started diver certification classes, the shop turned a profit.

Uncle Chris, Jill's father, had also played in the NFL, but no one ever paid for his endorsement. His career had lasted three years as a special teams guy before he got cut. He was blue collar, or so he liked to say, and never made more than a basic living. Perhaps that was why he seemed more human. For him, storybook endings belonged in storybooks.

Jon envied Jill her father.

Even as he thought that, his cousin popped out from the cabin. "Hey! Wall says I can't wreck dive!"

Mike threw him a look.

The brunette plopped on the bench beside him. "You're the captain, Jon. You make the decisions."

Jon sighed. "Jill, you're a beginner. You've barely logged two dives since certification."

"I was the best in class!"

In some ways, Jill reminded him of his father. No fear, no doubt. And no reasoning with her. "Acing a 'ditch and don' drill doesn't mean you're ready for wreck penetration. It's vastly more dangerous."

He caught the look she sent Mike. His partner treated her like a kid sister, and often took up her battles.

But not this time. "Mermaid, you probably ought to control your buoyancy better before we take you into an overhead environment."

Watching her face, Jon knew she didn't see the problem. Just like his father—it never occurred to either of them to weigh the risk, to consider that they might fail.

That a failure could be catastrophic.

Reaching under his seat, he plucked out the book Nita had sent, *Revisits: Theory of Soul Returns to the Earth Plane.* Randomly opening it, his finger stabbed a passage, and he read aloud. "Experience, the goal of life, teaches walk before run, glide before fly. Patience then is the true virtue."

Mike burst out laughing. "The Universe has spoken!"

"I hate it when you do that," Jill told him. "Wall's never wreck-dove either, you know."

"Wall's been diving for seventeen years. I think he's ready."

She actually flounced on her seat. Or to be fair, it might have been the motion of the boat. Jon tucked the book away, and she pulled it out again.

"Would you like to read it? I can wait."

Mike guffawed. "You're both a little old for fairy tales."

Jill shoved the book away.

Noting her red cheeks—too red to be from the wind and too quick to be from the sun—Jon sent her a wink. "Many cultures believe in some form of reincarnation. I think it answers many of life's inconsistencies," he told Mike. "You're welcome to read it."

The big guy snorted.

Jill stared out over the water. "Did you buy the paint to fix the 'R'?" She folded her arms, obviously knowing the answer.

"We can mend it another time."

It was a good ten minutes before she spoke again. "You guys really think that's a wreck?"

He found himself nodding, but she was still staring at the Caribbean water racing by.

"Oh, yes," he told her. "It's too uniform, too symmetrical. Got to be man-made."

"How old?"

"We'll find out."

"You're gonna need more manpower," she wheedled.

Mike looked over her slender frame and burst out laughing. She harrumphed in return, but her eyes glistened with answering humor.

At least she was coming out of the sulks.

∞

Kneeling in her pink shorty, Melanie scowled.

The thin wetsuit was still hot and uncomfortable, rendering a very expensive bikini invisible. Her gear littered the dive platform, mocking her. This same equipment had always attracted men in class, offering assistance and other things. Now she wasn't quite certain which piece went where.

Lifting the regulator, she eyed its hoses suspiciously.

"Don't forget your B.C.," Jill called sotto voce from the cockpit, for all the world as if she were trying to help without anyone knowing.

"My B.C.'s right here."

Mike, who'd taken a swim to cool off, vaulted onto the platform, drenching her with cold water.

"I meant attach your air to your B.C.," Jill said, ruffling her all the more.

"I know, I know. Go soak your...equipment."

Two muscular arms surrounded Melanie, reaching to connect the line to her tank.

"B.C.—Buoyancy Control, princess," Mike murmured in her ear. "Don't you remember my lectures? Or were you too distracted?"

She froze. In class, she had been rather fascinated with Mike's physique. He wasn't her type—she preferred a little sophistication—but there was a sort of raw animal feel to the man that was hard to ignore. She'd admired him the way you admired a panther in a zoo: from afar and fully intending to keep it that way.

Flirting with others, Melanie never gave Mike the slightest sign. Or so she thought.

Now Mike withdrew as Wall dropped onto the platform, carrying her pink dive knife.

"Why, just your color," Mike told him. For a wild moment, it felt like two men battling for her attentions. Deliciously primal.

Then the muscle man moved on to help Jill, and Wall knelt over his own gear.

Lowering her eyes to the platform, Melanie was startled to see Mike's shadow suddenly sport a huge phallic appendage. Her gaze flew to the man, watching him attach that damned machete to his rig. Wall had said no one in their right mind would carry such a knife underwater.

"Doesn't that get in your way?" Jill asked.

The muscle man patted it. "Brought me luck on every wreck I've explored. It's my second favorite piece of equipment." Over the brunette's head, he sent Melanie a knowing look.

She ignored him to click in her air hose.

∞

Wall snapped the buckles about his chest and checked the security of his rig. The familiar routine never failed to make him smile.

He loved diving.

Reaching down, he lifted Melanie's gear and held it steady as she slipped her arms through. She looked nervous, and he realized she hadn't dove since her checkout dive.

"Make sure my gear's in order." He smiled warmly and presented his back.

Her hesitation was palpable. Finally, she moved, stepping closer, then stepping away. When she said nothing, he prodded, "Am I good?" He had to turn to see her nodding.

Demonstration was in order. Turning her about, he ran fingers along hoses to verify her tank was attached to her B.C., her regulator attached to the tank. Lifting her console, he showed her the computer panel. "Full tank." He smiled.

She nodded and reached for his own wrist computer. "Full," she said.

He touched her shoulder encouragingly.

In the U.K., Jill and Melanie would need much more diving experience to get certified. Americans liked to deride the British for being too stiff on rules, but the accident reports told a different story. His old dive master had used the term 'Cowboy' when describing it.

Jon rolled off the dive platform into the blue water, barely disturbing the surface. Next, Jill jumped in with a big splash, surfacing sheepishly with her mask askew. Jon's cousin might be more enthusiastic, but she was as much a novice as Melanie.

Wall pointedly clamped a hand over his own faceplate as he leaned back and fell into the sea. Belatedly, he realized Melanie remained alone on the platform.

She nervously stepped off, somehow catching a fin and tumbling awkwardly. She came up sputtering, sans mask and glaring at the world.

Retrieving the pink plastic, he handed it back to her.

"Our mission is to find a way inside," Jon announced. "Ought to be easy where she split apart, but Mike and I couldn't find a break in the coral earlier. Might even be a hatchway on top—or a hole in the side.

"Do not feel the reef with your fingers, even in gloves. It's razor sharp and can slice through neoprene. Use your dive knife if you see something worth checking out. Or get us."

The two young women caught Wall's eye. Jill eager, bursting to prove herself as she had in class; Melanie doubtful and nervous. Both would need careful supervision.

"I'm not too keen on diving threesomes," he said aloud.

Mike cocked an eyebrow. "What about threesomes above water?"

"Jill's a novice," Wall continued, unamused. "And with you two concentrating on the wreck..."

"Mike is Jill's buddy. I'm on my own," Jon replied.

"Safe as in her mother's arms." Mike smirked. "Don't worry about her. We're two warriors."

Wall didn't like it.

When he'd come to the U.S. six months ago, wrangling a special assignment from his boss after the Padstow incident, he'd found the Crusty Porthole and Jon Sadicor. He'd been delighted to see the sign in the shop about volunteers for the certification class. A perfect opportunity to become part of the Wilmington, Delaware, community.

Wall discovered, however, that American dive training was an order of magnitude less than the British Sub Aqua Club. NAUI and PADI, the two U.S. organizations, considered a person certified after a mere two open water dives. The B.S.A.C. required ten.

There were other such examples.

"No penetration, even if we find a way in," Jon continued. "We split up on the bottom. Wall and Melanie take the reef to the east. We three check the bit to the west."

Slapping a regulator into his mouth, Wall studied the circle of faces. Jon so calm, Jill obviously eager. Mike just as eager but less obvious. And Melanie—whose green eyes widened apace with growing apprehension.

Jon's hand lifted in the okay signal as he made eye contact with each diver. One by one, they signaled back.

They submerged.

Ghosts of the Past

The water line rose over Jill's faceplate. Sunlight muted as her own breathing rasped loudly in her ears, sending a tiny shiver down her spine.

Truth was, ocean diving felt deliciously scary. Halloween scary—lots of fun surprises mixed with a touch of adrenaline.

Wall handed Melanie her console, prodding Jill to fish for her own. She ought to monitor her descent.

The blonde suddenly kicked, reversing direction, and the Brit immediately rose with her. Jill glimpsed wide green eyes framed in a pink mask before the woman moved up out of sight.

She felt sorry for Wall. Melanie was not here for the diving, and the Brit would be very disappointed once he figured that out.

Surely he'd be disappointed.

Warm-water diving was an adventure, one she wanted to share with Jon and Mike. Mostly for the sheer fun, though there was a need to prove herself, prove she was just as intrepid as Jon often said. And to show her father, who'd merely shaken his head and prophesied sharks.

Well, she'd already seen her first shark.

Mike described worrying about sharks like driving your car and worrying the engine would catch fire. It happened—but rarely, and there were plenty of more likely problems to be prepared to handle. Actual shark attacks were rare, and smart diving made them rarer still.

Complications from breathing compressed air, on the other hand, were far more common. The molecules compressed as you sank. At thirty-three feet down, they shrank to half their size. Thirty-three feet more squeezed them half again. So a lungful of air taken at sixty-six feet underwater would expand to four times its size on the surface—bursting the lungs long before you reached daylight. It was an image she found very hard to forget.

Jon had drilled it into the class's collective mind, highlighting the need to rise and descend slowly, breathe normally. Never hold your breath. If you had to surface quickly, blow the oxygen out of your lungs the whole way up.

Consciously she inhaled while peering down at the shipwreck.

The two reefs just looked like reefs. Maybe they did mirror each other somewhat, and perhaps there was a near ninety-degree angle to one side. But an actual ship? She couldn't see it.

As her fins set in the sandy bottom, Jon peered into her mask. He always liked to make eye contact with the students. Mike tapped her shoulder, flashing the okay signal. Belatedly, she returned it.

They headed to the wreck.

∞

Hovering barely fifteen feet below the surface, Wall tapped his ear. Melanie nodded nervously.

He slowly grabbed his nose, mimicked blowing it. When she just blinked at him, he repeated the gesture.

Finally, the light came on. She imitated his movements, eyes widening when her ears popped. He gave her the okay signal, waited until she nodded, and then deliberately held his wrist computer close to his faceplate. Once she did the same, they continued their descent.

He checked her again at the bottom. Most beginners had a mixture of nerves and eagerness, but Melanie seemed all the former and none of the latter. Still, she returned the proper signal before they swam to the reef.

Pulling his knife from his ankle sheath, Wall poked it into a few holes, hoping to produce a lobster to make her smile. He found nothing. So he set to work, prying at the coral and suppressing a sigh at the damage to an underwater habitat. Oddly, no fish appeared to protest.

No fish appeared at all.

Above him, a large gray patch seemed already dead. Wall wedged his blade beneath it, pounding the handle to lever the piece free. Nothing happened.

He floated higher and tried again. Nothing.

PING. Someone rapped on a tank. Someone, Wall guessed, had found something.

Melanie clutched his arm like a heroine in a horror movie. After calming her, Wall beckoned. Together they swam toward the source of the noise.

Skimming the length of the second reef, they spied a rather pointed end—with a bouquet of giant anemones, delicate tan in color with pink tips waving in the sea.

Wall found himself smiling in delight—it was exactly the sort of vision that drew him underwater in the first place. He glanced at Melanie, swimming beside him to keep from sinking. Her interest seemed focused on her swimming.

A tiny fish peeked out from the tentacles. For an instant, the reef seemed to offer him this magical undersea posy.

The tentacles jerked, froze. The fish shot out over his shoulder and vanished.

The only thing moving now were the two pairs of flippers below the anemones.

The ocean floor dipped low beneath, where Wall led Melanie. Where Jill stood on the sand, watching the men above her.

Here the reef rose twelve feet up, jutting out to hang over their heads, allowing a clear view of Mike and Jon shoving a crowbar beneath one of the anemones.

The thing burst free, shooting over Jill's head before drifting slowly down to the sand. Curling in on itself, as if already dead.

A shiver ran down his spine.

More coral chunks broke free, bits of rubble drifting down around them, revealing a void in the reef. A black hole just large enough for a diver.

∞

The tremor shook his lair. He woke.

Breathing, stretching, he moved purposefully into awareness. Something was different. The spinning in his mind grew, stirring the water around him. It was not enough.

He'd been vaguely aware of something stirring him. Some—intrusion. Familiar and intriguing. It would take more than his usual little swirl of energy to properly see.

He sought a living thing. Finding and rejecting a conch and then a snail, his mind perceived the perfect host. He beckoned.

The creature approached; it hesitated. Being outside the lair, it lacked an entrance path, but the little vortex demanded. Insisted. And the creature frantically sought a way to obey.

At last a narrow crack appeared—a small opening too narrow to pass through unscathed. Scratched, hurting, the creature arrived.

Taking possession, the Vortex swelled with triumph. And waited.

∞

Jon shone his light inside the hole.

Within appeared a cloudy cavern—a silt-blanketed floor, dangling thick white threads, and floating debris. He arced the beam slowly, revealing more of the same.

A modern shipwreck ought to be more, well, modern. If this was a ship interior, surely it would be more recognizable. Portholes, lamps...something. Hell, even the footage of the *Titanic* identified man-made pieces.

Jill swam up beside him to clutch the edge and peer inside. An instant later, Melanie did the same. Mike and Wall floated closer.

Could this thing have been purposefully sunk to form a reef? If so, it'd be a dead husk. Worthless.

His beam stilled on a distant spot, where shadows swirled.

The great thing about diving with Mike was the way they read each other's mind. The big man was already pulling line from his belt reel to tie off round the overhead point. Jon moved to do the same, pausing only to hand off Jill to the Brit.

Wall glared back, shaking his head. Mike had it right—this guy hated altering the dive plan, no matter what the circumstances. But already Mike was shimmying through the opening, penetrating the wreck. Jon had to follow, for safety if nothing else.

Grabbing Jill's arm, he pointed to her and then Wall. She caught on quickly and nodded.

With a last swift look at the Brit, a last questioning thumbs-up, Jon glided into the cavern.

∞

Wall glared after the little man.

This was absolutely wrong. Mike was Jill's buddy. He couldn't just pass her off and leave mid-dive. They should stick to the plan, sweeping the exterior for other openings. Plan a proper penetration topside, around the table. But Jon's fins were already scraping past the edge.

For a moment, the pair vanished in the void.

Then two spotlights shot through the murk, revealing hazy forms floating inside. Silt stirred as the divers passed, reducing visibility even more.

Jill gurgled beside him, pointing eagerly, but a flashlight blinded him before he could make out what had spiked her interest. When the light moved away, and he'd blinked the residual flash from his retina, he detected a...fluttering.

Mike saw it. Drifting lower, he aimed his beam at a sort of pulsing half-buried in the silt. Wall had never seen anything like it, not in Britain or even in diving documentaries.

Mike drifted closer.

The Pulse seemed to breathe, swell. The full-on dive light revealed only a blacker black, a shadow within shadow. Cautiously, the big man reached out—

The Flutter jumped at him.

The light tumbled, bounced on the floor as the spiraling beam caught a glimpse of a giant shadow zooming toward the opening.

Toward Wall and the girls.

It hit him hard, slamming him backward. Tumbling heels over head, he thrashed to defend himself, though the thing was already gone. His breath rasped in his ear as his vision righted itself.

An eerie wail threaded the water. Realizing he faced the wrong way, Wall turned.

Overweighted, Jill sprawled on the sea floor beneath the hole, just now rising on her elbows. Melanie huddled beside her, seemingly okay. Both were gawking upward. He followed their look.

The manta ray soared overhead, a shadow between them and the surface. The damn thing had a twelve-foot wingspan, gliding majestically without any seeming movement. How the hell it had gotten inside...

Wall lost his thought in a wave of sheer wonder. Of all the ocean creatures he'd seen with his own eyes, this was the most awe-inspiring. He had to shake himself to tear his gaze away and drop down to the women.

Setting his fins in the sand between the two, he extended a hand to each. Jill immediately grabbed his fingers. Melanie did not respond, and when he touched her, she turned to stare blankly. With the blonde hair floating all about, she looked an odd caricature of fear.

He tried the thumbs-up signal to ask if she was all right. She didn't even blink. When Jill's prodding flipper drew no reaction, he grabbed the pink-clad shoulders to bring her mask to mask.

Slowly she focused on him. Slowly she nodded, even offering a tentative thumbs-up. He patted her shoulder in approval.

Checking the air gauges was just habit. Wall already knew it was time to surface.

∞

The sun was setting as the compressor ran full-throttle, pumping air into empty tanks.

So much attention to dive gear. Jill sighed. *So little attention to human needs.*

She'd really love a decent meal. Cooked by hand, with proper quantities of vegetable to accompany the protein. Calmly consumed around the table while they discussed the wreck.

Instead, a plastic tub of pepperpot stew perched on the galley counter, fresh from the microwave. Too spicy for her taste. And a leftover mound of the weird okra dumpling with green stuff to round out the meal.

All this excitement over a stupid wreck. She just didn't get it.

Jon and Wall agreed it had to be recent because wood didn't last long in tropical waters. If the *Sadicor* sank today, there'd be precious little worth finding. She'd seen Jon sell a salvaged porthole for a cool grand, but that had been old brass, British-made at the turn of the century. The last century.

This whole thing felt more like the time they'd found a safe off the coast of New Jersey. After weeks of plotting and two failed attempts to raise it, Jon and Mike actually snagged some sort of underwater explosive. It had worked too well, destroying both the safe and whatever was inside. All the dreaming had come to naught.

She knew this greedy eagerness; she understood the excitement. But for the life of her, Jill couldn't share it. Maybe if they'd found something more than a manta ray...

Wall ducked out of the compressor room, pausing to select a dumpling. "Did you enjoy today?" he asked.

"First dive was fun."

"But not the second?"

She shrugged. "There weren't any cool fish. Did you notice? It was like they got scared off."

Wall reached for a bottled water. "The manta was pretty cool."

"If you like being knocked on your ass."

∞

The sun had set rapidly, as it did near the equator. Dinner was done, such as it was, and the empty takeout containers littered the tiny galley below. Melanie had left Jill to deal with that.

Instead, she sat cross-legged atop the sailboat cabin, beneath an oppressive blanket of stars. The sky seemed just a bit too close here, trying to muffle the world below. She felt exposed, vulnerable. Scooting back from the edge, she found a bit of shadow from the mast blocking the moonlight.

She was still seething.

That stupid manta had scared the crap out of her. And Jill—and Wall. They could deny it all they wanted.

They should all be more understanding, more sympathetic. Mike had actually teased her, as if it were funny. And Wall had done nothing to defend her.

Speak of the devil. Mike stepped out on the deck below, carrying two dive tanks. He didn't see her.

Tomorrow, she'd develop another headache...and to hell with what Jill thought. Better to be bored topside than eaten by mantas. Wall could just go whistle for a partner.

At that thought, two masculine arms slipped about her from behind. Just when she was working up a proper annoyance, the Brit had not only found her, but for once used actions instead of words. Like a real man.

His legs pressed against hers on both sides. How had he gotten so close without her noticing? She relaxed against his chest, deeply appreciating the comfort.

A faint buzzing whirled in her ears. Melanie half-turned toward it, but his hands firmly turned her back, pulling her hard against his body. His fingers slid over to caress her nipple.

Teasing, demanding. One stroke igniting a fire she'd never felt before, with anyone, ever.

"You never touch me in public," she breathed as her head rolled to expose her neck. "I like it."

"Where's my B.C.?" Mike grumbled below.

Worried he would see, Melanie tried to push the hand from her breast. The fingers cupped her insistently as teeth nibbled her earlobe, spreading a pulsing sensation through her belly. "You can't keep your hands off me," she gasped, excitement overwhelming caution.

"I got it," Wall said, stepping out on the deck beside Mike.

Stunned, Melanie whirled.

There was only empty space behind her.

∞

Having helped Jill with cleanup, which amounted to stuffing paper plates in trash bags, Wall climbed the ladder topside. Slightly awkward, clutching three bottled beers.

Melanie had picked at dinner, quiet after the dive. Now she'd locked herself in the cabin, refusing to even talk about it.

He'd met her on the job, consulting at her company. He'd been delighted when she'd offered to help him adjust to life in America. Things probably would have cooled if she hadn't surprised him by joining the dive class. Naturally drawing a lot of male attention, he'd been the source of envy when the bikini-clad blonde stood at his side. He'd enjoyed it, which led to the next logical step of bringing her along.

That manta had startled them all. He certainly didn't hold it against her. Yet she'd accused him of that, clutching a crystal pendant to her chest while kicking him out of the cabin. He wasn't quite sure what he'd done to make her feel that way.

Stepping out onto the teak deck, he shrugged it off. The half-moon and its many star companions sparkled off the sea, providing an ethereal light that simply took his breath away.

Moonlight in the tropics. Beautiful.

"You're sure there's more?" Jon spoke to Mike, who perched atop the cabin. Both accepted a beer.

"That was definitely a passageway," Mike answered. "But it's clogged."

"Can we free it?"

Shrugging, Mike twisted the top of his beer. "Maybe. Won't be easy."

Wall sat on the bench opposite Jon, sipping from his own bottle. "A second level? How big do you think it is?"

"Big." Mike savored the word. "We've yet to search so much as the front cabin."

"Let's try to scope it out before we start salvage," Jon said. "Figure out what all we have to do. It'll still be there when we're ready."

"You take the biscuits when they're passed," Mike answered. "What's to say it won't disappear just as fast as it popped up?"

Wall didn't quite see Mike's logic. "You mean like another storm stirs the bottom? Are storms that common?"

"No," Jon replied. "Never seen so much as a raindrop."

∞

Below, Jill was wiping down the galley when the cabin door opened and Melanie stepped out.

The blonde wore the red sarong, baring her shoulders to show off her new necklace. "Do you think this works? Crystal's supposed to protect you from bad energy. And it is flattering, right?"

Feminine, Jill thought with a pang. She looked very feminine, demanding male attention. She'd get it, too. Sighing at her own petty reaction, Jill smiled. "In the absence of a ruby, you look great."

"A ruby!" Melanie vanished, returning with a tiny travel bag from which she unearthed a choker with a red gemstone. Clasping it about her throat, her fingers dropped to the crystal pendant.

"Rubies are my jewel! Craig gave me this, and you're right! It echoes the red in the dress." Frowning, she added, "Looks silly to wear them both, doesn't it?"

Jill had to agree. "It's really one or the other."

For a moment, she thought Melanie would remove the ruby. Then with a shrug, she tugged the pendant over her head.

"So you're feeling better?" Jill asked after a moment.

"Yes." Stepping into the tiny bath, Melanie turned her head, then swept her long tresses into a coil. As she secured them with a pin, she smiled at Jill. "Shows the neck better. And...a genuine ruby would be more powerful than just a crystal. Wouldn't it?"

Melanie's hair maneuver awed Jill. She knew women could do it, of course, but she somehow imagined it took a lot more work.

"Why are you worried about crystals?"

"I...just..." The woman sighed. "Just a silly daydream. Does this place affect you, too?"

"Sure. It's the tropics. Can you teach me to do that? I've never been able to do stuff with my hair."

"Your mom never taught you?"

Jill shook her head. "Nah. Mom was more into sports and stuff. Not really the type for makeup or fixing her hair. Anyway, she wasn't available most of the time." The confession hung in the air, but the blonde didn't notice. Or didn't care.

Turning her head side to side, Melanie inspected the coif before squeezing back to make room for Jill. For a wild instant, Jill hesitated, then she forced herself to step in before the mirror.

The woman gathered her mass of unruly hair and artfully twisted. "All you need do is shape it to best show your features, then pin it in place."

Jill nodded, though she had no idea what Melanie had done. "I'll have to get some of those. Pins, I mean."

The blonde considered, then slipped away to her cabin. A bare minute later she was back with a hair-clasp to deftly secure her handiwork. "If the coil isn't perfect, so much the better."

Jill stared in the mirror. A poised, sophisticated woman stared back. Catching Melanie's reflection, she smiled.

Instead of returning the gesture, the blonde studied her face. "Is it strange? Being Jon's cousin?"

"Because he's black? Jon's the best guy I know. Want an ale?"

"I hate beer."

Jill could feel Melanie examining facial features, clicking them off one by one. The skin is too brown, the nostrils flare too much. Since elementary school, Jill had endured that same scrutiny from friends and strangers alike. Though by the time she got to college, most people were less observant—or mixed-race parents were more common.

Of course, in elementary school, both her father and her uncle were in the NFL. In college, no one knew who her famous uncle was—she never told them. And her father...well. He'd never really been famous.

"You could be stunning, you know. You have good features."

Jill gawked at her.

"You just need to…to act like you're attractive. People think beauty is all surface stuff, but it's not. If you're confident—if you move like you're beautiful—people sort of take you at your own evaluation. Exude a sexy attitude—just a little. You'll find that men start watching you."

Jill had to clear her throat to speak. "I don't want to be watched."

"Not even by Mike?"

"No!"

"Oh." Melanie inspected her reflection, smoothing a blonde strand behind her ear. "Too bad. His type is perfect to cut your teeth on."

Giving her hair a final pat, she floated gracefully to the ladder and paused. "If not Mike, who did you want to fix your hair for?" She climbed without waiting for an answer.

For myself, Jill muttered through gritted teeth. Whatever Melanie thought, she had no interest in Mike. She'd known him since she was twelve. And anyway, he was the dive shop Casanova. He treated her like a kid sister, which was just fine.

So why did she want to fix her hair?

For an instant, the image of Wall's smile flittered through her mind. She firmly squelched it.

The cooler called to her, and she considered drinking a beer, but Jon had warned about consuming alcohol while diving. Even though, she acknowledged, all the men had grabbed a bottle. Maybe, for once, she should do what she wanted and to hell with Jon's advice.

Unearthing a bottle of warm water instead—Mike refused to share valuable cooler space with mere water—she headed for the ladder.

∞

When Melanie stepped out onto the deck, conversation stopped. Her lips twitched, but she pretended not to notice.

Most men had certain buttons that were easily pushed. Simply show the proper amount of skin in the not-quite-proper setting. Bikinis on a beach blended in with all the other females, but answer the door in a bikini when the guy picked you up, and you got his attention.

On an evening like this, a simple sarong with a bit of cleavage and a split skirt flashing a glimpse of thigh should keep the Brit's attention where it belonged. And if others noticed...well. That was collateral damage.

She nodded at everyone, settling gracefully beside Wall.

"So what's the plan for tomorrow?" the Brit asked as his arm wrapped around her shoulder.

Melanie nestled against him. To her amusement, Mike's eyes lingered on her décolletage, her throat. She'd figured him for the type to love a choker.

But when the muscle man looked up, he was smirking. Giving her the slightest 'tip of the hat' gesture, he then ignored her altogether.

The son of a bitch thought she'd dressed for him.

"We explore," Jon was saying. "There's got to be a way to penetrate farther. We just have to find it."

Jill popped out of the cabin, settling on the deck floor when there wasn't any seat space. With her hair hanging straight—she'd pulled it back down—she looked more like a gangly teen than part of the adult conversation. She even had that rebellious vibe going.

"You can squeeze in here." Melanie scooted closer to Wall, leaving a small gap.

Startled, the brunette shook her head. "I'm not the touchy-feely type."

Amused, Melanie found herself looking up to gauge Mike's reaction, only to find him waiting to meet her eyes.

He held them as he spoke to Jon. "Dynamite. Open that blocked passage right up. Let's don't fart around."

Melanie was becoming far too aware of the muscle man, she decided, as Wall stiffened beside her.

"Explosives?" Wall had a wealth of caution in his tone.

"Don't panic," Mike smirked. "I know how to use them."

Jon replied. "Let's explore a little further before we start blowing things up."

Frowning, Jill studied the big man's face. "You think there's something down there!"

"It's an undiscovered wreck." Mike grinned. "Worth seeing what she's got, don't you think?"

The *Sadicor* was almost forty feet, Melanie sniffed. Its salvage wouldn't amount to more than a pile of junk.

"C'mon, Jon, let me help," Jill turned to her cousin. "You'll need everyone exploring. We've got enough reels."

Melanie felt Wall's chest swelling with protest.

Jon got there first. "For the tenth time, you're a novice, Jill. I know it doesn't seem like much, but entering an underwater structure is a whole level of magnitude more dangerous."

"We're just checking out that first cabin tomorrow." Mike grinned. "With the Brit here, the cabin's gonna be pretty crowded anyway. You and the princess can pitch in by feeding us."

It was time, the thought flashed through Melanie's mind, to wipe that smirk off the muscle man's face. "So we feed you and apply iodine to your sure-to-be-many scratches. What do we get for that?" she asked. At his confusion, she added, "What's our share?"

She had, indeed, wiped the smirk off his face. "Your share?!" he spluttered.

"I'm giving up ten days' vacation for this. If there's a treasure chest down there, I want my share."

"Jon will take care of us." Melanie wasn't sure if Jill was trying to play peacemaker or defending her cousin. "Jon and Mike always do."

"You mean they'll haul in a ton of cash and offer us free dive gear."

Wall touched her arm placatingly. "It's doubtful she'll yield anything of value. Anyway, plenty of time to figure that out."

"There's nothing to figure out." Mike spat. "I'm not slaving away so the blonde here can wear real rubies."

Her hand covered the gem protectively. "This is real," she snarled, feeling genuine fury wash over her. "I bet legally we're entitled to something. You have to pay us our worth."

"Twenty dollars. Same as any whore."

Her fingers curled into claws as Jon leaned in between them. "It's a valid point, Mike. Wall can be a big help, if he's willing to enter the wreck. And Jill and Melanie can do other things. There's a lot to be done."

"Minimum wage stuff." Then Mike noticed Jill's expression and softened. "Except for you, mermaid. You get a percent or two."

"If Wall goes into the wreck, that's worth...ten percent," Jon suggested. "Don't you think?"

"No way in..."

"Greed is the wrong vibration for what we're doing," Jon insisted. "We don't need that. It's bad karma not to be fair."

Mike rolled his eyes. "And the bi—the blonde?"

"Let's say five percent now for both women." Jon smiled at them all.

From nowhere, angry words welled up in her throat, eager to burst free. Melanie firmly pressed her lips together, clutching the ruby at her throat. What the hell was the matter with her?

Forcing herself to relax, she realized the others held their breath, worrying over her reaction. Wall's hand was stroking her shoulder, while muscle man Mike's eyes gleamed dangerously.

It was all she could do not to laugh.

∞

He was somewhere dark and distant, with only echoes of sounds. Echoes of fear. His hands lifted to his face, and he saw they were shackled.

"No!" Wall cried, reaching out, but his fingers closed on empty air. Something precious had been taken from him.

A booming laugh added to the confusion. "You double your gift, senora. Two for the price of one."

Melanie joined the laughter, leaning back against a bearded man. The ruby sparkled on her throat, dangling above a daring neckline of old lace.

The man's arms enclosed her possessively.

"You can't keep your hands off me," she breathed.

A whip cracked, splitting Wall's cheek. In a haze of pain, he watched a small gray cloth fall away. It was precious, that cloth. He must get it back. All depended on his getting it back.

But the gray vanished in a black void.

∞

"No!" Wall sat up, panting.

He knew he was safe, knew he was in bed, but his body took a moment to catch up with his mind.

Moonlight painted the stern portholes, the tiny curtains rippling in the night breeze. Dancing across the bed, the pale beam revealed Melanie sleeping beside him. The curtain shadow created a pattern on her bare throat, echoing the old lace in his dream.

His cheek stung.

Stumbling out of bed, he grabbed his discarded shorts, donning them before easing out of the cabin door.

It took a minute to find the galley light switch, and the single bulb seemed inadequate with all the other lights off.

Aspirin, he thought. Or whatever substitute was offered. Opening a likely cabinet, he only found herbal tea bags.

He gave up. In four steps, he bumped into the dining booth and sat down hard.

"Clumsy, Trevor."

He heard his father's voice. No one had called him Trevor since he'd arrived in America. He doubted anyone this side of the pond even knew his proper name.

Noticing the red shorts he wore reminded him of his mother. Five daughters to indulge her desire to wardrobe shop, and she chose to buy for him. Ignoring his preference for comfortable clothes, unable to grasp that he couldn't wear business suits in his technology career, she insisted on bestowing ridiculously expensive attire from Harrods.

Early on, her choices made him stand out.

He'd explained this, but she simply agreed. "It's what people wear when they can afford to, dear."

With his father's constant correction of his tendency to slouch and her ever more startling wardrobe notions, he'd felt a sort of amused exasperation; his parents were so concerned with appearance they never saw the man he'd become.

Wall had never let his exasperation show until four months ago.

It was just after Padstow. He'd left the dive trip the next day, showing up at the family home before he'd even considered. His mind knew he'd done everything correct; that no one could have changed the outcome.

But some part of him ached with guilt.

His mother gently prodded him; his rebuff was gentler still. She'd later knocked on his bedroom door, clutching her maternal answer to all of life's pain. This particular version being red shorts, with the hundred pound price tag still attached.

He'd kissed her cheek and booked a flight to the States that evening.

"Wall?"

His eyes jerked toward his closed cabin door, even as he realized the voice was not Melanie's.

Jill emerged from the dark, clutching an old blanket about her shoulders. With the threadbare cover and tousled curls, she appeared all of twelve years old. "You all right?" She frowned.

The last thing he wanted was a two a.m. conversation, but apparently his demeanor didn't give her the hint. Of course, Jill was impervious to hints.

She stepped closer, peering into his face. "You cut your cheek."

"I know. It's nothing."

"It's the tropics," she replied. "Jon says you've got to take care of cuts in the tropics." She suddenly stooped, sliding a storage bin out from beneath his feet. Startled, he watched her unearth a first aid kit and set it on the table before him.

"Any aspirin in there?"

Plucking a bottle of Betadine and a cotton ball from the contents, she peered inside and produced a packet of Tylenol.

He tried to decipher the expiration date and failed. The girl misinterpreted his look.

"We don't have iodine," she said.

It took him a moment to recall Melanie's reference to applying iodine to the men's injuries.

The blanket restricted Jill's arm movement, so she adjusted it, freeing her arms by tucking it sarong fashion around her. Tramping off to the galley, Jill squirted Betadine into a cup and diluted it with water.

Setting the pills aside, he clamped his lips firmly shut because he wanted to be alone; because he was impatient with her intrusion. And because, as he watched her bare shoulders—her delicate neck and flawless skin—desire rose within him.

Raw, physical need. For a girl whose temper reminded him of a twelve-year-old. What the hell was the matter with him?

Then Jill was before him, leaning close to dab his cheek with cotton. Instinctively, he jerked away.

She huffed and gave him a look. Moving closer, she allowed no room to retreat.

Despite himself, he grinned. "Thought you weren't the touchy feely type."

"It's different when you need help." Her nose wrinkled up in a vaguely familiar quirk. "Touching for a purpose."

She wasn't casting aspersions on Melanie, just quaintly defending herself. A respectable answer. Not quite a twelve-year-old after all.

Logic and lust around the same woman. Lord, he must be getting old.

Swabbing at his cut while clicking her tongue, he was reminded of his mother all over again.

"How did you do this?" she demanded.

"Shaving."

She never took her eyes from his wound. "You shave at night?"

"Upon occasion."

As he saw her take this in and ponder it, Wall had to suppress his smile. He never knew what most women were thinking, but Jill's thoughts marched across her face one after the other.

Red surged in her cheeks when she finally remembered Melanie in his bed. Christ, he hadn't meant to upset her.

"Jill..."

He suspected that she stooped as much to hide her embarrassment as to replace the first aid kit.

Unfortunately, she had to kneel at his feet to do so—practically between his knees. With her breasts pressing against the blanket, threatening to spill over the thin cloth, she caught him completely off guard. Obviously, she had no idea the temptation she offered.

When she looked up, he felt a tender amusement—familiar somehow. *Déjà vu*, he thought, and wondered where the hell that came from.

Jill stood, bare feet padding back to the galley. Seeing her toes somehow invested the moment with a startling intimacy.

"Melanie gonna dive tomorrow?" she called over her shoulder.

He had to clear his throat to speak. "Let's leave that to her."

Rinsing the cup, Jill shut off the tap. "But she demanded her share of the salvage. Surely she's planning to help out."

In the heat of his dream, Wall had forgotten that. His beautiful girlfriend had revealed a mercenary streak, and now Jon's kid cousin displayed some very adult curves. An unsettling night all the way around.

"She'll help," he heard himself say.

"Jon and Mike are good people. If they do find treasure, they wouldn't keep it all to themselves."

Wall sighed. Curves or not, Jill was still so damned naive. "I know that. So does Melanie, really. But discussing these things now sets the expectation. There's no surprise. No disappointment."

The brunette's lips trembled. She had more she wanted to say. He sought to cut her off.

"It's time we went to bed, mermaid." Wall stood up, deliberately stretched.

She gazed up at him—her eyes suddenly reflecting some new emotion. Or it may have been the poor lighting.

With a quick nod, he retreated to the safety of his cabin.

Raising the Dead

THE CARIBBEAN SUN burned mercilessly this morning.

Jill lounged on the cockpit bench, cradling a mug of coffee. They had diving to do today; treasure to find. The idea that she'd get a piece of it—even if it was just old beer bottles—made this a very interesting day.

Feet scraped on the ladder. She turned to see Melanie climb out on deck.

"Good morning," Jill said.

The woman sat down, rubbing her temples. Somehow, she looked more like the nervous blonde from dive class than the femme fatal from yesterday.

"You feel all right?"

The blonde nodded, which surprised her. She was half expecting another headache to prevent her dive. "Just didn't sleep well."

"Really? I'm sleeping like a baby here. A 'hardly awake when my head hits the pillow' sort of sleep." She watched Melanie close her eyes and breathe.

Jill was just turning back to her own thoughts when the woman spoke. "Are you dreaming down here?"

"No more than usual."

"Vivid dreams though? More vivid than back home...bright color. Strange ..." Melanie trailed off.

"You mean nightmares of diving?"

The blonde shook her head. "No. I saw a man..."

"Ladies," Mike popped through the doorway. "Let's go diving."

∞

Mike hauled two plastic trashcans up the ladder and then down onto the platform.

They were heavy in the heat, and by the time he was done, sweat trickled into his eyes. But that meant it glistened on his chest as well, which was a turn on for certain women.

Like the blonde.

"Trashcan Divers." Melanie smiled, as if just realizing the term referred to stuffing gear into large plastic trash baskets. B.C.s and regulators, wetsuits and fins, all fit within and were easily carried with the large handles provided.

"Jersey term." Jill grinned.

"Delaware term," Mike corrected her. "Nothing good ever came out of Jersey."

Jon, whose grandfather was born in that state, gave him a passing punch in the shoulder. "Wall, you take the girls and explore every inch of the second reef," he said. "There's got to be a way in."

"That's worth a good fifty cents." Mike plucked the side mount for his tanks, watching Jon's eyes roll. "Each."

"Would you leave off? Finding a way into that part of the wreck would help. And any time they spend exploring the outside is time we can spend on the inside. You can't argue with that."

Mike could easily argue with that. He had argued it late last night. This was a waste of time because two novices and a British idiot could only play at exploring. He'd need to do it all himself later.

Jon always hesitated about making decisions, especially when people's feelings were involved. It was the single thing that drove Mike crazy.

They'd met in fifth grade, when Mike had been passed from his mom to his grandmother. Supposedly his mom had found a new job, but he'd known even then she was an alcoholic. She'd hit you with a two-by-four if she thought you touched drugs, but whiskey, she oft explained, was legal. Moving away from her to Delaware had been a godsend.

Often people told him how wholesome the Midwest was—supposedly America's heartland. All he remembered was a filthy farmhouse with windows rattling at the shrill rants of a drunken woman.

Now Jon was earnestly instructing Wall. "The broken side—where she split in half—must have openings. Use your dive knife to poke around."

Great, Mike thought. *Three idiots chipping away at the reef. Three hours of bottom time totally wasted.*

∞

The water felt like silk this morning.

Warm, sparkling, and unbelievably calm. Wall could actually see all the way to the little island nearby. It tempted him to swim over and explore the shoreline.

Instead he prodded at coral while keeping a wary eye on the novices.

He'd never liked diving in threesomes, and doing it with novices just asked for trouble. Jill tended to rush ahead without checking with them while Melanie lagged behind. Neither thought to watch him, let alone each other.

They'd settled in the gap area between the two reefs, obedient to Jon's suggestion. The coral grew thick, however, showing no sign of an opening, which didn't make sense if this was truly a ship broken in half.

Tinged in gray this morning, the reef felt less inviting. He prodded a few holes expecting lobsters or other sea life but found nothing.

No living creatures at all.

Out of the corner of his eye—Wall floated in a spot where he could keep both women in peripheral view—he saw Jill paddle a few feet along without so much as a signal. The girl had tried to signal Melanie earlier, but the blonde was too nervous to see her. Consequently, Jill didn't bother now.

Extending his flipper, he tried to nudge her. She was just out of reach.

A sharp tapping filled his ears. A signal from Jon or Mike.

Jill looked around, puzzled; Melanie seemed scared.

Wall floated higher, seeking a vantage point, but all he saw was barren reef. While the tapping was clear, the noise hinted at no direction. Sound traveled faster underwater, and human ears could easily be confused.

Jill swam up beside him, but Melanie remained. They had to drop to get her attention before checking out the signal.

Swimming the length of one reef, they saw no sign of the men. They turned and swam in the other direction.

At the very end, Wall spied movement, and he led the others down toward the sea floor near the start of the coral. With a sweeping check of the two novices, he looked up.

It was an odd shape—more human than fish—tilted oddly, narrow end at the sprit, swelling in the middle, and tapering again where it attached to the point the sand and wreck touched. Unmoving.

Wall's belly clenched as if a fist grabbed his middle.

He jumped when Jill swam past, losing sight of the thing for an instant. When he looked back, he saw Mike and Jon plying crowbars to coral.

The apparition was gone.

∞

Jill frowned. The entrance hole had shrunk.

The two remaining anemones had moved down, blocking the narrow entrance. They were animals, she recalled. They could travel, but slowly. And shouldn't they have moved away?

Mike was digging a crowbar beneath one, prying. For an instant, the giant creature quivered, tentacles waving in protest. Larger, more vibrant than its companion, the anemone was the reigning king of the reef.

And Mike was determined to dethrone it.

Jill found her fists clenching, rooting for the anemone. Inevitably, the giant lost. The disc of tentacles popped free and floated away in the current.

And somehow the reef ceased to be. The last anemone fell away, as if it couldn't go on alone, and the shape beneath was sleek and smooth and symmetrical.

A ship's bow, complete with a severed spar jutting out to point the way. A broken bowsprit.

Jill swam past Wall—strangely frozen in place—to grab the rough coral edge near Mike as he shone his light into the now larger opening, revealing a flattened, level floor beneath the silt.

It really is a ship.

A second beam flashed. Jon was already inside, exploring a far corner. Mike bumped her, grinning into her mask. Jill couldn't see the grin of course, but well knew that crinkling at the corner of his eyes.

Then he shot over the lip through the hole.

For a moment, nothing. Wall and Melanie joined her, one on either side. When the Brit's fingers formed the 'okay' sign, she rolled her eyes with her answering signal.

And then two dive lights flashed the interior. She caught a glimpse of flipper, a bare leg, and a knee-high bulge. For an instant she ducked, half-expecting another manta ray. Rather than fly, the lump haltingly slid a little closer and stopped.

Mike was pushing it, she realized.

A beam shifted, revealing the lump's metal edges and boxy structure. Padlock.

Dear God. It was straight out of Pirates of the Caribbean. They'd actually found a treasure chest.

Melanie gurgled—at least Jill thought she did. Glancing at the woman, she saw a weird flickering shadow surrounding them both.

The manta ray swooped past, circled, and glided straight at them.

As it drew near its wings stretched wide, hovering like a pterodactyl pouncing on its prey. Directly behind Wall's back.

When Wall gave her a look, she jerked her head at it. The Brit turned and froze.

Jill tried to recall anything about rays. She knew there were various types; she knew a stingray had killed someone famous. Maybe this wreck was its lair, and it disliked their intrusion.

It didn't look as if it wanted to eat them.

Bubbles erupted beside her. Jill guessed Melanie had just seen the creature.

Wall floated toward it as if to defend them. Jill doubted they needed defense, but the gesture impressed her.

Then his gloved hand reached out, and he touched the thing. The dark creature turned puppy dog before her eyes, enjoying the attention, actually pushing its head into Wall's palm.

The ray moved nearer to Melanie, as if it wanted her to pet it as well. The blonde jerked back fearfully. The thing seemed annoyed.

Jill was reaching out when the manta vanished in a whirl of bubbles.

In the same instant, Melanie clutched her regulator, her overweighted body dropping as soon as she let go of the coral.

Wall swooped down to snatch her console.

Oh Lord. She's out of air.

Checking her own console, Jill still had half a tank. She fished around for her spare regulator, sank to the bottom and offered it.

Flailing wildly, the panicked woman didn't see her.

Jill stepped closer—Wall shoved her out of the way.

He yanked Melanie's mouthpiece free, thrusting his own spare between her teeth.

Her flailing slowed as she sucked deep.

She then erupted in frantic thrashing, clawing Wall's own mouth piece off his face and losing it in her frenzy.

The Brit retrieved it, firmly shoving it in Melanie's mouth. She clutched the piece with both hands, calming as oxygen filled her lungs.

The man then snagged his octopus rig and tried it. Jill could tell from his reaction there was no air.

As she floundered around for her spare—she'd lost it when he pushed her back—Wall hooked the blonde's B.C. to his. Looking at Jill, he jerked his thumb upward. She'd barely nodded when he rose up, taking Melanie topside.

Astonished at his own lack of air, Jill followed.

On the way up, he snagged Melanie's useless regulator floating between them and set it in his mouth. Apparently, this time oxygen flowed.

They burst through the surface, and Jill ripped out her regulator. "Geez! You guys okay?"

She watched him spin Melanie around, stroking her face. The woman still clutched his regulator as if her life depended on it.

"Melanie." He shook her slightly, then caressed her cheek. "You're safe, honey."

Jill swam closer. "Melanie?"

The green eyes blinked; narrowed. A spark of fury flared within them, so startling in its intensity that Jill physically recoiled.

"Let's get you out of the water." Wall ushered them toward the *Sadicor.*

∞

Melanie huddled miserably on the dive platform.

Wall had removed her gear and peeled the wetsuit from her quaking limbs. He'd also tried to get her inside. Shock, he'd said, offering hot tea and a "lie down."

She wanted nothing more than to be alone.

Truth was, Melanie didn't feel fear now. She felt stupid, exposed for a fool. She felt furious at herself; at her reaction. Furious that it had to be her to run out of air.

All this time, Jill thought herself better than everyone else, and it turned out she was right. It wasn't fair. It wasn't fair that the guys liked that—Mike, Jon. Even Wall.

It wasn't fair that she looked such a fool when she could have died.

Voices drifted through the sailboat's open windows.

"Why did you stop me?" Jill's tone held no sympathy whatsoever. "I had air all ready for her!"

"She was panicking, Jill."

"Well if I'd given her air, she'd have been fine."

"She'd have clawed your face off."

At least that stupid bitch hadn't been the one to help her.

"I could make her some coffee..."

"No," Wall's low rumble barely reached her ears. "Leave her alone for now." The voice trailed off as they moved away.

They sounded awfully cozy together.

"Stupid bitch," Melanie mumbled aloud. "Just wait till you're in trouble, Jill. Just you wait."

Behind her, between her shoulder blades, she felt the tiniest prickling of—something. It hummed with her anger, stiffening her spine.

Chilling her core.

She wanted to turn around, but her body froze in place. Breathing deeply, she forced her head to slowly pivot...

Mike and Jon burst through the surface. "*Whooo hooo!*" Mike shouted to the sky and saw her. "*Whoo hoo, princess!*"

Melanie completed her turn. The platform behind her was empty.

∞

"How did you do that?"

Plucking a piece of chicken from the plastic tub, Wall glanced up at the brunette.

"You breathed out of a dead regulator. Melanie had no air."

American dive training. "And Jon says he teaches you guys. Compressed air, Jill."

Her expression remained blank.

He sighed. "What happens as we ascend?"

"It expands...so the air grew in her tank!"

"Something like that. Enough for a few breaths."

Taking a big bite of chicken, he realized he was starving. Diving did that. In fact, many things tasted fantastic on a dive boat that once on land, he wouldn't dream of eating. Cold fried chicken had to be one of them.

"How should I have helped Melanie?" Jill persisted. "If you weren't there, I mean."

His amusement faded. "Best thing would be attracting Jon or Mike's attention. Bang on your tank. If no one else is there...I suppose you wait until she's calmer. Not flailing so wildly."

"Wouldn't she be dead?"

"No—not immediately. Probably your best chance."

Jill didn't understand. "But if she stops flailing, doesn't that mean she's dying?"

Wall closed his eyes. This was a particularly difficult area for him. "Don't risk your life for property; don't risk it for a life that can't be saved."

"But she could be saved. All she needed was air."

"Someone panicking like that; someone bigger than you, while you're in such a vulnerable environment...no. She'd have knocked your regulator out, clawed your face;

torn off your mask. Once unconscious, you had a chance to save her. It's not considered sensible for you to drown as well."

"Considered sensible?"

"I saw a boy drown in Padstow." He hadn't meant to talk about it. The words just popped out of his throat. "Caught in a rip tide. He swept by me, close enough I could see his face. Lifeguards ordered me to stay clear. They said I'd have been caught as well if I tried to help. Nothing I could do."

He was looking at his hands. Nervous, he realized, of looking at her. He didn't want to see her reaction. Wall could feel her, though, motionless beside him. And then her hand lifted, as if to touch him.

Jill, being touchy feely. She pitied him.

So much for his appetite. Tossing the chicken aside, he left.

∞

Emerging from his cabin, Wall turned to find an armload of rubber and metal hooks thrust in his face.

"Here." Mike shoved again when he didn't accept them. "Your afternoon work, partner." Hoisting a tank over his shoulder, the muscle man clambered up the stairs.

Wall gazed down at the rusted hardware, a cut from any piece of which would scream tetanus shot. Dragging the thing with him, he awkwardly climbed to the deck.

"You've used a lift bag before?" Jon prodded as Wall freed a hook from the doorway.

"Of course he has," Jill snorted, wiggling into her wet suit. "Quit the mother hen stuff! We can lift the chest."

Lift the chest? He and Jill—a novice diver who couldn't control her own weight—let alone that of something else?

Doubt must have shown on his face.

"If you want your share of the salvage," Mike told him, "do your fucking share of work."

"We've got this," Jill shot back.

Ahhh. Her way of supporting him. And despite his brain urging otherwise, he couldn't very well contradict her.

Instead Wall gazed down at the rubber armload and tried to recall anything he'd read on lift bags.

∞

Huddled in her cabin, Melanie clutched the crystal pendant to her chest, which was damned silly. It was supposed to protect her from evil spirits—not heartbreak.

She hurled it across the room and winced when it struck the door. She dreaded the running footsteps—he hadn't been easy to kick out the first time. When Wall didn't come running back, her anger evaporated.

From the open window—porthole, she corrected herself—she heard him talking to Jill after the others had submerged. "I don't know anything about lift bags."

"Easy," Jill said, huffing between syllables. "Just hook whatever you're lifting and use your air to inflate it."

Melanie knew that huffing sound well. The brunette was tugging her gear on. They must be nearly ready to dive.

"Oh, shit—Wall! Your octopus rig broke. You don't have an extra mouthpiece."

Wall chuckled. "I'll manage."

His thread of amusement drove Melanie off the bed, out the door, and up the ladder.

She practically leapt out onto the deck.

"Melanie! You coming after all?" Reaching for her B.C., Jill eyed her doubtfully.

Melanie shook her head.

"How do you feel?" Wall asked. No endearment this time.

"I—I'm okay."

She perched on a cockpit bench, surveying from on high as they donned B.C.s and buckled weight belts.

A memory from class rose in her mind: when she'd put her weight belt on first, Wall had admonished her embarrassingly. The weights must go on last. In an emergency, when you couldn't work your gear to inflate, the last resort was dropping your weight belt to reach the surface. Putting it on last meant it would come off, not snag in your B.C.

The splash brought her back to the present. Wall and Jill floated in the sea, swishing spit around their masks and arguing about her entering the wreck.

They look like a happy couple, she thought with a tiny stab.

Jill noticed her watching. "We're lifting the treasure chest, you know."

"Likely filled with someone's clothes," Wall told her. "Ruined sludge now."

Jill rolled her eyes.

"Wall is right," Melanie murmured. Not because she believed it, but to needle Jill.

Jill merely grinned. "We'll see. Ready to salvage?"

He returned a serious look. "Stay by the opening, okay? When I go in, you stay right where I can see you at all times."

"Oh, for the love of—"

"Okay?" He cut her off ruthlessly.

Jill finally nodded.

Chomping down on mouthpieces, their eyes locked. Wall gave the brunette a look; she gave him one back. He spit out his regulator to laugh aloud.

Jill's eyes twinkled merrily in response, and together, their heads popped under the sea.

Melanie stared at the ripples left behind. She hadn't come up here, she acknowledged, to see them off. She hadn't come to let Wall know she was okay. Spurred by their shared laughter, she'd felt jealous and miserable.

And they'd laughed again and left her all alone.

∞

Wall peered into the wreck.

His light played along the top and then the bottom, revealing little. Floating debris and thick silt on the floor. He traced the beam up a white string dangling from the ceiling, a ghostly cobweb in a corner, finding nothing more.

In truth, the interior looked more like a cave than a cabin.

Snatching a glance at Jill, he pulled himself over the edge and through. The void engulfed him, blanketing him alone with his own raspy breath.

His first wreck penetration.

A ray of light danced beneath him. Jill's, he realized.

Turning, he saw her clinging to the splintered edge of the hole, flashlight tilted straight down to spotlight the chest. He'd swum right over it.

It squatted just beneath the opening, as tall as his knee, more than half a meter wide. In the torch beam it appeared wooden, though that seemed unlikely. No coral covering had protected it.

Then his light struck the dangling padlock guarding the contents, and the explorer in him rubbed his hands in glee.

Now to get it through the hole.

∞

Jill watched, offering suggestions through her regulator as the Brit worked. He never heeded her—and she realized there was a good chance he hadn't heard a thing. Oh, well.

The treasure chest gleamed beneath her dive light as Wall shoved it round sideways, in preparation to get it out. When she caught sight of the padlock, excitement surged through her stomach.

This was why Jon and Mike loved wreck diving. The chance—the slightest chance—of finding treasure. And this trunk had to be valuable. Otherwise, why the lock? They'd have to celebrate tonight, whatever lay inside.

And to think she'd get a share. Maybe enough to pay off her car.

Wall strained to lift one end up onto the hole edge. Jill reached in to grasp a handle, but he waved her off impatiently.

Then the chest itself plugged the opening.

It slid an inch through, grating harshly against the coral edge. The scraping hurt her ears.

The side handle wiggled in her face. Grabbing it, she braced her legs on either side of the hole and pulled.

The thing remained stuck.

Putting her back into it, Jill heaved with all her might.

Slowly, very slowly, the sunken wreck gave up its prize.

She felt the rough scrape, the reluctant shudder. When most of the chest emerged, it suddenly shifted, tilting down. Losing her balance, she sank ass first into the sea floor.

Crack! A bit of coral snapped, and a dead anemone fell away. Jill scooted back awkwardly as the trunk fell, hitting the bottom in a blast of sand.

Wall popped his head out of the wreck, reminding her of a silly cartoon. Then their eyes met, and she knew he shared her feelings. They'd just plucked a treasure from a shipwreck.

Maybe treasure enough for a new convertible.

Wall drifted over, making a show of checking his air gauge before sticking it in her faceplate, prodding her to do the same.

The British, she could hear Mike's snide murmur, *are way too much into rules.*

Fishing her console from behind, Jill was pleased to see she still had over a half tank of air.

∞

Unhooking the lift bag from his belt, Wall examined the damn thing again. Mike's contraption consisted of tired rubber and rusty hooks, and he didn't want to injure himself. Why Jon and Mike—owners of a good dive shop—didn't buy proper lift bags, he'd never understand.

This, he'd been told, was a two-hundred pounder, which meant it could lift two hundred pounds of weight. If the chest was too heavy for that, then they'd all retire on the contents.

Six hooks total dangled from the opening, set evenly around what was basically the lip of a rubber balloon. Placing the first hook was easy—he snagged a side handle—but the rubber wouldn't stretch far enough to place a matching hook on the other side. He finally opted to latch three on the single grip—hooking the first, skipping the second, so that the three hooks were evenly balanced around the bag opening.

Truth was, he'd never used a lift bag. All his dives had been to sightsee—he'd never needed to send stuff to the surface.

Satisfied, Wall next grabbed his octopus regulator. Mike had checked it earlier and found nothing wrong. He wedged it between hooks and rubber so it could fill the balloon.

No bubbles. No air flow at all. Mike had missed something.

So Wall took a deep breath and used his own mouth-piece.

Jill swam nearer, eagerly watching. To his amusement, she thrust her spare regulator in beside his. Well, she had the air to contribute, and with the trunk seeming so heavy, it could well take a full balloon.

Exactly how much would fill it he had no idea.

Bubbles erupted around him. Startled, he saw Jill's wide eyes framed in her mask, fixated on him. No—fixated on something past his right shoulder. He thought fleetingly of Jon and Mike, but her reaction belied that.

Nervously, he turned.

The manta hovered inches from his faceplate.

Wall jerked backward, hastily slamming his mouth-piece back between his teeth. Breathing, gasping, he stared.

The creature didn't stir. Black eyes gazed unblinkingly, the solid pupil making it impossible to tell if the creature watched him.

Slowly he lifted his free hand.

The ray scooted into his palm like a dog seeking affection. Wall scratched its ear—or where an ear ought to be. The ray liked it.

Jill stepped closer. It was only that—seeing her spare regulator tucked back in place and an odd shadow flickering around her that made Wall turn back to the lift bag.

The balloon soared upward, gathering speed as it flew. Of course—the air would increase in volume, driving it faster. For an instant he worried he'd done the thing wrong.

Bump. The manta actually nudged him, demanding attention. Apparently, Jill's alone wasn't enough.

He complied.

∞

Melanie lay on her belly, warming her back and paging through a silly book Jill had lent her. She'd already finished her magazines and had nothing else to read. Somehow, she'd expected to be busier on a tropical vacation.

Jon had forbidden bringing smart phones, saying there was no reception, and they'd easily get damaged. For the umpteenth time, she wondered why the hell she hadn't tried it anyway...

The water exploded in gray rubber.

For an instant, she thought a whale had breached. She leapt to the cabin doorway, poised to duck inside.

The thing hissed, bubbles boiling the sea around it. The hiss rose to a high-pitched squeak. The bulge flattened, and the whole mass subsided back under the waves.

She clung to the door frame handles, anxiously watching the ocean. But whatever it was, the thing had gone.

∞

Wary, Jill retreated a few feet. Something about the manta's sudden demand for attention just felt so odd.

And in retreating, she saw shadows whirling around her. The chest. It must be on the surface by now. She looked up.

Fifty feet above, the dangling box seemed trapped in gray and bubbles. Slowly, it broke free.

And then it floated downward. Straight down, gathering speed. Aiming for their heads.

Water slows motion, Jill told herself even as she kicked backward.

The damned thing wasn't tumbling off a cliff. But that chest was heavy, and—dear God—would drop on Wall's head.

She launched herself at the Brit, knocking him toward the wreck. She felt a weight scrape the back of her calf just before it struck bottom.

A blast of sand engulfed them. Jill couldn't move her leg.

Through the whirling dust, Wall appeared, faceplate to faceplate. She nodded to let him know she was okay, frowning when she saw his shaking arm.

Only it wasn't him. She was trembling so hard her mask shook. Hopefully he wouldn't notice.

The manta, she realized, had vanished.

Jill tried to stand, but her leg wouldn't move. Turning, she saw her fin trapped beneath the chest, and a dark thread rose from her calf.

Blood. She was bleeding.

Oddly, Jill felt nothing. She'd never have known she was cut if she hadn't seen the blood in the water.

Blood in the water. Sharks.

Yanking with all her might, Jill couldn't free herself. She clawed at her foot, struggling to slip out of the fin. Jon could damn well retrieve it for her later.

Her breathing loud in her ears, she gasped when Wall leaned in to check her face. His eyes calmly inquired.

She angrily pointed at the problem before scanning the sea for great whites.

The Brit freed her fin.

It was all she could do to ascend at a safe speed.

Pandora's Box

"I know all about the barbecue," Melanie informed him over her shoulder. "Mike told me."

She lay on her stomach in the red silk bathrobe Wall had given her. Sneaking a glance, she saw his expression—confused, a little hurt—as his head poked out from the shirt he'd just donned. She kept her head down, pretending to read her book in the face of his frowns.

He couldn't believe she'd refused to explore the island with him. And she couldn't care less.

Earlier, when the man had surfaced, he'd shouted for Melanie to find the first aid kit while he fussed over Jill; he'd practically carried her up the ladder. Even the brunette had told him it was just a scratch.

And when he'd finished treating the injury, damned if the two hadn't taken another lift bag and dove back down to get the chest. Leaving Melanie all alone again, still demanding to know what happened.

Now his hand caressed her, but it was too late.

"Wouldn't you like to get off this boat?" he asked softly. Cajoling. "Come to the beach with me."

Way too late. "Take Jill," she spat out. "You spent all day with her. Why stop now?"

She felt him tense. The caress died.

Suddenly Melanie wanted to reach out to him and apologize. She had no idea why she was so angry, but he really didn't deserve it. Marking her passage in the book, she looked round.

Just in time to watch the door click shut. He was gone.

When she glanced down at her book, she shivered.

Her finger pointed to the passage, "Strife beset the doomed crew."

∞

Hands on the ladder, Wall hesitated.

He'd seen Melanie's face, her unhappiness at being left alone. He'd tried to make it up to her. What more could he do? Mark it lesson learned, and try not to count the remaining days.

Emerging into sunlight, the scent of some exotic flower caught his attention. They'd moved the *Sadicor* near the island, and its spiced breeze urged him to step on solid land. Explore a little Caribbean above sea level.

"You have to swim for it." Mike intruded on his mood. The muscle man squatted by the salvaged chest, idly toying with a screwdriver. "Jon used the inflatable to ferry Jill over."

Wall nodded. "Thought we were leaving the chest for later. Letting it drain."

Mike met his look. "I'm guarding it. Temptation can do strange things to people."

Resentment flared, a surprisingly strong wave of it. Wall had to master the urge to snipe back. Yanking his fresh shirt off, he tossed it on the seat before stepping onto the rail.

Mike smirked in triumph. "Remind Jon I need the bastard boat to set up the barbecue."

Wall dove in and struck out for the beach.

∞

Jon loved Sadicor Isle.

It consisted of a single giant rock and a lagoon. The rock housed two caves—one upper, one lower—the latter only reachable underwater. Beyond a few lizards and tropical shrubbery, there was little else, which was why the place remained uninhabited.

Having discovered the island when Jon was eight years old, Ray Sadicor had returned occasionally only because Jon begged. It had been named anew every trip, from 'Treasure Island' to 'Pirate Hideaway,' but nothing had stuck until Jill used the Sadicor label. The nearby coral reef made it an interesting day trip, but many more spectacular dives dotted the map.

To Jon, however, there was magic in secret caves and deserted beaches.

As a kid battling buccaneers or exploring underwater caverns when he was supposed to be scrubbing the deck, this was a private Disneyland. Treasure washed up in the form of empty crates and bottles. Geckos changed color, and the sideways-tilting palm tree must surely grow coconuts someday. Neither his dad nor family had shared his enthusiasm.

But Mike had.

At the age of twelve, with a famous athlete for a father, Jon had suffered in school. He was small by any standard and bullied unmercifully. Taunts about his dead mother drew the most reaction from him, so naturally these became the weapon of choice—until Mike Burke arrived. Back then he wasn't any bigger than Jon, but something about him kept the bullies away. One day he caught two boys shoving Jon on the playground and literally knocked their heads together. One lost a tooth.

Mike was suspended three days. On the fourth, he shook hands with Jon, and no one ever bothered either one again. From that day on, Mike followed where Jon led, scowling threats at anyone who stood in their way.

Jon discovered an unexpected business savvy in himself, which helped launch the Crusty Porthole, their dive shop.

Mike's strengths proved more mechanical. He could fix any car or construct a functioning dive compressor from scrap metal. The man liked using his hands to build solutions to problems, even if the problems only existed in his own view. He jury-rigged his gear for wreck diving, set special exercises to sculpt his triceps, and kept the sailboat *Sadicor* in prime functioning shape.

The big man once told him, in a rare introspective moment, that Jon's honor and his belief in Mike drew an answering loyalty. Unlike Mike's own mother, Jon saw the best in him.

Jon valued Mike's purity. Mike was Mike—no hidden agendas and no ulterior motives. If he wanted something, he told you. If he didn't like your words, he said so. And he was fiercely loyal to his friends. With so many in the world who wanted to get close to Jon because of his father, Mike preferred him.

Now, as Jon led Jill up the rocky path to the upper cave, he spotted the muscle man across the water, on the platform by the chest. His partner was standing guard. Totally unnecessary; totally Mike.

"Just how far is this cave?" Jill demanded. She was struggling in her sandals and trying not to let him see.

"Not far," he grinned.

In some ways Jill was cool—in her diving and her appreciation of a good adventure. But in other ways, she could act just like the silliest girl. He'd warned her twice about the sandals.

"I've always loved this place," he said, hoping to take her mind off her feet. "Felt an affinity—you know? I must have been a buccaneer in a previous life."

"A pirate?" she asked, trying to navigate the last few steps.

They had reached the slender ledge that hovered twenty feet above a raging ocean. Jill pressed back against the rock wall, staring at the crashing waves below. He'd forgotten that the far side of the island faced windward, with an oddly shaped channel trapping the sea's currents.

The entrance to the underground cave was just there. For a diver underwater at slack tide, the water was safe and calm.

"A buccaneer—it's not the same thing," Jon told her. "You understand something of reincarnation now. Conservation of souls, just like matter and energy."

Dropping to his knees, he brushed the covering vines aside. "I sailed the open seas, commanded a swift ship with a cunning crew. Feared throughout the Caribbean."

Jill pointed beyond him, to the smaller hole not buried behind vegetation. "Isn't that a better entrance?"

"That's the 'Turtle.' It drops to the lower cave. Drop being the operative word." Sweeping the vines aside, he ducked low and crawled.

Not hearing the sounds of her following, he tossed over his shoulder, "Good thing you're not Melanie. She's too girlie for this."

Jon grinned at the hesitant shuffle and reluctant scrape. In some ways, his cousin was so predictable.

The rock tunnel curved in on itself before opening up to reveal a large cavern. Faint light seeped in from some hole overhead, though not enough to see beyond a few feet. He flashed his beam across the back wall.

"Just as I remembered." He smiled. "Maybe a little smaller. Been a while since I've made the trek up here."

Helping Jill to stand, he suppressed a grin when her fingers hastily raked her hair to dislodge any insects.

His light caught the ledge along the rear rock—a ridge just wide enough for a boy to lay down with his arms folded behind his head and daydream. "My bunk."

Despite her aversion to bugs, a warm gleam shone in her eyes. "I had no idea you'd such an imagination."

Old crates still clustered around a rock-ringed campfire spot that when lit, as he well knew, sent the smoke up and out through the ceiling gap.

Dusting off two crates, he sat on one. Jill gingerly perched on the other.

"I had such stories," he said, warming to the memories. "There was a sea captain who lived here. Dark, bearded, and angry."

"Why was he angry?" Jill shivered.

Come to think of it, Jon had no idea. "Something about a crew that had mutinied." He must have seen it in a movie.

"That's a little odd for an eight-year-old playing games," Jill told him.

"I was ever precocious." He grinned.

∞

Wearing a hastily-donned bathrobe was a mistake.

Melanie discovered this as she tried to climb the ladder, her foot treading on the loose folds. She discovered it again when she popped out of the cabin to find Mike alone on the platform. "Where's Wall?"

Taking his time to lean back against the chest—and look her over from head to toe—Mike aimed the screwdriver toward the island.

She stepped to the railing and spied the launch on the beach. She wasn't exactly dressed for swimming. With a deep sigh, Melanie dug her hands in her pockets, just snatching the robe material from lifting in the breeze.

Mike, she realized, was still watching her, probably relishing her troubles with Wall. Well, she wasn't going to give him the satisfaction of running away like a scared little virgin.

She deliberately climbed down to the platform.

Feeling the delicate silk flutter against her thigh, she instantly regretted it. When she turned, he cocked an eyebrow as if to say, "Trying to entice me?"

Angry retorts rose to her lips. Melanie swallowed them before speaking. "So. Are we rich?"

It was Mike's turn to grimace. "The 'Universe' said we let it drain a while. I'll be on Medicare before we know what's in this bastard."

"What is this 'Universe said' stuff?" Feeling a...prickling...between her shoulder blades, her eyes noticed the chest itself. It was larger than she'd realized, constructed of iron. Or was it dark wood? A heavy padlock seemed to hint of treasure within, for all the world like a Hollywood prop.

"It's just Jon's way of avoiding decisions."

Maybe it holds a lot of treasure, she thought. Hadn't it proved heavier than they expected lifting it?

Moving closer, she dropped to her knees, caressing the worn top. "Why don't you open it now? You found it, after all."

The muscle man looked at her throat—where her robe had parted, she realized—and chuckled. "No dice, sweetie. We wait for Jon."

This idiot actually thought she was trying to play femme fatale.

The phrase flared in her brain, roiling through her conscious. Femme fatale—as if she would with him. As if she needed to with him.

She was so tired of his mockery.

Between her shoulder blades, the prickle expanded to a whirlwind of—determination. Enough of this cowardice, this backing away when he tossed down a gauntlet. He thought she was trying to manipulate him? She'd show him just how easy that was.

Leaning close, Melanie allowed the robe to gape. Her voice grew husky. "But you could, couldn't you? Pick the lock...close it again afterward? No one need ever know."

Shifting the screwdriver, he deliberately traced the nipple she'd half-revealed. "Now, just what are you proposing, princess? Maybe you can twist idiotic Brits around your little..." He pointedly gazed at her breast. "I'd take you up on your offer. So tighten that belt of yours and go back to your cabin."

She was more startled than he when her hand snatched the tool from his fist.

"What a hypocrite you are, muscle-brain. You want to see inside—an easy thing to do. But the little black man ordered you to wait." She poked him with the screwdriver, the metal tip imprinting his skin. "You're nothing but his lackey. And I thought you were the only real man here."

The words sizzled in the heat.

Melanie suppressed a hysterical giggle when Mike glanced at the island. The beach was empty. No one nearby to witness what they did.

"Be a man, Michael. No one is harmed here. Don't be such a fucking coward."

She flipped the screwdriver over and shoved the handle into his stomach. Both breasts were exposed now, and she no longer cared. She was amused at him.

Seconds passed. Then the screwdriver shifted, penetrating the padlock.

Leaning back to watch, Melanie's insides whirled in a vortex of glee. She never bothered to tighten her robe.

∞

Wall found the footpath off the beach exactly as Jon had described.

The trail spun around the rock summit, through green bush with large leaves and a carpet of yellow orchids, to rapidly climb forty feet to reach the peak. Before him lay a short walk to the rock ledge. He had but to travel most of that length, search behind the vines, and he'd find the tunnel.

After his fight with Melanie, it was a welcome diversion.

He saw what surely must be a toucan, with its sharp beak and scarlet and blue plumage making it easy to spot in a tree just below him.

Wall thought the bird lived only in South America—he'd have to ask Jon. His head was still turned when he stepped onto the rock surface.

Then he turned back and stopped short.

The ledge cut into a smooth rock wall, hovering almost ten meters above a raging sea. Unlike the lagoon and beach, the sea here contained furious white caps that bounced against each other, bashing the rock as if determined to break it down. Even so high above it, the spray dampened his legs.

All of which should have fascinated him. Instead Wall staggered, so dizzy from the view he almost lost his breakfast.

A second glance proved something was very wrong. Swallowing, he forced his gaze up to the opening in the stone, which was farther than Jon had described.

Straightening his back, Wall stepped carefully toward it. The swaying sea below spurred him on till he dropped to his knees, intending to dive through the hole.

The Turtle saved him. The knob at the top of the opening—with five protrusions for head and feet—marked the top of the chimney of the lower cave.

Thrusting his head inside, he saw little more than a black hole yawning beneath his hands. The impression was deep—a huge cavern. He'd nearly dove to his death.

Withdrawing, he carefully turned while avoiding glimpses of the sea below to finally spy the opening covered by vines.

∞

Even as his mind questioned what the hell he was doing, Mike plied tool to chest.

"Hurry," Melanie rasped in his ear, fingernails edging circles his shoulder.

The sun dimmed as if a cloud covered it or a mist rose up out of the sea. Neither had happened—the world just tilted dark somehow. Jon would have known the cause; he would have explained it well. But then he couldn't ask Jon.

"This is wrong," he said, pulling back. And the padlock fell open.

He watched it a long moment before plucking it free. His fingers clutched the chest lid as his eyes scanned the island, the beach. There was no one to stop him.

"You can't chicken out now," the blonde softly needled.

His hands lifted the lid against his mind's will. It screeched in protest, finally yielding to reveal a soggy dark mass.

Melanie slipped under his arm, grabbing at the stuff, pulling.

Layer after layer spilled across the deck; reams of oily gunk. Worthless. She was practically swimming through it, nearing the bottom, when he grabbed her arm.

"Jesus, enough!"

Eyes on the island, fearful of discovery, he stuffed it all back in.

∞

Waves of the muck landed on her, snapping her daze.

Revolted by the ooze in her lap, Melanie scuttled backward. Mike gathered it up, cramming wads of it back in the trunk.

Out of the dark mass, something solid tumbled onto her thigh. Sort of round, hard. Sharp. Her instinct was to brush it away before the red gleam caught her eye.

"Mike." She gasped.

"Put it away, goddammit! Adam should have strangled Eve!"

He hadn't seen it. He was too busy watching the shore, furiously thrusting gunk back in the chest.

That we have stolen what we do fear to keep! she thought, and she wondered why that phrase sprang to mind.

Scrambling to her feet, she saw ugly brown patches spreading across the red silk of her robe. The need to get clean, maybe rescue the garment before the stain set, sent her scurrying up the ladder.

Which was difficult with the thing in her hand.

Climbing over the bow, she turned back to face him, opening her palm. More dirt clung to her hand, revealing the sharp red edges, glittering in the sun. "Mike, this fell."

A ruby. A beautiful ruby, the width of her thumb.

His muscles strained as he slammed the lid shut, fumbling to replace the lock. "Just go," he hissed, eyes riveted on the island's deserted beach.

She couldn't just take it. "But..."

"Get the fuck out of here!"

So she did.

∞

"And you're sure nothing's dangerous?" Jill demanded.

Her cousin nodded, which she only caught because she was watching him carefully in the poor light. "Honestly, just a few insects that you have to look for to find, and the occasional lizard. No snakes, no bats. You're safe." Jon balanced the flashlight on its end, creating a halo of illumination flickering about them.

"Scorpions or spiders?" she asked suspiciously.

Her cousin's teeth gleamed. "Absolutely no scorpions."

Which meant there were spiders. She'd have questioned him further but for Wall's shout. "Jon!"

"Crawl through. We're in here."

Best to drop the insect questions. She didn't want the Brit to think she was afraid. She forced a smile as Wall's head popped through the tunnel entrance.

Bizarrely shadowed, just for an instant, Wall's face was all hollowed eyes and open mouth. Just for an instant, her stomach dropped.

Just for an instant, she felt terror.

"This is bloody brilliant," he grinned, crawling closer.

The hollows vanished, and he was suddenly just the British guy with all the rules. She watched him claim a crate, folding his tall form to an awkward perch.

"I used to hide here after a day of diving with my dad." Jon grinned. "Played with pirates and sea captains...sword fighting, swashbuckling. Treasure hunting."

There had been something profoundly familiar, Jill thought, about Wall's hollowed eyes. An echo from a childhood chimera, best forgotten.

"Mike told you we think there's another level to the wreck."

"Doesn't seem likely," Wall told Jon. "I mean, given the proportion of the two halves."

"Likely or not, it's there. Definitely a second level buried in the sand."

Her terror receded, there yet lingered a...disquiet. Instinctively, she shifted closer to the men.

"We found a hole in the deck. Flashlight revealed a big, hollow area. Has to be part of the wreck." Jon's eyes twinkled in the odd light. "That's a man-made room. A fully enclosed, big room."

"Sounds like a cargo hold."

"Exactly like a cargo hold." Excitement rose in her cousin's voice. "The cargo hold of a large, wooden vessel. An honest-to-God cargo vessel...that no one has ever explored. We should know more after we open that chest."

Suddenly she recognized the fear. When she was little, Jill had been terrified of being in the dark. No...of being alone in the dark. Her father later told stories of his getting her late at night when her mother would have left her to cry. Such terror in her cries, he'd felt it cruel to leave her alone.

"So you might have struck it rich."

"We all might have struck it rich."

So why this fear—or memory of fear—now? She'd not felt it in years. In forever, really. Only a fleeting impression of watching her father's back, watching him retreat. Leaving her all alone...

"So," Wall mused. "That's why Mike was standing guard."

Jon's grin subsided. "Did Mike have his screwdriver?"

Wall nodded.

"It's time to go set up the barbecue." Leaping to his feet, her cousin stepped to the opening.

Wall shifted to follow.

Jon's words stopped him. "You two stay and enjoy. We won't eat for hours."

Jill stood up, by no means anxious to remain. "Jon..."

But he was gone.

Her hand reached for the flashlight and hesitated. She realized she couldn't take it to find her way through the tunnel. That would leave Wall in the dark, and the idea of feeling her way made her shudder.

"If we are rich," Wall told her, as if they weren't stuck alone in this horrid cave, "I might just buy myself a sailboat."

Feeling a bubble of fear rising within, she firmly swallowed it. Whatever had stirred this stupid childhood memory, it wouldn't get the best of her.

Clearing her throat, she asked lightly, "Isn't that cliché? Don't all Englishmen sail?"

"We're an island race." He smiled down from his superior height, and instead of being annoying, it somehow reassured her. "What about you? What will Jill do with her share of the treasure?"

She had to think about it. Because, she knew, she didn't actually believe it. "Travel, I suppose," she told him. "I'd kinda like to see Europe."

Nodding, Wall stretched his legs out before him and knocked over the flashlight. It wobbled as Jill jumped to save it. She failed.

It crashed and flickered out.

∞

The cave was pitch black.

"Sorry. Always been a tad clumsy," Wall murmured. He fumbled around the cave floor and found the light. When it didn't click on, he shook it and tried again.

The light blazed forth to reveal Jill's tense face, her eyes squeezed shut.

"Jill?"

One eye opened, and she started breathing again until she saw Wall's narrowed gaze.

"Are you all right?"

She nodded quickly, too quickly. "I just don't like this cave." She leapt up and practically dove for the tunnel. Her knees struck the rock floor painfully. "Can I have the flashlight?"

Wall brought it to her, studying her the whole time. "Jill, in class, did you pass your blacked-out mask drill?"

She finally looked at him, her face belying her words. "I am not afraid of the dark."

"You didn't answer the question."

Jill snatched the flashlight from his fingers and crawled through to daylight.

He followed. Emerging in the dazzling sun, he saw her striding along the ledge. "You can't dive with nyctophobia."

Jill reached the dirt path as Wall stood to pursue and—dizzy at the sight of the crashing waves below—had to lean against the granite cliff.

∞

"Silt gets stirred, currents whip the sand off the bottom. Visibility can go to naught very fast."

Jill whirled. "I'm not afraid of the dark!"

The Brit gazed not at her but the sea below. When he looked up, she thought his face pale. They locked eyes an instant. Then Wall straightened his shoulders and walked the ledge. Worried, she waited for him.

He reached her side. "Something happened in there."

He was too tall, she decided. It made her feel small, and that wasn't fair. Too many men in her family were larger than life. "Uncle Ray cured my fears a long time ago."

"How did he do that?"

"Not by doing horrible things," she flared. She resented that look, the one on his face now. Skepticism tinged with sympathy.

Why was she so disturbed in the cave? The feeling had come out of nowhere. She couldn't even fault Wall for his concern. "Uncle Ray told me when you're scared of something, go ahead and do the thing regardless. You can't outrun fear 'because it follows you everywhere.'" And Uncle Ray was right, she realized. "You can't choose what you feel, but you can do what's right anyway. When fear sees it's irrelevant, it dies."

The doubt in his eyes faded, and for an instant, there was a new expression. An unfamiliar expression, but she sensed understanding was just coming.

Jill marched off before it got there.

∞

She really ought to tell someone.

Cabin door locked, Melanie lay the ruby on the faded bedspread. It sparkled in the sunlight as if it hadn't been underwater for years.

It presented a conundrum, as her mother would say. The only person she could tell was Mike—and somehow, that opportunity had passed. He'd be furious, mostly because he wanted to pretend he'd never opened the chest.

To tell anyone else was to get him in trouble.

Best to tuck it away in her jeans pocket before Wall returned. Stuff the denim in the back of her drawer and wait for the right moment to slip it back.

But Wall was ashore with Jill, and she liked looking at it. Watching the light gleam through the facets, the tiny red line of refracted sun shimmered on the wall.

Melanie stripped off her dirty robe.

The cabin mirror was small, but she caught sight of her nude breasts, long blonde tresses coyly hiding her nipples. Mike saw her like this, she thought.

And he did as she bid.

He'd opened that chest for her.

In the midst of Wall's attitude with Jill, of her worry she was losing his interest, Mike's reaction was a balm. Wow—her femme fatale routine had risen to a new level.

There was also a tinge of guilt, but that was quickly swept aside. As she'd told him, no one was harmed. No one would even know about it.

The glistening gem drew her eye, and her hand stretched over the bedspread to grasp it. Ruby, her own special stone. Her birthstone.

The skin prickled down her back as her fingers touched it and quickly withdrew.

Instead she took a shower to wash her hair, dressing in the sarong that draped her curvier figure nicely, just to bolster her confidence, to show Wall her assets, worth so much more than a tomboy's.

As she stood before the mirror, admiring the red against her skin, she glimpsed something beyond her shoulder. A sort of whirling, like a mass of dancing motes in the sunbeam. No, it moved faster than that, like a mini-twister. As she peered at it, for just an instant, she saw a man within the haze. Bearded; leering. Boldly admiring her body as Mike had not dared.

When she spun round, only the dust motes remained, flickering above the gemstone. How stupid. She'd left it lying out on the bed. Someone could have seen.

Hastily, she rooted through her drawer, found her jeans, and thrust the jewel in a pocket before withdrawing her hand.

The thing somehow stuck to her fingers.

She sat on the mattress, staring at it. Red glowed from within, pulsing like a heartbeat. Almost alive.

Melanie threw it back on the bedspread.

Without thinking, she grasped the crystal pendant off the dresser and held it up to her heart. She held her breath, feeling silly.

The air rushed out of her lungs in a weird gasp.

Still clutching the pendant to flesh, her other hand lifted the cord over her head. It would go nice with the sarong—matching the primitive, island touch. And maybe protect her, if from nothing more than her own foolishness.

The ruby on the bed glittered enticingly, showing streaks as scarlet as the shades in her dress. Such a beautiful gem.

Could she switch it for the one on her choker?

Craig had given her that necklace. Craig of the cheap deal, the man who never spent more than he absolutely had to. His ruby was small and flawed. Not of good quality.

Unlike this one.

She caught her reflection in the mirror and saw a nervous woman of thirty years old. Femme fatale indeed. She couldn't even keep her boyfriend away from a puny, mixed-race tomboy.

The pendant dropped back to the dresser as she snatched the gold necklace in its place. Deftly she pried the choker setting, easily freeing the smaller gem. Surely the larger one would not fit. But it did.

Melanie rose triumphantly from the mattress, fastening the choker around her throat. When she checked herself in the mirror, the large ruby twinkled provocatively above the cleft of her collar bone, sexily emphasizing the spot.

Femme fatale indeed.

Something about jewelry high on the throat always pleased men. Probably because it looked like a collar; like a slave collar. Implying the female wearing it was pliant and obedient to their wishes.

If they only knew.

∞

When the cabin door shut behind the blonde, the swirling dust motes enveloped the crystal pendant, shaking and rolling it off the dresser.

The threadbare carpet cushioned its fall.

Whirling in a tiny circle, the necklace slid beneath the furniture, out of sight.

∞

Wall stepped from the sailboat cabin into the fading light.

It amazed him how fast the sun set near the equator. A flash display of pastel skies above earthly shadows, and the flaming ball dropped into the sea. He missed the English twilight, where the sun lingered, reluctant to leave.

Here it seemed eager to go.

Celebration scented the breeze, along with the hibiscus and teak oil. On the island, Mike was just setting the grill over a pile of driftwood.

Hibiscus, teak oil, and now he caught a trace of musk. Melanie had followed him up the ladder.

They'd just had a rather surprising hour. The blonde had thrown off her inhibitions and then some. He only hoped no one had heard them.

If they had, they were being very discrete. Jon and Jill sat on the platform beside the sea chest, laughing.

"You," Jon told his cousin, "have no imagination."

Jill folded her arms. "Okay, maybe we are reincarnated. But there's no way all five of us opened this same chest a hundred years ago."

Wall swung a leg over the back of the sailboat, stepping down to the platform. Taking a seat, he left room for Melanie to join him. She didn't, choosing to sit closer to the chest.

Out of the corner of his eye, he saw Mike swimming toward them.

"Sure we did. I can practically remember it."

"Jon! The odds of all five of us being together in another life are..."

"Excellent, mermaid." Jon's grin encompassed them all. "We're a soul pod."

"Pardon?" The word burst from his lips.

Jon spoke over Mike's approaching splashes. "Soul pod. Souls tend to hang together—knowing each other and being at the same lesson level. We travel time and space as a clan, if you will. This reincarnation, I'm Jill's cousin—the last time, her wife. Or son. Or neighbor. We choose different roles for different perspectives. Different lessons."

Jill had to scoot back as Mike hoisted himself out of the Caribbean, rolling to his feet in one movement. Showering them all with seawater.

For once, Wall was glad of the interruption. Jon had spouted some metaphysical ideas before, but this was so wild it made him uncomfortable. He glanced at Melanie to share a "wow, is this weird" look.

She, however, focused on Jon. "Do souls ever...break away?" she asked, playing with her necklace. "From the pod, I mean."

It was Mike, plucking up his screwdriver, who gave Wall a disgusted look.

"Sure. A soul can accelerate its growth, moving beyond the others to a new pod."

"Or get left behind," the blonde said softly.

Wall felt the hair raise on the back of his neck.

"Left behind?" Jon stared at her. "Never heard of such a thing."

"Sure you have," Jill broke in. "It's called a haunting." And she shivered, as if she also felt her hair rising up from her flesh.

Silence shrouded them all, until Mike rattled the padlock. "Can we open this bastard now? Or do we need ceremonial crystals?"

Wall leaned closer, his anticipation now tainted with the specters Jon had conjured.

Jon gestured, and Mike thrust the screwdriver into the lock, which instantly sprang open.

Suspicious, Wall thought, frowning at Mike.

The same thought echoed on Jon's face.

The muscle man tossed the lock onto the metal platform, grabbed hold of the lid, and heaved. When nothing happened, he planted his feet and heaved again.

Nothing.

Jon joined him, latching onto one side as Mike shifted to the other. They strained, pulled. The chest protested loudly.

"Don't damage it," Wall warned, just as the top flew open.

Mike reached in to lift a soggy mass from the trunk, raising it higher and higher. Standing, he pulled it up shoulder height.

Wall pressed back against the boat's stern, revolted.

∞

Melanie gasped.

The sludge dropped away from the thing Mike held, revealing a black velvet dress from another era. It had white lace—pristine and delicate—embellishing a low décolletage.

Exquisite. She reached to stroke the material.

"Don't touch that!"

Startled, she glanced at Wall, then turned back to find Mike holding a horrid mass of brown sludge. He tossed it into the sea.

"Mike wait. There could be something caught up in—"

"There's nothing," Mike told Jon, peering back inside the chest. "Hello." He plucked out a gray square thing and unwrapped it—the gray was a frayed cloth—to reveal a small box. The sort of thing usually holding jewelry.

"Now this is more like it." Tossing the cloth aside, he offered the box to Jon.

The dingy gray repulsed Melanie, and she was grateful when Jill picked it up. Although the girl did so reverently, as if she treasured it.

Jon's fingers flipped a simple catch to open the box.

For an instant, Melanie saw her ruby choker lying on a creamy satin. When she blinked, the box interior was empty.

"*Fuck.*" Mike spun back to the chest, furiously digging through waves of sludge. The sludge spilled out as it had before, a living thing eager to escape. Finding nothing more, he finally sat back on his heels. "*Fuck.*"

Jon studied the box, turning it over. "There's writing here."

"Tiffany's?" Mike leaned in.

"Too faded ... too ..." Jon squinted. "I think it says Isabelle."

Melanie shivered.

Mike kicked the worthless chest. "Bitch must have gotten our treasure."

Dive in the Dark

THE GRILL LAY DISMANTLED, the fire stoked, blazing against the velvet night. The stars, so close in the Caribbean, ran shy from the flames, though the moon stood fast.

Wall felt the tension in his shoulders ease; his muscles relaxed. His lips curved in a contented smile. A good meal shared with friends, a warm night, and a tropical sky. What more did a man need?

"If you really could buy anything, you'd travel?" Jill laughingly demanded. "What about a new house or a beach condo? Even a red Ferrari?"

Conversation was the answer. He might miss his texts on his phone, but to actually sit and talk, hear the inflections, see the gestures. Real communications, and this particular one threaded with rich dreams.

"I want to meet people," Jon answered his cousin. "Traveling, I can meet a lot of people."

"You could travel fast in a Ferrari," Wall prodded.

"But I'd be isolated. A car only holds two." Leaning back on his elbows, the little man stretched his legs out toward the sea. "The only thing real in this life is people. Not places, not things. People. I want to meet as many as I can."

Jill caught Wall's eye. She knew he was just stirring the pot with his question. That surprised him. He somehow hadn't expected her to see it.

"I'm gonna buy a Corvette," Mike declared. "Don't want to see Europe; don't wanna live in a fancy house. I'm gonna drive a sweet black convertible. No—a red one. With black leather upholstery."

Even Mike was playing the game: what to do with the treasure lying on the sea floor less than 200 meters from them. Only Melanie refrained. Perched on a log, she merely chomped into her fourth chicken leg.

And he'd thought her a simple salad kind of woman.

"You rent a stupid studio apartment," Jill stabbed a finger at Mike. Sitting cross-legged, the shred of gray cloth 'artifact' that she'd rescued lay on her thigh. "Surely you're gonna upgrade."

For a moment, Wall watched the blonde tear into the meat, her teeth bared in a startling grimace. His visions of a satisfying conclusion to the evening faded.

"You can pick out something for me," Mike conceded.

Jon burst out laughing. "You really want Jill choosing your perfect bachelor pad?"

"Pink leather furnishings?" Wall offered.

More laughter.

"I'll put in a shark tank," Jill grinned.

"In the media room." Mike's eyes lit up at the thought. His gaze turned to the sea, to the area where the wreck lay. "This little beauty's really gonna pay off."

They all smiled warmly. All but his girlfriend. Avoiding her ravenous display, Wall caught Jill's hand stroking the gray material.

"Mermaid," he winced as the nickname slipped out. "That thing's worthless. Just throw it away."

She shook her head, the long dark tresses fluttering around her face. "It's my first ever artifact." Turning to her cousin, her eyes took on a hopeful gleam. "So. We diving?"

Jon nodded and must have noted Wall's surprise. "Night dive. Remember?"

"I thought you were kidding. Don't we need all our bottom time for the wreck?"

"This is only thirty feet down. We should see some amazing things after dark."

"Tomorrow, let's do the stern," Mike broke in. "If we could find a passage to the lower level there, it could help pin the location in the bow piece. Maybe even get a clue what broke the bastard in half."

A peel of laughter jarred the night.

Wall turned—they all did—to see Melanie's eyes glittering eerily over a chicken bone. "You still think its two pieces?"

"We men can manage to count that high," Mike snorted.

Tossing her shredded meat aside, she rolled forward over her folded legs, thrusting a greasy finger into the sand to sketch. When she sat back, the rest of the group leaned in.

She'd drawn a side view of a ship, with two square box structures on deck, one fore and one aft. Leaving an empty gap area between.

"Ain't never seen nothing like that," Mike scoffed.

"Sure you have," Jon spoke slowly. "A Spanish galleon."

Melanie hopped to her feet, darting over to the leftover food containers.

"That's not possible," Wall barked, his mind denying the sudden sense the diagram made. "A galleon would be centuries old, not decades. That's not physically possible."

Mesmerized by the drawing, Jon traced it with a finger. "Many galleons in the Caribbean."

"Like the *Atocha*," Mike murmured, his eyes suddenly afire. "Just ask Mel Fisher."

Wall's mind whirled. He was no physics expert, but the idea of wood surviving so well in warm water did not add up. "I believe the *Atocha*'s remains were metallic. Guns. Gold. I'm pretty sure there's no wood. Or if so, just bits. A beam, maybe. Not a whole bloody ship."

Jon never took his eyes from the crude sketch. "Coral could have preserved it, or maybe the sand protected it for centuries."

Mike's face shifted oddly in the flickering light. "This explains everything! The gap...the perfect alignment. Lack of passageways below. This is our wreck!"

Jumping to his feet, he showered Jill with sand. "How far back does that book on Caribbean wrecks go?"

"We'll soon find out." Jon rose. The two hurried for the launch.

"Hey! Don't strand us!" Jill called.

Deep in conversation, the pair strode past the small boat to wade out into the water, then dove and swam for the *Sadicor.*

Melanie tossed her half-eaten wing aside. Sending Wall a look sparkling with—something—she trotted after them to dive into the sea. Despite her nice dress, despite her gold necklace.

Wall found himself locking eyes with Jill.

"Melanie figured it out?" Jill gazed after them with wide eyes. "Of everyone here, master divers, wreck divers. Melanie figured it out?"

That was the least of many questions rampaging through Wall's mind.

∞

A halogen shone from just beneath the sea, the only light in a very dark night. The stars had winked out earlier, as if abandoning their part in this venture.

Jill regretted ever pushing for a night dive.

The waves tossed them about like flotsam, forcing them all to work to remain near each other. The ledge to the upper cave looked on from up high.

Jon had called this slack tide. Thank God. She couldn't imagine what it must be like otherwise.

"Melanie's with Wall; Jill, you're with me," Jon told them. "Stay with your buddy, ladies." His underwater light tilted, blazing across the circle of faces. Like a watery version of the campfire.

"What about Michael?" Melanie purred.

Jill wondered if the woman was drunk, though you weren't supposed to drink when scuba diving.

"I'm my own backup." Mike patted his rigged tank redundancy. His grin faded as he met her eyes, maybe detecting her concern. "You'll like this, mermaid. You're finally gonna see those colorful sea dancers." His fingers opened and closed in a fluttery gesture.

She'd forgotten she'd ever begged to see those.

Melanie slanted her a pointed look.

"Living feathers that dance in the water," Jon explained—though Jill doubted Melanie cared. "This is one of their favorite spots."

"Sea snails," Wall added.

Did all Brits have this ability to take the extraordinary and make it so mundane?

No one spoke for a minute as water splashed and gear adjusted. Jill suddenly wished she could call it off.

"No wetsuit?" Wall asked Melanie. "Thought you were always cold."

"You would think so," the blonde murmured.

Jill must have imagined the emphasis on "you."

Movement ceased until the only sound was the sea.

I begged for this night dive, she reminded herself over and over, like some sort of mantra. *I love diving.*

"The lower cave's pretty cool," Mike offered, his regulator inches from his face. "Sure you guys don't wanna check it out? All we gotta do is crawl through a short tunnel and surface."

"You guys crawl in and out of places all day," Jill found her voice, anxious to speak before anyone could say different. "I just want to see lobster and octopus."

"Can't you see that during the day?" Jon frowned.

"You somehow managed to scare off everything by the wreck." Deliberately, she spat in her mask, running her finger around the plastic before rinsing it in the water. Truth was, she wanted to get this over with. Truth was, Jill felt the dark night weighing down on her.

There was a memory, trying to break through. A childhood nightmare—heaven knows where it came from—of being trapped in a dark place. Dark and damp, with an odor. A stench of decay...

Like the cave, she suddenly realized. Maybe that's what triggered her fears again. That made perfect sense. No need to freak out.

Yet she felt no relief at the thought.

"Sure you want to do this?" Wall asked, looking directly at her.

Beside him, Melanie's eyes sparkled.

Jon must have thought he spoke to the blonde. "It's not that deep—barely thirty feet. And I promised the mermaid."

Feeling the woman's eyes riveted on her, Jill hastily grabbed her own dive light and switched it on. "Let's do this."

"Can't have enough light, can you, Jill?" Melanie murmured with a devious giggle.

Others adjusted masks and slipped regulators between their teeth. Jon looked around the circle, making eye contact with everyone.

Waiting for her signal, she realized.

She quickly nodded.

They submerged.

Descending at night was different.

Jill had always felt herself dropping into a new world just waiting to be explored. Now a black abyss gleefully sucked them down, without any promise of letting them go again. Even with her cousin right beside her, she felt alone.

Just like her dream.

Jon's mask tilted down, his dark eyes shining with eagerness. Anticipation.

I'm just feeling remnants of a childish nightmare. She firmly pushed her fears aside.

Her fins set down in a soft white bottom. Talcum powder clouds puffed out, swirling around her legs. She was the only one to touch the sand. Everyone else floated with perfect buoyancy control. Even Melanie.

The other dive lights snapped on, beams shooting out like light sabers in a movie. Wall and Mike actually crossed them in mock battle. She saw Wall check Melanie's face an instant before Jon checked hers.

He led her toward a coral cluster.

In Jon's harsh halogen, the coral looked brown, ugly.

Dead, she realized.

No fish darted within, no anemones fluttering their tendrils. Her cousin plucked dead seaweed from the gray surface.

Everything couldn't be dead.

Sweeping her light over the bottom, over the rock barrier beside her, Jill saw nothing. She arced her light all around, even toward the open sea. There was no trace of Spanish dancers, no lobster or octopus. Just a single gray sea fan alone at the base of the cliff wall.

Her fingers touched it in sympathy, and the fan crumbled. Its dust spiraled away in a single thread, swallowed by a black hole in the cliff.

Crouching, Jill shined her light inside. Something seemed to flicker within.

It must be the lower cave.

Pink flashed beside her, startling her. Melanie's mask leaned in to bump hers, the framed green eyes sparkling with devilment.

"What are we waiting for?" she murmured.

Jill's blood ran cold, for the words were as clear as if spoken on the surface.

The blonde launched herself through the opening. And as her pink bathing suit vanished in the void, Jill realized the woman hadn't even turned on her flashlight.

∞

Wall prodded a conch shell, the only sign of life he'd seen down here. It slowly rolled to reveal a shattered, empty underside. Honestly, he'd expected their dive lights to attract lots of attention. Predators hunted in the dark, and shy creatures emerged, feeling safe after sunset. He'd never been on a night dive not rich in wonder.

Something flashed in his peripheral vision. He looked up, finding an empty space.

Where was Melanie?

Whirling, his dive light found the rock cliff, with Jill on her hands and knees beside it. She'd thrust her head into a hole half a meter in diameter.

And he knew.

He shot over next to the brunette, pointing, but of course she didn't see.

Jon and Mike appeared, gesturing, questioning him.

As they should, he realized. He was her buddy.

Jill withdrew, pointing at the hole.

It made no sense. Had Melanie been sucked inside? Could an odd current have pulled her, maybe disorienting her with fear? She'd never have deliberately gone inside.

His flashlight swept the sea around them, even checking the surface. Whatever the cause, Melanie was nowhere in sight. And Jill kept pointing to the cave.

Jon grabbed the brunette's facemask, steadying her and forcing her to look at him. She quieted, though Wall could sense her exasperation. The girl was not hysterical.

Jon pointed at Wall, then stuck his index fingers together, an old signal of "get with your buddy" or "buddy up."

Jill couldn't possibly know what he meant.

Bubbles poured from her mouthpiece as she thrust out her arm, pointing at the cave.

Mike cut the discussion by swimming through the opening. Jon waved Wall to follow.

He thought it best that Jill surface with Jon while he went on with Mike, but there was no way to communicate that, and speed was vital. So he entered the cave.

The tunnel was narrow and long, longer than the upper cave entrance. Milky threads dangled in his torchlight, hinting at ghostly spiders. He glimpsed Mike's fins ahead as the rock seemingly swallowed the man.

The fins vanished, and the tunnel emptied into a large basin. Already above him, Mike rose to the surface.

Jill appeared at his side. Wall checked her eyes and sensed her nervousness, yet she nodded gamely.

They both lifted their consoles, tapped their air valves, and ascended.

Wall burst through the surface a second before Jon's shout. "*Melanie!*"

Lifting his dripping torch, Wall aimed it on the far wall. Far wall indeed, as it was easily twenty meters away. He tilted the beam higher to find a dome-shaped ceiling five stories over his head. Somehow, the arc and the echoing silence reminded him of a cathedral, albeit with stalactites clustered at the shimmering apex. Small in diameter, long in length, they were a mass of calcium spears aimed at their heads.

Scraping sounds echoed as Mike leapt out of the water. "*Goddammit, where are you?*"

Even when Jon leveraged himself onto the dry shelf, shedding gear as he rose, Wall remained treading water, fascinated by the dancing sparks reflecting off the cavern walls. He was past the impression of a cathedral. Now he thought vaguely of a Hammer horror movie.

"Oh, God," Jill whispered beside him, reminding him of his responsibilities.

Together, they struck out for the side.

Wall vaulted out first, dropping his gear before lending her a hand. "Jill, what happened?"

"She just swam in."

Circling a tall cluster of stalagmites, he discovered an opening to another chamber, only slightly smaller than the first. Jon and Mike were already there, twin lights scanning the stone floor as if expecting to find her lying unconscious.

He stepped through the opening.

"I'm here." Faint, raspy.

Pinpointing the voice, he swung his light to a far corner.

Melanie stood calmly at the back, her light pointing up to a hole in the ceiling. "I wonder what's up there," she said.

"Bloody hell," Wall bit out. "What are you doing here?"

She lifted a puzzled brow. As if she'd merely gotten a little ahead of the group, rather than violated every tenet of safety.

Jon and Mike stepped in silently beside him, awaiting her answer.

"Jill indicated the cave. I thought you all had gone inside. I just followed." Her voice echoed, along with the sound of water dripping.

Wall finally found his own voice. "You thought I swam into a cave without you?"

Remaining where she was, her light still on the hole, the blonde spared him a single glance. "That was silly of me, wasn't it?"

Jill's piercing scream split the air.

∞

Women. Mike clamped his mouth shut, because if he spoke, he'd annihilate Wall and his blonde bimbo.

She stood at the back, innocent as they always were. Late for dinner? Not their fault. Spent too much? Not their fault.

This one actually left a night dive to go play in an underwater cave. She stood there now, pretending she'd done nothing the fuck wrong.

At Jill's scream, he sprinted.

The mermaid sat on the pool ledge, dive gear piled behind and frozen rigid. Eyes riveted on a spot by her thigh.

Suppressing his grin, he advanced, expecting to see a nearby gecko—as he knew she hated lizards. If it was a spider, he fully intended to squash—

He saw the snake, and his gut twisted. Hearing steps behind, Mike gestured to halt.

"Don't move, Jill," he whispered sotto voce.

She sent him a furious look. Of course she wasn't going to move.

Mike eased around to his discarded gear, where his machete lay attached to his B.C.

"That's a fer-de-lance," Jon hissed.

"Didn't figure it for the garden type." Moving slowly, his fingers freed the latch and grasped the hilt. Sliding his blade from its sheath, he was positioned behind the reptile, but he needed three steps to reach it. Jesus, where the hell had that thing come from? In all his years here, he'd never seen any snake, much less one so deadly.

Easing closer, he slowed his step. The neoprene boots might protect his ankles, but if the thing struck higher... At least it wouldn't strike Jill.

In reflex, he gestured for her to hold still. Her jaw clenched in answer. One thing about the mermaid—she had courage. Although behind in some of the more feminine traits, she'd always had guts.

Mike crept within striking distance. Raising the blade, he hesitated. If he screwed this up...

"A snake," Melanie spoke from the chamber entrance.

Jill twitched.

The serpent hissed.

Mike swung.

Its severed head splashed into the pool.

He quickly speared the wiggling body, swinging it away from her and holding it high.

Jon moved close to study the markings. "Definitely a fer-de-lance," he said, confirming what Mike already knew. "Central and South American. Never heard of them around here."

"Poisonous?" Jill whispered.

"Big time," Jon said.

Mike watched Jill hug her knees with shaking hands. Jon, like himself, thought of the mermaid as tough, strong. A younger version of themselves. But right now, she needed a hug.

He gave his partner a nudge, but Jon didn't get the hint.

"Everybody lived," Mike finally announced, tossing the carcass to the far side of the cavern. Squatting, he patted her shoulder before shoving his machete into the water to clean his blade.

"Bad luck to kill a snake," Melanie said.

"Tell me," he asked the cave at large, "isn't blonde hunting season somewhere between deer and quail?"

∞

Jill watched the big blade thrust into the water as Jon's feet appeared on her other side. She heard breathing again. The others must have held their breath as well.

She couldn't seem to make herself move.

Mike's hand scrubbed the gore off his machete.

Jon touched her back. "You okay?" he asked.

Unable to do anything else, she nodded.

The scream had erupted pure and unsummoned, even before she'd identified what the gleaming fangs beneath glittering eyes were. She'd have clawed her way backward, except her frozen limbs refused to heed her brain.

She'd have died.

"It's over," her cousin murmured, his soft voice cutting through her racing thoughts. "You're okay."

Having taken two tries to stand up, Jill wasn't so convinced. Her stomach rebelled at the idea of remaining in this cave another moment, but then she wasn't anxious to get back in the water either.

And when she looked at Melanie, she saw the same cold, reptile look. The blonde scared her more than the snake.

Through the fog that seemed to envelope her, the blonde's explanation of 'I thought you were here; I followed you in,' made no sense. The men took her to task without the severity she deserved.

At least that Jill thought she deserved.

"As we're here, can we explore?" Melanie asked.

And they all strode away with the blonde.

All except Wall. "Are you really okay?"

Jill nodded.

"Jill, what exactly happened?"

Rubbing her arms, she spied the tremors in her fingers and quickly dropped them back to her side. "I saw the cave opening. Melanie appeared. She...she said, 'what are we waiting for,' and vanished."

"You mean she gestured?"

Jill shook her head.

His face shifted, skepticism mingling with concern, because her story sounded crazy. She knew it was crazy—absolutely insane.

So she said nothing more.

After a few seconds, he stretched down a hand, offering to help her up.

She grasped it quickly so he wouldn't notice how she shook like a frightened rabbit.

They trailed the others into the second chamber.

Jon's beam lit up the far wall. "The hatchway," he said, as if introducing royalty.

Jill had heard about it, of course, but now, gazing up at the smooth surface, trying to shake off the numbness, she appreciated the story for the first time. A slick rock wall raised forty feet high, actually sloping back on itself. To climb it was to hang suspended by your own muscles the last few feet. The top opening was apparent by the void, spattered with white pinpoints.

A hatchway to the stars.

"That's the hole on the ledge? The one marked by the turtle knob, past the upper cave tunnel?" Wall asked.

Jon nodded.

Halfway up—if you made it that far—your body would be poised above a wicked cluster of stalagmites, ten foot spears just begging to impale an unlucky climber.

"You never scaled that." Shaking off her fog, she stepped close to touch the surface, slick and smooth, polished by the sea in times long past. "Jon. You're crazy."

"I did it...all the way to the top without a safety harness. Couldn't do it now to save my life." He turned to Wall. "My father and his brother, Jill's dad, bet each other who could make it to the upper cave first. A race, with the sailboat as the prize. Dad dove in the pool without even donning his gear. Uncle Chris dove after him but wound up returning for his tank. It's a long way down and back to the surface outside on a single breath of air.

"I was seventeen and knew I couldn't beat either of them swimming. But I could rock climb. I slipped three times before managing to pull myself through the opening, just as Dad stepped onto the ledge. I got to the tunnel first."

Jill gazed up the expanse of rock, the sheer height making her dizzy. "You scaled this? No wonder Uncle Ray gave you the *Sadicor*. He must have been so proud."

A slow grin spread across Jon's face. "He was livid."

She'd never understand men.

Eventually, they returned to the pool, donning gear amid prodding dares. Mike was of a mood to challenge Wall's standing as club champion at holding his breath underwater. Wall refused, siting his obligations as the blonde's buddy.

An acrimonious vibe threaded the jesting, further tainting the night. Jon finally hustled them all back to the

Sadicor, where Melanie continued her claim that Jill had waved her into the cavern. Somehow, Melanie's misadventure became Jill's fault. Wall didn't blame her, so he said, but his advice suggested he believed most of his girlfriend's tale.

When she was finally alone in her tiny cabin, crawling into her bow-shaped bed, Jill left the lamp on, in the same way she'd done when she was eight years old. Muffling the noise in her pillow, she sobbed her heart out.

It was a tossup whether her nightmares would feature crazy blondes or evil snakes. Instead, Jill dreamt of a cave filled with people. Moans of pain and panic echoed endlessly through the dark.

A tall man with curly hair tried to comfort her, murmuring, "Don't be afraid."

"I'm not, as long as I'm with you." She stroked his face; kissed his cheek.

He put something soft in her palm. "From the holy man's cloak," he whispered. "It's sacred."

Rough hands grabbed her, yanking her away. She saw Jon, but his skin was ghostly pale. He looked at her with pity even as he bore her away. The cloth fell to the floor, trampled by his heavy boot.

Wall reached to help her, but a whip cracked and his cheek split. So he let her go.

And she was swallowed by the dark.

Snare

With the sun smacking her in the face, Melanie woke.

Her eyes hurt, Wall's snoring hurt, and the *Sadicor's* rocking was affecting her stomach. She sat up, maneuvering her way out of the bed and out of the room. Jill usually had a pot of coffee going far too early for a normal human—and thank heavens today was no different.

Of course, the downside to that was Jill herself being awake.

The brunette climbed down the ladder with an empty mug as Melanie poured. "Morning," she said, far too loud.

Melanie winced, managed a nod. She felt like she'd been drinking tequila. She couldn't remember drinking tequila.

Apparently, the same thought occurred to Jill. "Were you drunk last night? Is that why you went in the cave?"

There had been a dream with a cave. With men...and one bearded man in particular. He'd given her a ruby...

Melanie glanced at the counter, and there it was. The ruby choker, cushioned on a folded paper towel. Wall had removed it last night, concerned that she'd worn it diving. Jesus, she'd actually worn gold jewelry diving. They'd left it out to dry.

Leaning close, she couldn't find any damage. "I went into a cave?"

The brunette threw her a sharp look over the coffee pot. "You claimed I waved you in."

Melanie reached for the jewelry, struck by a wild thought. This thing needed to go, as far away from her as possible. She could take it up the ladder and toss it over the side. No one would ever know.

Her fingers trembled. She was actually scared to touch it.

"Jill." She grasped the edge of the towel it lay on and shoved it across the counter. "Get rid of this."

The brunette looked at her suspiciously.

"Please." She couldn't find the words to explain, but she knew, deep down to her soul, that the ruby was bad.

Jill's brown eyes narrowed. Melanie held her breath.

The girl slowly wrapped the paper towel around the gold and bore it away.

The pendant, Melanie told herself. Today she would wear the crystal pendant.

Except, as it turned out, she couldn't find it.

∞

It was astonishing, Jill thought, just how much her cousin and his partner could eat. Diving seemed to double their capacity.

The five had gathered round the dining booth. Mike wolfed down toast; Jon shoveled in oatmeal. Wall, empty plate before him, sipped a cup of coffee.

And Melanie sat quietly in the far corner, withdrawn in every way. She hadn't eaten, but then she'd devoured a whole chicken last night. Admittedly, Jill didn't like the blonde, but somehow now she felt sorry for her, even after last night.

Something was most definitely wrong.

"I just don't believe it," Wall was saying. "The physics makes no sense."

"Screw physics," Mike said. "You have to overthink everything."

"Easy enough to verify." Jon leaned in between the two men. "Check the gap area. Has to be flat, even. Some sign of decking."

"If it is a galleon"—Mike's eyes gleamed—"there ought to be an opening to the cargo hold."

"Cargo hold…" Jill found herself exchanging looks with Jon. Her adventure last night had eclipsed thoughts of Spanish galleons and treasure chests.

"The West Indies Fleet," Jon spoke softly. "Spain used convoys to transport luxuries around the empire. Just read about it last night." His smile encompassed the table. "They also called it the Spanish Treasure Fleet."

"So maybe a whole cargo of gold." Maybe they really were rich.

"Could be full of gold, silver, jewels," Jon said. "Could also be tobacco, sugar, or silk, which wouldn't be so valuable after a century underwater."

"I like our odds," Mike rumbled through a full mouth.

Jon slanted him a look. "Even if it were sugar, the captain must have had coin with him. For purchases and such."

The words hung in the air, full of promise.

Then Jon stood. "Wall, you and Melanie together. Jill, you're with me. And Mike, buddy—you're on your own."

"Just the way I like it." He grinned.

Leaping up, pushing to escape the booth, the men missed Melanie's wide eyes and stiffening shoulders. It wasn't reluctance. It was closer to terror.

Wall's fingers clasped the blonde's arm.

To Jill's surprise, she went with him.

∞

Melanie felt better in the dive prep.

Wall was attentive and gentle. He even caressed her cheek when she assembled her gear properly. Mike winked at her; Jon patted her shoulder. Even Jill smiled.

She'd somehow been forgiven for last night. They all thought her confused, recalcitrant. Mike had even called her brave, though she didn't quite remember it that way. Vaguely, vaguely, she recalled getting back at Jill. For what she couldn't say.

Submerging proved easier today. She held her console in front of her face plate, allowed a small stream of bubbles out of her B.C. They sank together, looking at each other over instruments, laughing over foolish gestures. No need to clear her ears this time—a first. It must be the money, she decided. The anticipation of wealth. Even in Wall, that anticipation ran high.

Everything was perfect.

Except that they sank past fifty-two feet. At exactly fifty-five feet, she and Jill stood on the ocean bottom while the others hovered.

Melanie glanced around, startled. The bottom still looked even with bumps here and there. Ruffled sand from the currents shifted the soft powder. None of the others seemed to notice the depth change, or maybe they just didn't care.

Wall tapped her arm, pointing, and she looked. If she hadn't a regulator tightly clamped between her teeth, her mouth would have fallen wide open.

The space between the two halves of the wreck now rose out of the sand by inches, looking very much like part of the wreck. Coral had receded somehow, revealing the even, flat surfaces belonging to a man-made structure. Even the protruding bump was obviously a bowsprit.

This was a damned big ship. How had the others not known?

Maybe the change had been gradual. Maybe in diving every day, they hadn't noticed. She'd skipped a full day and probably not been very observant when she had dived. After all, clearing ears and keeping up took all her attention. Still, the bones of this ship before her looked nothing like the pair of reefs she remembered. Did their diving kill the coral? She'd have to ask.

She'd also make damned sure of her share.

Wall touched her, and she swam with him to the wreck.

Jon and Jill worked atop the gap area, the midpoint between the two raised housings. Their fingers busily brushed through the traces of sand, fins gently propelling them onward. Mike examined the side of one reef facing the gap.

Wall led her to the other reef.

The familiar feeling of fear was gone. And without it, Melanie found herself able to really see things, such as the dead bits of coral still clinging to the wood, flaking away when her gloves touched them. Behind the flakes a solid structure stood erect. If she squinted, she could almost make out individual planks of timber.

Surely there had to be some sort of doorway here. Of course, that's what the others were seeking.

Wall yanked out his knife, using the handle to chip away at the coral. On the opposite side, Mike plied his crowbar. Melanie reached for her own dive knife, struggling with the strap to free it.

A loud scrape, slow and drawn out, surrounded them.

They turned to see Jill straining, feet braced against the bottom, pulling something with all her might. *No, not bottom*, Melanie corrected herself. *Deck.*

She pushed off to join her, feeling a small thrill when she realized Wall was behind her. She was leading him.

Closing in, she saw the brunette tugging on something, trying to pry it from the gap deck. Jon set beside her, adding his strength to hers.

Mike joined them, feeling beneath the sand first to find their quarry. Nudging Jill out of his way, he bent his knees in weightlifter fashion and heaved.

The entire wreck groaned furiously. If not for her regulator, Melanie would have licked her lips.

∞

A thick black ring tilted upright out of the sand, and a chill ran down Wall's spine.

A handle, he realized. *A handle to the cargo hold.*

He hadn't really believed, never allowed himself to fully believe before. He only toyed with the notion, idly considered a thing or two he might purchase.

But he never actually believed.

Mike and Jon ceased pulling. Mike now wielded his crowbar, Jon holding him off so he and Jill could clear sand away, looking for edges of the hatch.

Wall knelt to help.

Melanie made some movement. Swiftly he checked her, but the sparkling eyes within the pink mask reflected the same excitement everyone else shared. She actually knelt to help.

As she dropped, he caught a flicker behind her. Something in the distance swam away toward the broken bowsprit. Something large.

It disappeared before he could make it out.

Frantically Jon's hands brushed silt, revealing a dark crack running parallel to the upright ring. The edge of the hold door. Mike drove his crowbar in and thrust down, trying to lever it.

Wall slipped beside Jon, grabbing the ring as well. Bracing feet by the opening, they yanked, muscles straining.

Nothing. Not the slightest give or the smallest promise of future yield.

That shadow-thing shot by again, circling back to the bow. Possibly the manta, but Wall kept a wary eye out. He hadn't forgotten the hammerhead.

Jon startled him by grabbing his arm, urging him to stop. Wall did so the two men could clear the rest of the doorway; perhaps they could even find a more promising angle.

There wasn't room to help, so he watched, floating higher and drifting sideways. His mind also drifted, wondering if the manta had made a home in the wreck.

If mantas make homes, he thought. He had very little experience of rays.

Keeping Melanie in view, he'd angled just far enough to see the bowsprit. Something dangled below it, seemingly caught rather than hovering free. Something dark and crescent-shaped that he'd glimpsed once before.

He swam closer.

Light from the surface shifted, and he saw an old man, hands bound to the sprit. His body was thrust backward against the bow. His head lolled, revealing a large strawberry mark on his cheek.

Rheumy eyes lifted, brimming with anguish...terror. Those eyes focused, pinning Wall with accusations.

"Wall?"

Jolted, Wall spun awkwardly to see Melanie hovering beside him, green eyes wide within her mask. In question, not in horror. She was checking on him, like a proper dive buddy.

And he'd understood her—as he never understood anyone underwater.

Not attempting to answer, he spun back to the bowsprit. But even before his eyes could focus, Wall knew the thing was gone.

∞

Melanie surfaced to Mike's shout of triumph and Jill's delighted whoop.

For the first time, she let out a whoop of her own.

They'd found a treasure ship. She just knew it. She was rich, whatever her share. She'd be wealthy. Wealthier still if she ended up with Wall.

Far wealthier, the thought flashed through her brain, *if I hook up with Mike.*

She shook that last notion away and climbed the ladder.

Mike and Jon discussed options and made plans. There was another way inside the front section, so they thought, within the bowsprit cabin they'd first entered. They'd go back inside.

And if it failed, other options abounded.

"So you're going into the wreck again." Jill rolled her eyes. "That means I'm left without a dive buddy, unless Wall—"

Wall shook his head. "I'm with Melanie," he said. And looked right at her, smiling warmly.

Melanie smiled back. "I'm definitely diving. We can finish uncovering that door."

"We need you inside, limey." Mike snatched up a tank, heading to the compressor room. "You want a fucking share, earn your fucking share."

"Melanie and I can buddy," Jill declared.

Wall immediately protested. Two novices, and the men were not around if trouble arose.

"They'll be fine," Mike growled.

Jon seemed to agree, adding, "Let's see if we can clear that passageway Mike found."

Melanie grinned. She felt no fear whatsoever and marveled at it. "I'll dive with Jill," she decided.

The great feeling continued. She consumed two hot dogs and made plans in her head. Plans for the dive, plans for the future.

Mike filled tanks. Jon unearthed a better dive light for Wall. For the first time since setting foot on the *Sadicor's* teak deck, she felt ready; eager. Confident.

Until she took Mike his lunch.

He huddled at his bench behind the compressor, red muscle shirt stretched over his ripped chest as he plied a screwdriver. She smiled and set the plate at his elbow.

Then he reached for a folded paper towel. The ruby choker lay within it.

"I don't like other people in here," he growled. "Let alone stashing their shit. Get this out of here."

Melanie shook her head. She really, really didn't want to touch it.

Mistaking her reaction, he tossed the screwdriver aside, snatching the necklace and thrusting it at her. "It'll get messed up in here, princess."

Stepping back, her retreat was stopped by the cold compressor against her spine. Her eyes slid off his—noticing the books on the shelf: *Wrecks of the Caribbean* and *Revisits: Theory of Soul Returns to the Earth Plane.*

She glanced back at Mike and saw his expression, realizing he was as drawn to her as she was to him.

Impulsively, she leaned over the necklace. She meant to kiss him, but somehow it was her teeth that caressed his lips.

She felt more than heard the click of the gold clasp at the back of her neck. Panic flared for a heartbeat.

Trapped, she thought, and knew she'd made the same bad choice again. Fleetingly, she wondered where that idea came from—what it could possibly mean.

Big hands grabbed her hair, and the muscle man was kissing her with a thoroughness Wall had never dared attempt.

All thoughts fled as she twisted in his grasp, demanding even more.

∞

Mike climbed out of the sailboat cabin, balancing two full tanks on one shoulder. As no one was looking, he set them down to rub his protesting muscle. Truth was, carrying these heavy tanks wasn't quite as easy as it used to be.

But other things were looking up.

During the beginner dive class, the blonde had been one of two very interested females. Being the instructor always attracted the women, and owning the shop hadn't hurt. At the time, Mike hadn't pursued Melanie. There was a tasty redhead to thoroughly enjoy before her husband returned from a business trip. And anyway, it could turn awkward with the Brit assisting the pool training. When class was done, however, he had turned his full attention to her. Melanie rejected him, to his surprise.

He was startled not because all women went for him—though a surprising number did—but because he recognized her attraction to him. She had a good girl veneer, but a bad girl core. Wall, he well knew, couldn't handle her.

Her timing was typically female. Any hint of her new allegiance would wreak havoc on the salvage, upsetting Jon and God knows what else. And Nita—who tolerated Mike's little forays on the mainland—wouldn't stand for it here. The blonde would just have to cool her jets till they got back to Delaware.

Stepping closer to the stern, he saw Jill cross-legged on the platform, busily screwing her regulator to her tank. Preparing to dive with Melanie.

"Jill," he called.

She sprang to her feet, grasped the tank he lowered, and settled it down on the metal with a tinny clang. She reached for the second tank, but he waved her off, carrying it down himself.

"Maybe you should skip this dive, mermaid. I'll make it up to you later. Promise."

She gave him that look where her nose wrinkled, like a puppy being teased. "But we're earning our percentage. Helping you, clearing the gap, checking for other entrances."

Mike could hear activity behind him as the others gathered, preparing to dive. He spoke so they wouldn't overhear. "Stay here instead. Blondes can be...unpredictable. This one more than most."

If anything, the nose wrinkled more.

"Just be careful." He sighed.

She nodded, but with that "yeah, yeah" nod teenagers give their parents when their mind had already dismissed the discussion.

Melanie appeared at the bow, eyes sparkling as if she'd heard.

Before he could react, Jon hopped down the ladder, snatching his equipment to assemble. "Shake a leg, Muscle Man. Where's our British hired help?"

"Sounds like our butler." Mike attached his tank to his B.C.

"A butler?" Wall swung his leg over the stern, swinging down to crowd the platform. "You Yanks have strange ideas about the British."

As Wall maneuvered, Mike caught an odd reflection in the metal tank on his back. He saw his own hand, and for a moment, it was severed at the wrist.

Hoisting his gear in place, Mike leaned backward and dropped into the sea. *Just a trick of the eye*, he told himself as he realized he was checking his hands. *Why the hell let it bother me?* He donned his fins in the water, pulling himself along the platform to Jill. "Just remember, you gotta take care of yourself first," he told her softly.

Jill fired up. "You told me she was fine. That last night was just confusion and my imagination."

On the opposite side of the platform, Jon rolled into the water. It was almost show time.

"I'm just saying be careful. Don't risk your life to save another, as the Limey says. Especially a blonde life."

Jill harrumphed and turned away.

Mike spit in his mask and dipped it into the water. His disquiet grew, reminding him of Nita for some reason. She'd no doubt tell him it was his psychic sense warning him.

Except Mike didn't believe in a psychic sense.

Jill tugged her reluctant wetsuit into place and rose to get her gear. Melanie jumped lightly down onto the platform, sitting squarely in front of Mike.

"Ladies, remember your dive buddy rules," Jon announced in his best instructor voice. "Watch each other and watch your bottom time. Gap area only. No going farther afield."

To Mike's surprise, Melanie slapped her gear together fast, like a veteran. Seeing his interest, her lips curved in a wicked smile.

"We'll be fine," she murmured, producing a plastic sandwich bag.

Startled, Mike saw the ruby necklace gleaming within.

She stuffed it between her breasts with red-tipped fingernails, leaning closer to offer a tempting view. With her shoulders angled, he realized no one else had caught her act.

"I still don't like two novices—" Wall began.

"We're not sitting in the sun while you men have all the fun," Melanie cut him off. "Right, mermaid?" And she smiled at Mike, reminding him of that smile in the movies.

The sexy curl of the lips the hot female bestows on the male just before she vamps out and sucks his blood.

He shook himself to literally shake off the stupid thought.

"Sadicor!" he yelled, turning in the direction of the wreck. "Let's do this."

∞

Nita had finished with her last appointment for the day.

The large woman's husband had been angry. Wasted money, he'd said. The large woman knew better.

Cleaning the room, tossing the sheet into the laundry basket, she reflected on the result. The woman who had seen her own sister pull the trigger had finally realized she'd always hated her sibling for killing their father—in Nazi Germany.

Past lives revealed present life answers, often to questions you didn't know you had. She'd seen it time and time again, watching tears of the heart bathe the cheeks as they washed away a lifetime of resentment and fear.

She had seen the understanding suddenly bloom, lifting a person up out of darkness and ignorance. Knowledge truly is power, she knew. It helped you understand your feelings, to more easily overcome them. Even more important, it helped you forgive yourself for those feelings.

Some on the island thought she preyed upon weak people, silly tourists or needy women. Ignorance blinded the doubters. Or fear, as there were those who thought it insane to toy with past darkness.

For the most part, she'd accepted that foolishness as part of her calling. None were so blind, her mother often and loudly explained, as those who refused to see. Her mother had died before the age of forty. Nita wondered if the disdain of so many had shortened her life.

Naturally, her thoughts turned to Mike. He had that same trait as her mother, a genuine unconcern for others' opinions. He was Mike, and the world could choose to love him or hate him as it willed. He honestly didn't see what difference it made.

She'd been worried about him, about that blonde on the *Sadicor* with him. The woman had clung to the tall man, suppressing her true desires. That, Nita foresaw, was a path to trouble on a small boat.

Closing her eyes, she checked in with Mike. She thought about him, sought his feelings at that moment, wherever he was. He felt—determined. Excited.

He'll be here tonight, she realized. He didn't even know it yet, but he'd be here tonight.

Slowly, inevitably, an idea blossomed.

∞

Jill watched the three men prepare to sink below the sea.

Heads turned to each other, exchanging approaches and ideas.

Mike sent her one last concerned look before slapping in his mouthpiece, and the water swallowed them all.

She felt abandoned.

"Shall we?" Melanie murmured, eyes sparkling know-ingly. Already in her gear, the blonde slipped backward, easing into the water without a splash. She looked as confident as the men.

For an instant, Jill thought she glimpsed bright red—like blood—between the woman's breasts.

Realizing she was last—something Jill had never been in class—she buckled her B.C. while trying that roll entry Melanie had just performed. Her fin caught in a slat and flew off, slapping the water before her face.

Blinded, she wiped her eyes to see Melanie giggling.

"You okay?" the blonde asked sweetly.

Jill tugged her fin back on. "Let's go."

They descended.

The wreck lay poised on the sand like an artist's drawing of a wreck. With the last remnants of coral now faded to brown, the ship appeared fully constructed of wood planks. The deck area between the two cabins, though still bathed in a thin sandy layer, now sported the rectangular edge of the cargo hold, perfectly framed.

How had they ever doubted this was a galleon?

Melanie's pink form shot downward past Jill's mask, startling her. Divers were supposed to descend slowly, giving the body a chance to adjust to the pressure change. And the ears—Melanie always had trouble clearing her ears.

Until now.

Jill alighted beside her, near the black ring handle. When the woman made no movement, Jill pointed to the cabin on the stern half and then swam to the one on the bow. They still sought doorways.

The inside wall of the structure was crusted with dead coral. Pulling out her dive knife, she tapped the handle against it as she'd seen Mike do. But dead or not, the stuff clung to the surface, denying any entry. Either this was a different type of coral, or it was in a different part of the death cycle.

This is useless, Jill decided. She turned to see if Melanie had had better luck.

The blonde was nowhere in sight.

Turning completely around, Jill saw no sign of her.

Keep calm, she told herself, *follow procedure.*

She swam higher, looking over the wreck. As her eyes swept the area, she ceased swimming and sank back down to the gap. Annoyed, she firmly suppressed a spurt of fear, grabbed her console in one hand and air valve in the other, and rose.

The wreck looked quiet, deserted, and it was getting smaller. Jill realized she'd put too much air in her jacket. Grabbing the valve, she reversed direction.

Something flickered near the bowsprit.

She lost sight of it as she dropped. It was only a flash, but there was no other sign anywhere. She kicked her feet and swam toward it.

Rounding the edge of the wreck, the ocean seemed eerily still. No sound of the men, and no sign of the blonde. She glanced at her gauges—still plenty of air—and realized her hand was shaking.

I must be cold.

As she cleared the bow, a flicker—a pink flicker—shot into the hole. The same shade of pink as Melanie's gear.

Surely she wouldn't go in there. That must have been a fish or something.

Except no sea life had been spotted near the wreck in days.

Jill finned her way to the hole, grabbing the edges. She saw nothing inside.

And then an odd purr enveloped her.

Jill whirled, eyes sweeping the Caribbean above her and behind her. She was alone.

Fumbling with her dive light, she tugged it free. The beam shook as she scanned the inside. *I must be very cold.*

Three taut ropes stretched through the ghostly stillness, disappearing into the black void. The ropes of the men, she realized. If she yanked on one...

Something fluttered at the edge of the beam.

She heard purring again, this time ending in a whimper. The flutter increased, becoming a whirl. Catching a flash of pink, she heard one distinct word.

"Help."

Jill hauled herself over the rim and inside.

Dark enveloped her, disorienting her. She didn't even know which way was up until her feet set down against the floor.

Glancing behind, Jill saw the opening. She released her breath and turned toward the spot of the flicker.

The whirling was still there, growing weaker. Worried, Jill walked toward it in her fins. She aimed her beam.

Two glittering eyes stared back.

The manta shot straight for her, knocking the flashlight from her hand. The beam rotated wildly as it fell and bounced off the floor, revealing the giant ray streaking toward her again.

It slammed her. Jill somersaulted, losing her mask and regulator. In the final bounce of the beam, she glimpsed the creature shoot through the opening before the light died.

Pitch black.

She shoved against the floor, trying to free her face from the silt, one hand frantically clawing for her mouthpiece.

A throaty whimpering echoed in her ears, and she realized it was her own.

It's the panic that kills you. Jon had said that in class. *Losing your air, losing your mask, you can survive all those things. If only you didn't panic.*

Jill pushed up on her knees, forcing herself to move slowly. Deliberately.

Upright, her fingers sought her B.C, then she reached behind her, scooping as she'd been taught. As some of the students used to joke about. But she felt nothing, no hose nor regulator. Her hands brushed her jacket again, and this time she felt the spare.

Her octopus rig—the second regulator clamped to her jacket. Fumbling, she freed it and slapped it into her mouth.

She savored a long, deep breath.

We're living, she told herself, echoing some movie memory. *We're living, gentlemen.*

Now she had time.

She looked around. Without her faceplate, things would look different, but in truth, the loss of mask didn't matter because everything was pitch black. She was completely disoriented, with no idea how far in she was or in which direction lay the opening. Only her knees resting on the floor told her which way was the surface, which did her no good because she had a literal ceiling.

Panic welled in her throat, and she forced herself to swallow it.

There's oxygen, she reminded herself. *But how much?*

Her hand flailed around for her console of its own accord.

Snagging it, she brought the thing close to her face, finding it hard to read without her mask and her eyes stinging. She had less than a quarter of a tank—and Jesus, if the gauge wasn't visibly dropping before her eyes.

On inspiration, she tilted the panel to see if its light helped. It didn't. Jill tossed it aside, her eyes sweeping the area, trying to find a lightening in the water. Surely the opening must be lighter. The silt couldn't be stirred up that much.

But no matter where she looked, black void surrounded her.

Well, she couldn't stay here. Forcing herself to turn around, she felt something brush her face, and she jerked back.

Okay, she thought, deliberately taking a calming breath—God knows how many of those she had left. Her hands swept the area before her, trying to find a wall, and she crawled forward.

Again, something flicked her cheek. She flinched, startled that it didn't give, and reached for it.

A rope, she realized. A firm, steady lifeline, leading from one of the men to the outside of the wreck.

Relief swamped her, but she shoved that aside as fast as she had the fear. Peering in both directions, she could not guess which would lead her out and which way would take her deeper inside.

Her air approached critical.

Wrapping fingers around the line, Jill drove forward. Thoughts of keeping her head against the rope while using both hands made sense, but her hand refused to let go. So she continued, feeling the floor before her and crawling. Feeling, crawling.

Then her hand felt a wall. Her fingers slid up it, finding an opening. The rope led through it, arcing up. The way it should if the rope was tied to the bowsprit. But the water before her was as black as ever. Shouldn't she see light?

Shouldn't she turn around?

The mere thought of turning—of crawling that distance again—made her stomach clench, and then her breath spluttered.

Her air tank was running dry.

Eyes closing, she pitched forward through the hole.

When she opened them, daylight surrounded her. She was outside the wreck.

Her feet paddled frantically, hands stabbing her air valve.

Will there be enough air to lift me? she wondered.

The surface loomed too fast. Jill blew all the air out of her lungs and broke through into the sunshine.

She was shaking so hard, she couldn't swim to the platform.

∞

Jill sat on the platform, legs dangling in the sea. A single drop of water escaped her hair, trailing down her nose to gather at its tip, and fell back into the Caribbean.

She'd managed, after an eternity, to climb onto the platform. Telling herself that Mike kept a spare tank ready, that she'd grab it and go back for Melanie. But as soon as she cleared the ladder, her legs had collapsed.

What in the name of God had happened? The wreck hadn't just silted up. The whole interior went dark. Pitch black, even right in front of the opening.

And where is Melanie? How much air could possibly remain in her tank?

Bubbles peppered the sea at her feet. She barely registered them.

Three heads popped through the waves, masks lifting and regulators yanking free.

"You can dive, you limey!" Mike pounded Wall's back as Jon struck out for the platform ladder.

"Being sensible doesn't mean lack of ability, you bugger." The Brit removed his fins, slapping them onto the platform. "Where's Melanie?"

Jill couldn't find the energy to speak.

Another flurry of bubbles, and the blonde rose from the sea with mask in hand, her mouthpiece trailing behind in a frothy cloud.

Locking eyes with Jill, she trilled with laughter.

"You took your time." Wall frowned. "Where the hell—"

Jill toppled into the sea.

∞

Vessel San Dicaro, west of Saint-Domingue, 1648

He stood tall and lanky, as did all in his family. Unruly hair and too much humor, or so his father said. He had no humor now.

Quash leaned his head against the planked wall. He felt weary, bone-numbingly weary. There is a point where a man quits fighting. Drowning, sinking, his body finally surrendered. Often, the muscles acknowledge defeat before the mind can fully accept it.

"We cannot fight them," he whispered in reply. "It is death to fight them."

"To accept this fate is death," the warrior answered. "He is the one they speak of, the Sadico. He gains pleasure in torture."

The warrior stepped out of shadow, an angry stump where his hand had been days before, beaten more savagely than Quash had once thought any man could be and still draw breath.

Yet he looked more alive than Quash felt.

The vessel pitched in the ocean, waves thrashing in the storm, echoing the violence on the ship.

All nightmares are shamed by this day, he thought.

In the long flash of lightening, he watched two sailors haul the old man across the pitching deck. The strawberry on his face marked him as the one who'd been kind to Juba. His hands bound, a grinning sailor threaded a rope through those bonds. Others tossed the end of that rope over the spear that pointed the way of the ship.

The bowsprit, the white men called it.

The captain strode through them all, hauling the girl behind him. While the old man watched, the Sadico tossed her to the deck—a child of barely nine summers.

And the Spaniard fell atop her. The storm of the night screamed at them brutally, thundering protest. Yet louder still, he heard her screams.

And he saw, when the captain raised his face, the red glistening on his mouth. The warrior had named them animals, and here now was proof. The Sadico had bit her ear—as her father had done to him hours before.

The old man with the strawberry erupted, fighting furiously to reach her; to save her. To kill this devil. He had no chance, of course. The white man's rope always held fast.

"A warrior does not fight because the odds favor him. A true man fights because he cannot accept what is thrust upon him. He wins because he fights for a righteous cause."

The laughing sailors yanked the line, jerking the old man over the railing. Two men lashed him to the pole, where he would ride through the heart of the storm till his flesh tore away and his bones slipped from the knots.

"We can't allow this, man. We are warriors!"

"We are dead men," Quash whispered.

Possession

all sat in the sailboat cockpit, a cold beer clenched in his fist.

Well, cool beer now. It had warmed somewhat. He set it aside in one of the holders Americans seemed to pride themselves on.

"What do you think happened?" he asked.

Jon made no answer. The man stood beside him, firmly clutching the wheel as if somehow that would determine the outcome, sailing the *Sadicor* back to Antigua.

Jill seemed physically fine. She'd told them an odd, hysterical tale of being trapped inside the wreck searching for Melanie.

The blonde had told a different story: having dutifully worked the gap as she was bid, she turned to discover Jill had vanished. She claimed to then methodically scan the area, rise to the surface, and mount the platform. Upon finding no Jill above sea level, she dove back down to the wreck to search some more. She'd been so worried, she said.

Jill's story made no sense. She described seeing Melanie struggling inside the wreck, except it wasn't Melanie. The interior had silted up, which was likely with a novice floundering around, but so much so that the brunette couldn't tell where the opening was. Physically shaking, at times incoherent, Jon had finally coaxed her to lie down.

It made no sense at all, yet Wall believed Jill's version.

Perhaps it was the blonde's calm explanation, her thorough reasoning, and her flawless procedure. Too well-reasoned, too sensible for a novice. And there was genuine horror in Jill's voice. True, she had often begged to enter the wreck—but to do so alone, with her buddy missing and her mentors out of reach? She couldn't be that rash.

And while Jill was shaken, verging on hysteria, Melanie had been coldly amused.

"What do you think happened?" he asked again. Wall had demanded answers earlier, receiving nothing intelligent in reply.

"There's a doctor on the island." Jon gripped the wheel in a wrestler's hold. "He's a friend of mine. He'll know what to do."

Wall could only hope he was right.

Wrapping his own fingers around the warm glass bottle, he raised the beer from its holder to his mouth. The flat, watery beverage did nothing for his mind or his stomach. He hated American beer. Wall grimaced, firmly setting the beverage aside.

"What the hell happened?" he murmured.

Jon sailed on.

∞

Nita saw the *Sadicor* slip into her berth.

Her heart gave a tiny leap, and she realized that fact ruefully. Mike was supposed to be a diversion, not an obsession. Enjoy being his girl in port, she'd decided, as long as she kept in mind the man had other ports.

Well, he was here now. Back sooner than he'd said.

Nita grabbed one of the new pocket shirts, a large one in a sky blue print to set off his eyes. Impulsively, she snatched a crystal from the plastic bin, inserting it inside the tiny compartment as she ran.

She'd avoided her two aunts, something easily done and preferable to arguing. Her mother's mother, a woman she'd never known in life, was not so easily fooled.

"Where do you go, Nita?" the crone demanded, appearing on the path before her.

Nita stepped around her, though she could easily walk through. Well, not so easily, as it felt cold to her skin and always angered the woman.

"My man docks his boat. I go to meet him."

"The crippled warrior is not your man."

At her words, a chill touched her spine. Her grandmother—but she refused to call her that—always sneered at Mike. Her words held no sneer now.

"He will be, someday," Nita responded.

"Do not do this thing."

Nita hurried away, along the path between the two houses, only to be confronted again at the gate.

"Child, do not do this thing," she said. "Go consult your aunts. Go consult your own heart."

For an instant, Nita wavered, but only for an instant. Then she raced on, through the crone and past the gate. The former could not follow outside the center.

I probably won't even go through with it, she told herself. Her hurry now was because of the blonde.

That woman clung to the tall man in hopes of inducing marriage. Once she accepted that plan would never succeed, she'd switch to Mike. Hers was the nature to both desire and disdain the earthy types. Such women could never be happy until they dealt with that conflict.

Nita reached the wharf in less than twenty minutes, yet to her surprise, Mike stood alone on the deck. He gazed at the taxi stand, which was simply the place Ernie the driver waited whenever he caught sight of a boat coming in to dock.

The taxi wasn't there. Either Ernie had started early at the pub, or he'd already taken some fare to St. John's.

As she stepped close, she saw the muscles in Mike's face. He'd clenched his jaw, eyes narrowed even though they gazed away from the sun. Her warrior was not happy, and that alone was enough to worry her.

"Michael?"

The blue eyes reluctantly shifted. When his muscles smoothed into a smile, Nita released a breath she hadn't realized she'd been holding.

"We hadn't expected you back so soon," she offered. When he didn't take the bait, she asked, "Everything all right?"

He gazed a moment longer before his lips parted. "Jill had an accident. She's fine," he added before her gasp died. "Jon's taking her to the doctor. What's that?" He indicated the cloth in her hand, deterring further questions.

"A gift. A pocket shirt. My own design. I had twenty made."

Nita stepped carefully to board the *Sadicor*, but Mike forestalled her, blocking her way to take the shirt from her fingers.

"That pocket's set a little off, isn't it?" He held it aloft, pretending to admire it before laying it on a cockpit bench.

"The shirt pocket's set over the heart chakra," she explained. "You place a crystal inside, for protection or to enhance your energy without needing to wear a pendant."

Mike burst out laughing.

Behind him, the blonde appeared. Her silky blouse fluttered enticingly in the breeze, dancing about the two bottles of beer clutched in her hands. She cocked an eyebrow at Nita. "I didn't know there were three of us."

Mike turned.

"And I think we're just out of beer," she purred, tucking one arm around his.

To Nita's delight, her warrior disengaged himself, knocking a bottle to the deck in his haste. It rolled to stop at the woman's foot.

"You can drink both," Mike told her, hopping off the *Sadicor* to wrap Nita's arm around his. "Thank you for the shirt, sweetheart," he told her warmly. "I'll wear it tonight."

The blonde glowered at them both, genuinely surprised, Nita realized. "I thought we were all going to the casino," she pouted. Not a sexy pout, but more with the look of a disgruntled child.

"We"—Mike nodded his head to indicate Nita—"are going wherever Nita wishes to go." And turning his back on the blonde, he escorted her away.

Nita didn't dare glance back. Enlightened beings did not grin so triumphantly.

∞

Melanie stared after them.

When the *Sadicor* had first docked, and Jill was bundled off to the taxi, Melanie had pretended to sleep. She pretended when Wall cracked open the door and pretended as she felt his gaze upon her body.

She'd grinned when he left.

The Brit was too tepid, and she'd come to realize she deserved more. She deserved a hot, sexy animal. She deserved Mike.

So she waited, watching through the porthole. When Wall had jumped to the wharf, she had leapt to the dresser, chosen just the right clothes, and applied just the right touch of mascara and lipstick. The bed loomed behind her, brushing her thighs as she swept her blonde strands into an alluring twist.

She pictured Mike in that bed, unruly dark hair dangling about his chiseled face with shades of tanned skin, minute shadows hollowing the cleft in his chin. And those deep sea blue eyes, the only color in his profile.

Now beneath the hot Caribbean sun, she felt chilled. He'd rejected her. She hadn't been rejected in years. Mike should have stepped back when she appeared; he should have enjoyed two women battling for him. Or better yet, he should have shooed that black bitch away.

Instead Melanie now stood alone, like a cheap hooker who'd demanded too high a price.

The worst part had been seeing Nita suppress her triumph.

Flouncing on the bench, Melanie shoved the stupid shirt out of the way and felt the hard lump.

Buried within the blue print, inside a tiny pocket, her fingers unearthed a glasslike cylinder. *What is this?*

Trying to guard the man's heart.

Her neck prickled, feeling the familiar whirring behind her. Anger rose with the whirls. No wonder Mike had rejected her. Nita had cheated, using a sneaky trick to trap the man.

Melanie had no epiphany standing there. She had no real plan at all. Clutching the crystal, she climbed down the stair-ladder, flung open the cabin door, and snatched up her necklace.

The ruby dropped off easily. It wasn't the proper ruby after all—it had fallen into her hand from the treasure chest that held no other treasure. No one knew it existed.

Racing back to the steps, she vaulted up, popping outside as the sun hid behind a cloud. She slipped the ruby into the pocket and tossed the crystal overboard.

Melanie opened the beer still lying on deck, toasting the air before drinking deeply. The magic woman would not sleep with her man tonight after all.

∞

Dr. Mallory's place was a true island house. Painted a crisp white, it had more plantation shutters than simple wall, and numerous ceiling fans stirred the air.

Jon waited in the library. Although short on shelves, it had many books. Bathed in a sort of cluttered cleanliness, it seemed as though someone meticulously dusted the stacked piles without ever so much as straightening them.

Spotting an old tome labeled *Reincarnation Operating Principles*, he plucked it up and opened to a chapter titled 'Gatherings' just as the doctor appeared.

Mallory's age was somewhere north of thirty-five, his body reed thin and meticulously groomed down to his pointed goatee.

"No ill effects, my friend."

Jon sighed.

"In a bit of shock," Mallory continued, "but she'll recover. Don't push her to dive. Wait until she's ready."

"So Jill's perfectly fine."

"Save for her temper," a girl said.

Jon turned to find a ten year old in a red dress, gazing at him over a handful of medical instruments.

Dr. Mallory shook his head at the child. "You don't need to speak to do your work. Jon, this is Ammie."

Jon offered a swift smile, but Ammie merely walked away.

Dr. Mallory noticed the book in Jon's hand. "Still pursuing that foolish study?"

Jill emerged, face pale but less dazed. "Another regression book?" she asked, noting the book's title. And frowned at the doctor. "I thought it was you who got Jon started with that."

"When he sought answers, I pointed out the path. Now that the barking dog is silenced, it's best to let the sleeping ones sleep."

Ammie snorted and crossed the room to dump her burden in a sterilization unit.

Jon agreed with Ammie. The profound results of regression spoke for themselves. He couldn't conceive how Mallory would ignore such success.

The brunette's lips twisted, and he well knew that look. With Jill, it was all or nothing. Moderation was an unknown concept.

"Dr. Mallory believes delving too much in the past is more dangerous that not delving at all."

"Dr. Mallory can speak for himself." The man smiled. "I believe seeking the answers to a current life problem is crucial. Regression goes to the heart of the trouble. But trying to learn more before these things are ready to be revealed revives long forgotten energies. By their nature, very powerful energies for the soul. Some things are best left buried to decay."

Ammie returned with a tray of drinks.

Jon watched the girl deliberately startle Jill before waiting in some amusement as she cautiously tried one.

"Lemonade," Jill told Jon. "But regression helped me. At least—I think it did."

"It did help you," Jon assured her. Her personal space issue had vanished, at least as far as he could tell. "It helped because a past issue had boiled over into this life. Seeing the source of it—why you felt it—enabled you to heal from a higher perspective."

"It did! It really opened my eyes!"

The doctor smiled. "You followed the thread of your recurring reaction to the source. But some practitioners use more powerful methods, blasting the victim back without necessity or thread to follow. The energies thus stirred can be...undesirable."

Seeing Jill's wide eyes, Jon shook his head. "That's just his theory...that ignorance is indeed bliss." He took a glass from Ammie's tray and smiled his thanks.

Ammie ignored him. "Now?" she asked, and it took a moment to realize she was talking to Dr. Mallory.

The doctor twitched his head, sending her away.

Jill was still disturbed. "What about the...soul pod stuff? Souls coming back together?"

"We tend to meet the same souls in each life, Jill." Jon said it with the same conviction he used to explain scuba diving procedures. "We travel together, if you will. On this side of the veil, we're kind of drawn to each other. Vibrate at the same frequency."

"Vibrate?"

The doctor smiled warmly at her now. "The Bible talks of the energy when souls gather in His Name."

Jon could see the doubt in Jill's face.

She snatched up her purse and set it down again. "What if these souls—the whole soul pod—shared a bad experience?"

"They'd just replay individual problems," Jon told her, closing the reincarnation book.

"Unless," Dr. Mallory said, "the vibration was both powerful and shared."

Jon stilled. "Energy vortex," he said.

"Karmic vortex," Mallory corrected him. "You're correct. Souls do tend to replay old issues. The bigger the issue...the more souls present..." The doctor shook himself, as if clearing the thought. "Wars have begun that way. Old grievances igniting new conflict."

Jill shook her head. "No. Surely nothing big carries over."

Beethoven's *Moonlight Sonata* suddenly disturbed the atmosphere, low and haunting, expertly played. Jon turned to see young Ammie at the piano, tiny fingers caressing keys, her face screwed up in concentration.

"Of course it does," the doctor told her. "Of course it does! Tendencies, feelings, preferences. They all come from earlier times. Even a few memories may seep through if we allow them."

Jon clasped Jill's shoulders, turning her toward the door. He felt the need to get out in the sunshine.

"Do you wish to borrow that?" Mallory asked.

Looking down, Jon realized he still clutched the book and that his finger had marked a passage.

Beware the gathering of men and earthbound souls. For doorways are blown open, and Hell itself unleashed.

Snapping it shut, he dropped the book and left.

∞

"Here," Nita said, and heard the excited timbre of her voice. This would never do—she needed to calm herself.

"You never told me." Mike kissed her bare shoulder.

Her fingers lifted the hidden latch and the beadboard panel creaked open, revealing the narrow doorway to the hidden room.

The ladies called it the windowless room. It lay in the heart of the home. Supposedly the old house and the new were identical, but the new building lacked this narrow space. It barely measured ten foot by eight, with some of that lost to shelving at one end. Tales claimed the plantation owners used it to hide during slave rebellions. In fact, Thomas Kerby, owner of the famous Prince Klaas—the slave he accused of planning a full island rebellion—had cowered from them in this very room.

Or so they said.

"You want to do this here?" Mike broke her reverie.

"Unless you're afraid." She winced as her words dangled in the air. It was a blatant ploy—and Mike's lifting eyebrow showed he knew it.

But he let her have her way.

The truth was, it startled Nita, the amount of thinking she'd put into this. How desperately she needed to prove herself, to show him reincarnation existed. As the big man swung open her folding massage table, she felt a qualm. Desperate energy was the wrong vibe for this experiment.

She placed four crystals around the room and lit the incense. It was a special blend she'd spent hours developing, with mugwort, celery, and jasmine. Plus that odd oil she'd discovered in town. Nita had avoided the usual sage and sandalwood, both of which would have protected them and kept the energy positive.

She'd feared they would reduce the power.

A single bulb dangled from the ceiling, a chain pull dropping so low, Mike's hair tangled with it. Its light was dim but badly placed. Instead, she lit four candles, one in each corner.

Table legs locked, Mike turned. "I can think of other things to do here," he murmured, tracing her jaw with his thumb.

Of all the men she knew, he alone had this touch, this ability to tantalize females. He never forced, never pushed, using instead an enticing aura that drew her on. Every step was her own choice. Precisely because of this, women went much further with him than they ever normally would. Even in the afterglow, a woman knew her choice. He was too potent a sexual male to need force. He simply offered.

And knowing that, it was a hard thing to regret. His reputation was as a womanizer, but he truly appreciated women. He delighted in them, loved them, if you accepted that his love never promised exclusivity.

Mike's secret was he respected women—as equals. He saw them as powerful, as sexual, as human as himself. He gave an honest choice, and his sincerity made it hard to refuse.

"Later," she promised herself as much as him.

Nita started the music she'd snuck in earlier—an odd African chant that demanded success rather than entreated it. Soothing despite the patter.

And lastly, of course, his shirt.

Mike hadn't wanted to go back to the boat to retrieve it—but she'd insisted. Fortunately the blonde was gone. Even more fortunately, Mike had donned it.

So now the fifth crystal lay upon his solar plexus, the one she hadn't mentioned because she feared he'd find it silly. Between the crystals, the incense, and the music, this regression should work.

It will have little choice. She smiled to herself.

Carefully, she manipulated the cloth so the pocket lump was set perfectly on the chakra. Nita avoided touching the crystal itself for fear Mike would feel it. She'd pushed far—too far, really. Best he not know about that till afterward.

In the distance, the old grandfather clock chimed the hour of seven. The sun had barely set, the stars just stretching themselves.

An hour of power, came the unbidden thought.

She switched off the overhead light.

Mike lay on the table, folding his hands and closing his eyes. "I'm hungry," he announced to the air. "Let's get this thing over with."

Yet seconds ticked away as she hesitated. She'd planned this for days, dreamt of her triumph in his seeing her ability. Wondered just what the regression would reveal about his past. Such an interesting past, she knew.

Don't do this, something whispered, even as her hands slipped to his shoulders, massaging. Soothing.

Kneading away any last resistance.

"Can you picture yourself on a beach, Michael?" she murmured. She always used the green meadow image— but different words seemed to rise from her depths. "The sand at your feet, the waves lapping at the shore. You're walking, heading to a cave."

As her fingers detected his hesitation, her eyes focused on the shirt bulge; the crystal on his chest. She instinctively willed him on, crushing any denial.

"It's in the distance and familiar to you. A cave you well know. Treasure awaits you there, Michael. Lying behind a golden key."

The air surrounding them crackled. Her eyes saw nothing, but she felt tiny sparks whirring, swirling. Just beyond the five senses, but not quite beyond the sixth.

"The opening looms in front of you now. Your feet stop before the dark within. But you're fearless, my warrior. Bravely you go inside."

Clenched muscles in his shoulders melted. She saw him enter the cavern.

"Your passage slopes down, spiraling deep into the earth. There lies adventure, Michael. There lies treasure. Stride on and learn."

In Nita's mind, she saw him striding. Fear made him cautious, as he felt something behind him. Stalking him. When he shifted his stance, she realized he'd readied a spear.

"Don't..." Her assurances of safety died, for he was not safe.

Something did stalk him. She sensed the image unraveling—the cave, the sea, even the dark. His whole world was unraveling.

Spinning away with hurricane speed.

The sheer power churned her blood to ice. Sensing such things always took will and effort, yet now she couldn't turn it off. His dark churned with her blood, becoming something not dark.

Something darker than dark.

∞

He sensed a tunnel.

All other ways had been demanded by him, created by him. He swelled, he pushed—and the path appeared at his command.

This one slipped into awareness. Distant, which made him wary. He never left this place—yet this tunnel promised something new, something special. A host with arms and legs, capable of doing more of what his essence screamed to do.

Gathering himself, compressing, sucking in all his fury, he knew he could do this. Gleeful with unholy joy, he leapt the gap.

∞

Nita sped round the tiny room, kicking the floor crystals over.

"Mike, no! Retreat!"

His tensing muscles smoothed, relaxing.

Breathing deeply, gratefully, Nita looked at his face.

The last thing she saw was two pinpricks of power, not light. Burning eyes of a pale blue. Watery pale and so hot they burned the skin, so cold they chilled the soul.

Then Nita saw nothing at all.

∞

The galley clock struck eight.

Melanie heard it, locked in her cabin with her ear pressed to the door. She also heard, through the creaking of the boat and the play of waves on wood surrounding her, his footsteps. Slow, careful.

Stalking.

There was a peephole of sorts. An odd gap in a patched hole. Through it, she saw the sweat glistening on his brow, damp patches on the sky blue shirt. His forearm muscles rippled, tightening. Her stomach answered, clenching enticingly.

The eyes, devoid of his usual thoughts, reflected others in their stead. When his fingers twisted the door handle, she felt it rotate against her hip.

The lock held.

He tried again. And then he pounded the wood, shaking the surrounding frame. Melanie stepped back, eyes sparkling. Her tongue moistened her lips. She was afraid, and the fear was delicious.

He struck again. Timber groaned, protesting. Surely one more strike would rip it apart.

That strike never came.

Through the gap, she saw him turn and lope off, like an animal on a new scent.

He'll be back, she knew.

∞

Spying the man at a distant table, Wall made his way through the casino crowd.

Jon grinned and waved at the vacant seat beside him. Wall fished two twenties from his wallet, received a short stack of red chips, and flicked one into the tiny circle.

Crisp new cards snapped as they were dealt atop the green felt. Jon drew a seven and eight; Wall fared better with a jack and eight. The dealer's card was a seven.

"You're looking good." Jon beckoned for another card.

"Looks can be deceiving."

The six of hearts landed atop his hand, yielding a total of twenty-one. Behind them, a woman in a low-cut black dress paused to watch.

Very low cut, Wall noticed when she leaned in further. He realized the dealer was waiting on his call, and he waved the man on.

The dealer turned over his hole card—another seven—and dealt himself a five for a total of nineteen. Smiling apologetically, the man whisked Wall's chip away.

"Oh, tough." Jon pulled his own winnings close as Wall placed another bet.

The woman in the black dress left.

Somehow, the fancy casino just added to the surreal air of the day. Wall found himself rubbing his split cheek, forcing his hand back down to the green felt.

"What happened to you?"

"Shaving accident."

Jon frowned, probably at seeing his cards. "Again? You need to be more careful."

Wall nodded. An hour earlier his razor had scored a slice in his cheek—when Melanie had bumped his arm. She'd apologized in a sweet tone that left him more suspicious than appeased.

"Melanie find the rooftop dancing?" Jon grinned as the dealer dealt him two face cards.

Wall got a face card and a six. "Headache. She took something and went to bed."

Jon collected more winnings, and Wall lost another hand.

"Can't blame her," Jon told him, as if knowing Wall did precisely that. "That must have been scary to surface and find no Jill. And then make herself go back down alone. It took nerve."

"She has a lot of nerve," he answered, hoping those words hadn't revealed too much.

Common sense said he should wait till they were home before officially ending the relationship, though his resolution had suffered with the arm bump.

Losing again, Wall pocketed the remaining chip. It obviously wasn't his night.

"Blackjack!" the dealer announced as an ace fell atop Jon's ten of spades.

Wall fingered his pocketed chip but decided to leave it there. "Where's Jill?"

"She's here somewhere." Beckoning a waitress, the small man pointed to his empty Guinness bottle.

The girl swept it away with a friendly wink and vanished in the crowd.

"She could be with Mike, but I doubt it. Mike likes to do a little prowling when we're here."

Somewhere, a lounge band launched into the song "Bad Moon Rising," raising the hair on his arm for no reason Wall could identify. "Prowling?"

"Female tourists." Jon split a pair of eights and turned them into two hands of eighteen. "Or Nita. She's becoming a real favorite. He needs some release tonight. Tomorrow's...a little stressful."

"So you're going through with it?"

Jon pulled in another pile of chips. "Mike's done this before. He may seem a little cavalier, but he knows what he's doing."

Cavalier. Why did Americans use that word when 'cowboy' was so much more accurate?

As the singer wailed, "There's a bad moon on the rise," Wall scooted his stool away from the table. "I'm gonna look for Jill."

"Try the roulette table. She usually watches for twenty minutes, to get the slant of the particular wheel, she says, and then places a single chip on red." Jon tipped the waitress as his Guinness plunked down before him. "Tell her we sail back tonight. Everyone on board by eleven."

Wall checked his watch: eight thirty. "I'll tell her."

∞

Nita woke slowly, swimming up through a void. Something resisted her waking.

At least part of that resistance was herself. She knew she'd done something terrible.

One candle sputtered, and another had gone out. Candles that should have lasted for hours. Rising to her feet, she saw the rectangle of kitchen light across the room. The hidden door now gaped open, flung wide as if something had escaped.

Something had escaped.

No protection. She marveled at her foolishness. She'd been so intent to prove her skills to Mike that she'd ignored most of them. She had acted with no regard for his own needs or his own wishes. And no thought to safety.

Something had come in.

Nita stumbled, rounding the massage table, and used it to steady herself. Reaching the bright light of the kitchen was a relief.

For all our sophistication, she thought, *we still yearn for the bonfire to chase away the terrors in the dark.*

The garden door stood open. When she stepped into the night, she saw the door handle had dented the siding. Such force had blown it open. She had to find him, she thought, even as her knees collapsed, even as she sank to the planks of the porch.

All this time, she'd worried about giving her heart to him and fearing his betrayal of her trust. In the end, she had betrayed him.

Shutting her eyes, she checked in with her solar plexus, sagging with relief to feel he lived, that he would survive, that he would wake in the morning and be in his right mind again.

But that future of them married, of them dwelling together in this house, no longer existed.

It, too, had vanished in the night.

∞

Wall threaded his way through the casino crowd, dodging excited craps players, lost patrons, and a woman in ridiculously high heels as she staggered from the bar. He saw no sign of Jill.

The body heat from the mass of people added to the warm night, so he climbed the two steps to the ornate French doors and slipped outside.

A stone-tiled terrace stretched beneath the stars, bathed in moonlight and offering a pleasant breeze. The Caribbean moon hung large and full over the sparkling ocean, and the exotic scent of frangipani teased his senses.

Very romantic, all in all. Only thing lacking was a lady by his side.

Moving to the balustrade, he allowed himself to play with the thought until he realized he was imagining dark hair instead of blonde. He sighed and leaned on the rail.

Watching the waves break on the nearby beach, the whitecaps visible beneath the bright moon, he relaxed. The rhythmic swishing lulled. Concern over underwater demolition diminished, if it was not entirely banished. After all, he'd be on the surface for the actual bang.

And it was easy to relax under a tropical evening sky.

He had the terrace to himself, save for a couple entwined a short distance away. They were heavily occupied.

He caught a glimpse of long dark hair, and a man's face buried in the nape of her neck. Decency made him turn away.

An odd gasp made him turn back.

The woman writhed, face jerking toward the light from the casino doors, her fingernails straining against the man's shoulders.

Trying to pry herself free.

"Jill!" Wall sprinted to her, seeing her tears glistening. Mascara ran down her cheek. He'd never seen her wear mascara before.

At the same instant, he recognized the man. "Jesus, Mike! You're hurting her!"

He yanked on one powerful arm to no avail. The big man didn't seem to notice him at all.

Could he be high on something?

Mike's head buried deeper in her flesh.

Jill cried out, beating on his back ineffectually.

Something inside Wall snapped.

Grabbing a fist of hair, he yanked it painfully, peeling Mike's face off her neck.

A wild blue pupil rolled and focused on Wall. There was no shame, no surprise, and certainly no recognition. Only pure rage.

The huge man snarled, a low guttural sound that stilled the heart and froze the blood. For an instant, he beheld an enraged monster.

Wall slammed his fist into the man's exposed chin.

Mike staggered back, releasing Jill. Immediately, Wall stepped between them, palms out in a placating gesture, but ready to do battle.

"Mike..."

Mike whirled and vaulted the railing to lope down the beach.

"Oh, God."

Wall turned to see Jill wobbling on her feet. He steadied her, slipping an arm about her shoulders to guide her to a nearby bench. "Jill, what the hell happened?"

She shook her head, staring at the patio tile. Gently, he turned her toward the light, lifting her chin to see dark spots on her bare shoulder, beneath her ripped dress. Another drop fell.

"Jesus! This is blood! That bastard bit your ear!"

She trembled violently.

Shock, he realized. He needed to get her back to the *Sadicor*. Or to a clinic? Ought there to be shot of penicillin or something for a human bite?

"He...he jumped over the railing. I was looking for Jon..."

"Mike jumped over the railing?"

"Why do you keep saying that?" For the first time, she focused on him, withdrawing a little. "That wasn't Mike! He spoke Spanish...had that...beard..."

Her face crumbled, fresh tears flooding her cheeks.

Wall firmly tucked her head against his shoulder and let her cry.

But there had been no beard. His knuckles still felt the contact of flesh on flesh, bare skin slick with sweat.

And that expression. Pure animal, devoid of any humanity. Jesus, he'd literally bit her ear, vicious enough to leave four bloody holes.

Drug-induced, possibly.

Mike Burke for sure.

Cargo

It was dark, still hours from midnight.

Melanie rose from the bed, staring at the cabin door.

Her image in the mirror caught her attention: eyes glittering above her bare breasts. Lips curled in a weird smile—the sort a cat wears when it's just devoured the canary.

I want my ruby, she thought.

For an instant, that thought startled her.

What the hell am I doing?

Her mind felt numb, trapped in a fog. It was some sort of dream, maybe over, maybe not. Trying to think, she broke eye contact with her reflection.

His fist struck the door, pounding and threatening. Demanding. The wood creaked in protest and splintered. His hand smashed through the hole and turned the lock.

Her weird smile fell back in place. Here was her gem.

Her arms reached out to welcome them both.

∞

Wall moved down a hazy corridor.

He was chasing something, or someone. There was a man ahead, with big shoulders and muscles on his arm. The man had brown hair, a little long.

No—he had black hair, very long and filthy. Wall knew him well. Well enough to understand he was not a man to follow.

But still he followed.

The man faded. The corridor shortened, now a tiny area with two doors. One led to the compressor room. Cracked open as it was, Wall leaned in to watch the odd lights flickering inside, punctuated with a sort of animal grunting. He ought to continue, but his hand spread out against the door.

It slowly swung wide, to reveal a dark cavern with flickering lights dancing on the metal machine. Beyond a web of dangling air hoses, he saw Melanie, bare-chested and facing him, moving rhythmically. The animal grunts came from behind her.

Mike's fingers dug into her shoulders, and the blonde lifted welcoming arms toward Wall. He pulled back in refusal.

Jon stepped out of shadow, embracing Melanie. His mouth devoured hers as she clawed the shirt from his back. Behind her, a bearded man now stood in Mike's stead. He threw his head back and howled.

Wall turned to the curtained door, the one to the tiny bow cabin. The one that couldn't be bolted.

Jill lay sleeping fitfully, whimpering as she tossed and turned. The sheet was wound tight about her, tangling her limbs.

He meant only to help, to free her. In his mind, he intended his hand pull the sheet loose. His fingers obediently grasped and tugged, exposing a breast.

In his mind, he saw his mouth brush her skin. He leaned down and tasted her, the faint trace of salt on smooth flesh instantly arousing him. Needing more, he pinned her down.

In his mind, he saw his teeth bite through skin. Drawing blood and fear, he declared his power over her.

Beneath him, she cried out.

Wall fell back, horrified. Still asleep, she arched toward him, begging, pleading. Her skin was still whole. He hadn't hurt her yet.

He fled.

∞

Wall shot up.

He was in the galley booth, lying as best he could in the hastily converted bed. The *Sadicor* itself was dark and silent.

He'd dreamt that he was dreaming. Who had such nightmares?

Squinting at his watch, he saw that it was after 4 a.m. The *Sadicor* had reached the wreck site in record time, and everyone now slept in preparation for the task ahead. He had chosen the galley bed. Why had he chosen the galley?

Jill.

She'd refused to tell Jon about the attack and had become angry when he'd pushed. No matter what he told her, the brunette was adamant it had not been Mike on the terrace.

Still shaky when Jon saw them later, she'd laughed about having too much to drink, and her cousin, eager to sail, had accepted her words at face value.

So Wall slept here to guard her door. And perhaps to avoid the implications of his own cabin's damaged door.

Looking now in that direction, he saw an odd flickering.

From the compressor room, he realized. His hands reached to leverage himself out of the booth to check on Jill.

Remembering the dream, he froze and forced himself to lie back down.

It was a while before he found sleep again.

∞

When the sun rose, his power waned. The returning strength of the warrior threw him out and sent him back.

No matter. They were all back, their very proximity feeding his will.

∞

Jill poured her coffee and spooned her sugar. As one hand stirred, her other crept up to her neck.

The tiny mirror in the bathroom cubbyhole had revealed a bruise on her shoulder, three pools of dried blood on her ear, and a fourth shallow fleck. At least her hair hid the damage.

Now, with the sun glaring through the portholes, Jill wasn't sure which memories were real from last night and which mere remnants of nightmares. Just like the old dreams from her childhood, when she used to fear the dark and fear having those whom she loved snatched away. It had been decades since she'd had those dreams.

When she tried to remember the face of her attacker, she saw only a beard. He was a stranger, yet somehow familiar. There was a wisp of a dream...

She drank too fast and burned her tongue. "Damn."

Wall popped up in the booth, scaring the bejesus out of her.

She spilled hot coffee on her fingers. "Damn!"

The Brit rubbed his head, blinking to clear his vision. "You've got to find more swear words."

Anger flared and died. He'd actually come to her rescue last night—that part at least was true. And now he looked just as she felt: bone-tired.

"Jill..." He was watching her carefully, she realized.

"Wall, it wasn't Mike. How could you possibly think he would do such a thing?"

"I know what I saw. I wasn't the one in shock."

That was an insult. She hadn't been some stupid girl fainting in the hero's arms. A nasty retort rose to her lips, but she bit it back. He didn't deserve insults. Wall had faced a monster to save her last night. This man, who Mike loved to call a coward.

So she kept quiet, watching him extricate himself from the narrow booth-bed. It took a full thirty seconds just to untangle his legs.

When at last he joined her in the tiny galley, he reached over her head to dig a coffee mug from the cupboard. "Anyone," he told her as he filled his cup, "would be in shock. Hell, I'm in shock."

She leaned away from him, the counter edge digging into her spine. Not because he invaded her personal space, but because she liked it too much.

"I'm okay. I am. But Mike didn't do it. Anyway, he's got an alibi."

The Brit stilled. His eyes widened, and she realized he saw the door. She thought he'd seen it last night – but perhaps he hadn't believed it.

The cabin door—the cabin he shared with Melanie— had a splintered hole the size of a fist.

Wall strode to it and peered inside. Jill knew what he saw: the bed with torn sheets, the pillow thrown across the room.

Even as he digested this, the door flew open, and Melanie stepped out, smoothing a huge sky-blue shirt over her bare legs. A shirt with an odd center pocket.

"Good morning," she cooed. "Mike and I had the littlest...accident...last night."

∞

The whole day had started wrong.

Jon found himself chafing at the delays, the odd currents suddenly swirling in the water. The odd currents suddenly swirling around his friends. Wall, normally even-tempered, fumed at something, something he would not discuss. Jill jumped a mile when he asked her about it, then frantically denied any knowledge.

Only Melanie smiled this morning. And he didn't trust that smile.

As for his partner—who should have been pushing him, demanding they go faster, insisting they do this—Mike was hungover.

Now the big man hunched at the booth table, an untouched bowl of cereal before him.

Jon slid a coffee cup under his nose. "Can you even do this today?"

Mike clutched his head in his hands. "I don't remember last night. You didn't let me drink, did you?"

Jon physically took one of those hands and wrapped it around the mug. "Drink."

One eye rotated in his direction. "Nita pissed with me?"

"Wouldn't be surprised. I was in the casino, Mike. Didn't know you needed a babysitter." He watched his friend a moment more, then sighed. "Shall we postpone? Till this afternoon, maybe?"

"No." Mike raised the cup, slowly pouring the entire steaming contents down his throat. Then he shook his head like a retriever coming out of the water. "No. We do the thing now. Won't take long—giving us plenty of bottom time this afternoon."

Relaxing, Jon grinned. His grin faded at the sight of the splintered door. "What the hell happened there?"

Mike eyed him questioningly then turned to follow his gaze.

"Bloody Brit. If he thinks I'm fixing stuff smashed during his little sex games..." Wincing, the muscle man rubbed his aching head.

∞

The launch motor cut out.

Jon turned to check that they were in position.

The *Sadicor* floated close to the island, set perfectly between the tallest palm on the beach and the launch itself, giving a rough reference point. Crucial today, especially as everything else seemed off this morning.

Mike slowly kitted up, lacking his normal energy. Beyond him, Wall seemed faintly...hostile.

Right, Jon thought. *If we're doing this, let's do it and be done.* "Maintain your position," he told the Brit as he grabbed his tanks. "Don't let her drift, and keep an eye on our bubbles. If we get a little off, follow us. I don't want to have swim for it once we surface."

Mike tugged a flipper over his toes. "We got ten minutes. Plenty of time."

"Electronic timer?" Wall asked.

The big guy opened the bag to produce a wrapped packet with a long wire-ish tube protruding. "Not exactly. The length of fuse is the timer."

Jon eyed it apprehensively. "You sure? Ten minutes worth?"

"That's what the kid said." Flippers on, Mike rooted around for his mask. "You know, ten minutes is a long time for something to go wrong...fish might eat it or something. I could cut this fuse in half..."

"*No!*" Both Wall and Jon stopped him.

Disgusted, Mike stuffed the thing back in the bag and set it down. He then threw himself backward into the Caribbean, his long machete scraping the launch as it slid.

"Why take that thing?" Wall demanded.

Pulling up over the gunwale, Mike grabbed the blue bag. "It's lucky," he said, attaching the bag to his B.C. as Jon donned his own mask.

Mike has done this before. It's not a big deal. Still, it took all Jon's willpower to roll backward over the side into the sea.

∞

Jon sank through a blast of bubbles. Mike must be jittery, or he was. Likely both.

Catching his buddy's eye, he saw his excitement shining through, the schoolboy thrill at doing something different and dangerous. Mike had only attempted this once before.

That time, they'd used too much dynamite.

They seemed to descend in slow motion, yet they reached the bottom all too soon. Sand whipped off the ocean floor, born away in swirling ribbons that wrapped around their bodies before vanishing into the distance. He'd never seen current this strong here. Already, it had swept the gap area clear, revealing what could only be a ship's deck.

A perfect square outline stood out. The cargo hold hatch. Mike swam straight for it and detached the bag. Reluctantly, Jon followed.

The current buffeted Jon, blasting him backward. Catching himself on the edge of the stern cabin, all he could do was watch.

Mike set the charge atop the hatch. Instantly, the ocean swept it up. The big guy barely saved the bundle before the sea would have claimed it.

The surge ceased, and he swam over as Mike thrust the explosive back in the bag and handed it to him. Jon felt greatly reluctant to take it. Slipping his arm through the handle at least kept both hands free to latch onto the cargo hold crack.

Mike swam away, disappearing in a funnel of sand.

A strong surge swung Jon's legs, yanking his fingers. He dug in, hands curling in claws. It won't detonate. It can't.

The last time Mike had tried this, Jon had questioned and probed till Mike's exasperation snapped. Without the fuse being lit, the charge couldn't accidentally go off. Still, fifty feet underwater in a record current, clinging to a piece of an old wreck with an explosive on his shoulder, doubt crept in.

Mike appeared, bearing three heavy rocks.

Again his partner laid the thing in place, this time anchoring it with the rocks. It seemed precarious, in danger of being swept away.

Maybe even, Jon had a sudden thought, *of being swept to the* Sadicor *herself.*

He tried to communicate this, but his buddy didn't grasp his concern—or he didn't share it.

Snapping an underwater stick-torch, Mike lit the fuse, and he calmly set his watch to count down the time. Jon rapidly did the same.

Shooting him a steady look—eyes brimming with excitement—Mike signaled 'up.' Jon released his fingers from the groove, already tumbling backward as he stabbed his air valve.

They ascended.

Reaching to clip the now empty bag to his B.C., Mike brushed his machete. Somehow, it wasn't properly secured.

The lucky blade sank to his fin—gently wobbled for a few seconds—and then slid off into the deep.

Jon winced, foreseeing time this afternoon wasted trying to find it. They wouldn't, of course. Eventually Mike would realize that.

Apparently, Mike realized it now. A swift check of the countdown, a quick dump of air, and the big man duck-dived in pursuit.

∞

Wall relaxed when the first diver broke the surface just beside the launch. As he reached for Jon's fins, however, there was no sign of his buddy. "Where's Mike?"

"I don't know," was the shaky answer. "Seven minutes till it goes off. He knows that. Only seven minutes left."

"Jon, how accurate is that fuse length? I mean, some kid at closing time cuts the thing. What's the margin of error?"

"Sweet Jesus." Jon frantically spun, clamping his mask back over his face so he could peer beneath the surface. "*Jesus!*"

Wall realized he was holding his breath and forced himself to let it out. "Let's get you in the launch. One less thing to worry about."

∞

He stirred.

Still depleted, he yet knew that they were near. Doing silly things in a futile quest.

Without thought he stretched out and found the manta ray. Possessing it was easy after last night's accomplishment.

If he could distract the one...

∞

Finding something on the bottom of the ocean floor was almost impossible, so Mike had kept his eyes on his blade the whole time. He now dropped to the sand beside it, grasping the handle before anything else could happen. He lifted it with genuine relief.

Not that he was superstitious or anything. But losing it, today of all days, would have been bad.

He was just reaching for the proper carabiner when the manta appeared. The damned ray nuzzled him, rubbing its head against his shoulder. Begging for attention.

Almost six full minutes remained, his timer showed, so Mike stretched out his gloved palm, allowing the creature to cuddle against it happily. There it stayed, body ruffling gently to maintain its position in the water.

Mike thrust the machete underneath.

The manta froze, seemingly stunned. Deliberately he ripped the blade down its center, making sure it was dead.

That's for Jill.

Reattaching his machete, he casually checked his watch: 4:07. Lots of time, he assured himself, even as he inflated his B.C. and rose. Cool as a Catholic nun.

When he thought he might be rising just a hair too fast, he breathed out all his air rather than slow down. Sunlight swelled, sounds rose in his ears. He burst through the surface.

"Where the hell have you been?" Jon shouted.

"Chill out, you pussy. We've got plenty of time." Yanking off his fins, he glanced at his watch before handing them over. "More than three minutes."

Jon snatched the flippers out of his grasp. "Island time, Mike."

Slowly the words sank in. Island time. The locals' lax, easygoing attitude toward the clock.

"Fucking son of a..." Mike grabbed the side of the boat, yanking himself up and clamping an arm over the gunwale. "Go! GO!"

Wall revved the motor.

∞

Lounging in the *Sadicor* cockpit, Jill heard the roar. She glanced over to watch Wall fumble with the engine, Jon springing to help.

"Something's not right. Hey, Melanie—something's wrong."

The blonde lay on her belly atop the cabin. Lifting her face to the sun, she smiled.

The motor dropped into the water and the launch leapt forward, roaring toward them.

Jill stood, watching Mike's body dragging dangerously in the water. Jesus—what were they playing at? If he lost his grip...

Then the boat was there, Wall wheeling it in a tight circle to bump against the dive platform. The engine cut off.

In the sudden silence, Wall and Jon huddled together over Jon's watch.

"Six, five, four, three..." Jon called off. Both men's heads bobbed with the count. "Two, one..." They all watched the water above the wreck.

A tiny puff of bubbles hit the surface, subsided.

Then nothing.

"Is that it?" Jill demanded. After all the hype, surely that hadn't blown a hole in anything.

"Wait for it," Mike told her, arm still clamped over the side.

Eagerly she did.

After a few minutes, Jon straightened. "I think that was it."

"Knew we should have used more explosive," Mike said, and then tried to move. "This bastard arm's gone numb!"

∞

Jill scraped the blob of mayonnaise she'd plopped on the bread.

"Don't tie yourself to a wood splinter," Jon continued. He'd been in full instructor mode for ten minutes running. "Find something solid and test it. We've got plenty of line, so don't make the mistake of feeling you have to tie off right at the entrance."

Slapping a slice of cheese atop her lunch meat, Jill folded the bread. Half a sandwich would do. She was too excited to eat properly anyway. She grabbed a bottle of water and headed to the table.

Jon, Mike, and Wall crowded the booth, peering down at Jon's inevitable sketches. The man was a frustrated artist, and he could never resist drawing things to illustrate a point.

"How far in do we go?" Wall sipped a soda, a sure sign he was planning to dive again. Jon and Mike would drink the occasional beer before a second dive, but Wall always waited until his diving was done for the day.

"That was a huge trap door." Jon grinned, tapping the deck sketch between them. "Got to be the cargo hold access. We drop straight through and cash in."

Wall shook his head. "Wouldn't a galleon have several levels? We may have a ways to go, and that's assuming she's intact."

Her cousin caressed his drawing. "They hoisted their cargo through that huge thing, which means we should drop straight into the middle of it."

Jill stared at it, irresistibly drawn to the image. If there really was gold, if that really was a Spanish galleon...

"You boys don't get all the fun." Melanie emerged from her cabin. "Jill and I want to dive too."

Silence. But a pregnant one, Jill knew.

"Not inside the wreck." Wall broke it first, looking to Jon. He didn't even bother addressing Melanie. "They're barely out of beginner class."

"You can't worry about 'overhead environments' when you just blasted away the overhead." The blonde laughed. A sparkly laugh, oozing with amusement and contempt. "And you can't insist we sit up here when the real fun's below. Besides, you'll need all the help you can get searching. Maybe carrying stuff."

Mike pondered and slowly nodded. "If we're not going any farther inside, it should be fairly simple."

"We don't know what's down there," Wall spoke to Jon. "I'm still new at this. There'll be other dives."

"You do overthink things, Brit-man. Let us at least go see this big crater you guys made. If you're afraid at that point, Jill and I can always surface again." The blonde grinned. "After all, Jill's the best diver in class. She wouldn't want to miss out on this tiny little adventure."

Meeting the sparkling green eyes, Jill felt the back of her neck prickle. She had absolutely no desire to go back inside that thing, and Melanie knew it. The woman was deliberately goading her.

How had she come to this? Fearing to try something that Melanie—the wimp of the dive class—eagerly demanded to do?

"They've got guts." Mike chuckled. "What's the harm in taking them down to the deck?"

Mike, Jill realized, was giving her that look of kindred spirits, that sharing of his intrepid nature.

"Two warriors," he'd once said.

How could she possibly confess to being chicken-hearted now?

Forcing a grin, she nodded. "Let's at least check out the damage you guys have wrought."

∞

Wall followed Jill into the compressor room.

He almost bumped into her back, she'd stopped so abruptly. Her hand yanked away from the reel on the peg wall. It took him a second to spot the gecko that had startled her.

"Jill, listen to me. Don't let Melanie talk you into this."

She stood staring at the lizard, hands clenched. He tried to step around to chase her dragon away, but the space was too narrow.

"I'm not afraid," she said rather pitifully.

"That bout of nyctophobia you felt in the cave is nothing compared to what you'll feel inside a shipwreck. Even if it starts out okay, it can silt up out of nowhere. The water adds to that feeling of being cutoff and alone."

"I don't have any fear," she said between her teeth. "I'm not afraid of the dark."

"Jill, don't be foolish. No one will think less of you for simply being sensible."

"If Melanie can do it, I can do it." The brunette shifted in her stance, eyeing the gecko warily. "At the very least, I want to look inside. Shine a flashlight and see. Maybe it's filled with gold."

"And if Jon beckons you deeper? Are you going to tell him no?"

"Melanie's right on one thing. You do overthink." Snatching a towel off a hook, she waved it at the lizard.

The gecko darted away.

Flashing a triumphant grin, she lifted the reel off the wall. "Dad always says you can't outrun your fears. You gotta face them head on." She squeezed past him and trotted away.

∞

Melanie couldn't wait.

Squatting on the dive platform, gear assembled, she snatched a hose from Jill when the brunette couldn't seem to click it in properly. She attached it in one fluid move and laughed aloud at the girl's expression.

So much for being the queen of dive class, you little half-breed. This was the ocean, not an indoor pool. And Melanie was feeling more at home here every day.

The others, though slow as well, were more eager. Anticipation leaked into their actions, making them clumsy, torn between desire for riches and fear of what else they might find.

Well, they should be nervous.

The little black man finally stood.

One by one, the others rose, still buckling B.C.s and securing masks while exchanging nervous, excited glances. Even the brunette had found a little gumption.

"Mike, you're Jill's dive buddy. Wall..."

"Mike's mine," Melanie informed them.

Jon's eyes swept from one to the other.

Startled, Mike shoved his regulator between his teeth, probably to keep from commenting.

The Brit looked at Jill. "You with me?"

The brunette, playing with her reel of line, nodded.

The stage, Melanie smiled, *is set*.

Jon lifted his thumb in the air, asking if everyone was ready. One by one, the others signaled "Okay."

For her answer, Melanie threw herself backward, flipping heels over head, and shot down into the ocean.

∞

The divers descended.

Bright sunlight filtered down with them, sparkling off her cousin's silver tank.

Jill watched it flicker and thought how very much like the other dives this looked. Same people in the same gear, tropical daylight haloing them all. Same muffled sounds, same exchanged glances. Yet the nervous excitement she'd always felt had changed.

I'm scared.

Looking down past her fins, she saw the ragged blast hole in the gap area. Sand and coral had been blown clean away, revealing the ship's wood deck. For an instant, she could almost see masts rising from cabin housing and sails fluttering in the currents.

How had they ever thought this anything but a shipwreck?

The galleon loomed up to meet them, her crater-wound an accusation. Hovering inches above the shattered deck, Jon and Mike exchanged nervous looks.

Or perhaps she imagined the nervous part.

Jon inverted, thrusting his head into the black void. Melanie floated a foot above the gap, green eyes dancing in her mask.

Perfectly buoyant, Jill realized with a pang.

She herself was still overweighted, still swimming hard instead of gliding like the experienced divers.

Watching Melanie's pink-clad form busily pulling her line, Jill hastily reached for her own reel. She wasn't sure where to tie to off and swept another glance at the blonde.

The woman had found an old black—dear God, it looked like a ship's cleat. It must be something else.

Jill tugged the rope from her reel, paddling toward a thick splinter of wood around the blast hole.

Wall stopped her. For an instant, she thought he'd refuse her entry, but instead he guided her to a solid piece of coral still clinging to the deck cabin. Together they attached their lines, testing them.

The others waited at the hole. Exchanging gestures, Wall peered into her mask. She gave him her bravest smile, or as much as she could manage with a regulator clenched between her teeth.

More signals, more gestures. Then Jon touched his B.C. and sank into the void.

The others followed.

∞

Wall glanced up.

The blast crater, so huge from outside, seemed to shrink rapidly as they spiraled downward. The dark seemed to swallow them whole.

Beside him, Jill remained calm. At least she returned an annoyed look when he leaned in too close.

His impression was a second level, a layer of deck punctuated with rotting holes and vertical beams. They passed through it quickly, falling into a vacuous cavern.

So much for not being in an overhead environment. Too late to do anything about it now.

Flashlights burst forth, narrow beams stabbing feebly at the black. The only thing clearly revealed was the faces of the other divers, eyes mirroring swirling emotions.

One part excitement, two parts fear, Wall thought ruefully.

Even muscle man Mike looked less assured.

They were well and truly in the belly of the beast.

Silt puffed in clouds around Jill's legs, her overweighted condition forcing her to stand instead of hover. Checking her face, he saw her annoyance and impulsively set his fins down beside her.

Her eyes widened. She nodded and looked away.

Wall swept his torch along the floor beneath him, then farther away. Silt blanketed everything, thick and heavy, like gray snow rising up to his knees.

Jon chose a direction and floated away, his beam sweeping side to side just ahead of him. Mike and Melanie chose a path at right angles, imitating his search technique.

A blast of bubbles prickled in the water, over Jill's head. Swiftly he checked her eyes, and she nodded. Naturally the girl felt nervous, but not panicked. She even pointed in the direction away from others, perfectly sensible. He nodded.

Ghostly clouds rose about them, stirred by their awkward steps. There were reasons divers swam.

Bumps sprouted out of the landscape. Swollen debris masses, like a mogul field on a ski slope. Navigating through, he noted the uniform gaps between. Too uniform, he realized.

The side of the ship stopped them.

Jill reached out to touch a lump. Hesitated.

He shone the light upon it, then slid the beam on to the next...and the next. Against the vessel's side the bumps were both taller and more uniform, creating a line in both directions, seemingly infinite, disappearing in the void. A chill tickled his spine.

Jill's fingers brushed the bump. Dropping to her knees, she started digging.

Maybe barrels, he thought. Possibly deteriorating faster away from the ship's side, thus the smaller piles. Would a cargo of sugar be in sacks or barrels?

Drawn to a prominent mound before him, Wall started clearing silt with his gloves.

At first there was only more silt. And then, almost teasingly, he found something hard and unyielding. Metal—heavy and thick. Black forged rings.

Chains.

Jill ceased, arms dropping to her sides. A voice in his head urged him to do the same, but his fingers didn't get the message. He watched his hands busily clear the gray powder, clasp a black chain. Pull.

His peripheral vision caught a distant flashlight falling. It struck the floor, bounced in a slow motion arc. Through its wildly careening beam, a diver shot skyward.

It must be bad. He needed to get Jill out of here.

But his hands refused to stop.

Silt fell away slowly, reluctant to reveal its secrets. More chain appeared, and something pale entwined in the black. Long, thin lines of white. The back of his neck prickled, his body understanding before his brain. And then a large pale globe popped free, rotating in his hand. Grinning at him.

A skull. A human skull atop a pile of bones and chains.

Wall rose up and away, adjusting his buoyancy without conscious intention. To the right, to the left, behind. They were surrounded. Macabre remains of iron and...

The sudden keening flayed his ear. Jill. Grabbing her, he forced her mask around to face him.

She knew, he saw it in her eyes. Horrified, but she met his gaze. Not quite in a blind panic. Hugging her felt ridiculous with the insulating neoprene and interfering gear—he wasn't even sure how his arms got around her.

Funny how training kicks in when the mind goes numb. Attaching a line to her jacket, he pointed up and squeezed his air valve. Their reel lines drifted around them halfway up. Wall could only hope they didn't catch on something.

Near the blast hole, he thought to check below. All he could see was one abandoned flashlight lying still, its melancholy beam barely penetrating the silt. No divers remained.

At least none with their lights on.

Somehow they broke the surface inches from the dive platform.

Jill breathed in deep gasps, her body racked with shudders, but when he plucked the mask from her head, the look she gave him was rational.

"My God," she whispered.

Jon hunched on the platform, strings of spittle dangling from his lips. Mike towered above him, as if ready to battle any who would harm him.

"Melanie," Wall said. "Where's Melanie?"

Mike glanced about as if expecting to see her. "You left her down there?"

"She was your bloody..." Wall's fist curled of its own accord, but he forced it to relax again and checked his gauges. To his surprise, he still had a quarter of a tank and plenty of bottom time. Pushing Jill toward the platform, he donned his mask.

"You can't..." Jill spluttered.

Blonde hair surfaced precisely at the ladder, as if she'd climbed it all the way from the cargo hold. Slipping her faceplate up on her forehead, Melanie burst out laughing. "Oh, that's some valuable cargo you found."

"Cargo?" Mike glared.

Jill's face was also blank.

Wall knew, of course, but he couldn't bring himself to voice it.

"Human cargo," Jon whispered hoarsely, clearing his throat. "Damn thing's a slaver."

∞

Being alone on a thirty-eight foot sailboat isn't easy. Not when four other people live there.

So Jill had swum to the tiny island before running along the lagoon beach, until the sheer weight of her heart dragged her down to the sand. Now she sat with her back to a palm tree, hugging her knees tightly against her chest.

The threatening clouds that had blown in while they were underwater suddenly burst. Rain struck her skin in prickling needles, and she didn't care. At least it was one physical sensation among a dozen raging emotions.

Why are we still here?

Jon should have weighed anchor as soon as the gear was stowed, as soon as everyone had calmed down. Instead, he and Mike sat planning their afternoon dive.

You can't dive on a graveyard.

That's what she'd tried to tell them. Though why anyone needed to be told that was beyond her. Don't disturb the dead.

Especially these dead.

And Mike had actually laughed, albeit with a trace of sympathy in his eyes. "That's what shipwrecks are, mermaid."

She'd waited for the others to correct him, to bring him to his senses. Okay, perhaps not Melanie. But surely Wall understood the difference between sailors going down with their vessel and this. All those people chained to their doom, rocking in the bowels of a galleon they hated, probably not even knowing what was happening. Left to die as the sailors jumped overboard, swimming to shore.

Abandoning the slaves to their fate. For some reason, she couldn't get it out of her head.

The sand around her puckered as the heavy drops struck. They marred the smooth surface, fading the pale sheen. The air chilled her, startling after the tropical noon heat, but she couldn't be bothered to find shelter.

She couldn't be bothered to move at all.

"Jill!"

At the British clip in the voice, she held still, keeping the tree between them. Trust him to bother her now, when any idiot could figure out she wanted to be alone.

He strode straight up to her, following her footsteps in the sand, she realized. So much for hiding behind the palm.

"Jill. You're soaked."

She had a snide answer, but when her throat opened to utter it, only a sob escaped. Gulping the next sob back, she shook her head.

He towered over her, crowding her. She didn't dare look up because, she suddenly realized, if she saw empathy in his face now, she'd completely break down. Why the hell didn't he have enough empathy to leave her alone?

∞

Wall squatted low beside her, trying to make eye contact. Stubbornly, Jill refused to lift her eyes.

Without thought he clasped her hand, lifting her palm to his cheek. He needed to see her eyes, see exactly what thoughts were hiding there. See those warm brown orbs with the golden halos.

Blue eyes, green eyes—colors he'd always deemed more exotic—hid things. They fooled you. Brown eyes were real, true.

Jill looked up, revealing all her misery. She was startled, he knew, and more hurt that no one shared her feelings than the actual plan to dive. If Jon had just taken the time to explain to her, make her understand.

Slowly her misery faded, replaced by a rueful smile. A gallant smile. On such soft lips...

He was kissing her.

Startled, Wall pulled back. He hadn't planned that, had had no such intention. He had come here with Melanie, even if no longer sharing her cabin. Jesus, he was here with Jill's cousin and adopted big brother. Any thought of pursuing her had to wait until they were back in Delaware. Wait until...

All his thoughts drowned in the pool of those brown eyes. When her hand touched his cheek, his arms claimed her.

With the cool rain countering their heated play, they made love.

Cartagena

Wednesday, October 14, 1648

ISABELLE CLASPED THE balcony railing.

It was hot, as ever in the city, but for once she didn't resent it. For news of her husband's death had not come as she'd feared. Indeed, Captain Sadico had had other reasons for his visit. Pleasurable reasons.

Even as she remembered last night, he emerged, striding through the doors as if he laid claim to her husband's home as well as her. Commander of a successful ship, he set his own rules, showing no concern that this house belonged to the governor. Fernando was away, pursuing his pursuits.

Whatever his pursuits were, they did not include his wife. Captain Sadico's did.

Isabelle drew her kerchief over her bare shoulders, a shawl from fashionable Europe that truly had no place in this heat. The captain slid it off, baring her skin for a long, lingering kiss.

He was a big man, dark and swarthy. As masculine as true Spaniards were. His black beard caressed, igniting sensations skin alone could not. Her husband was pale and puny beside this man.

"What is this gift you have for me?" she murmured.

The captain continued his assault, teeth teasing the nape of her neck. "It approaches now, Senora."

Marching below the balcony was a line of slaves.

"They are fresh from Africa, Isabelle. Young, hardworking. Healthy."

She'd seen slaves arriving from across the ocean before. Few could claim any of those traits.

"You may have your pick, sweetling. My gift for...a most memorable night. In the hope of future such nights."

"I prefer jewelry," she murmured.

"Rubies." He nodded, studying her throat. "When next I come, I'll bring rubies."

"I shouldn't accept such things without...payment."

"You may pay for them in other ways," he whispered enticingly.

Delighted, she turned to the Africans.

A slave can be scrubbed, she mused. *After all, they are not inexpensive. And to have my pick from the captain's purchases...*

Watching them shuffle by, heads down, she saw the sudden stumble of a female with her swollen belly protruding over her thin bones. A tall male caught her, moving faster than Isabelle thought the lazy beasts could move.

He must be her mate, she mused. *Perhaps he'd be a good choice, though his frame seems devoid of muscle.*

No, not him. The pregnant female.

One of the captain's men cracked a whip to punish the clumsy slave. Her tall rescuer jumped in front to shield her.

"I want the female." Isabelle pointed.

Captain Sadico burst out laughing. "You double your gift, Senora."

The male's cheek darkened. Split open by the lash, she realized.

"They bleed?" she asked.

The captain's arms encircled her, hauling her against his broad chest.

"Freely," he murmured against her skin.

∞

They huddled in the dirt beneath a cruel sun.

Seeing her shiver, Quash put an arm around his mate. Shivering in heated air was never a good thing. He could only hope it was not a chill but fear that affected her. The latter, at least, was reasonable.

He'd been afraid since the pumbeiros, the hawkers, had taken them to Luanda. All knew it was a bad thing to be taken. A very bad thing.

His last day on the soil of his birth, a holy man had walked through their midst. The man bestowed a name on each of them, even giving them a token to remember it. Quash and the others had later tossed the flimsy things away when the white masters were not watching. This holy man had placed salt on each tongue, sprinkled water upon them.

"You will now go to the land of the Spaniards," they'd been told. "You will learn the things of the Holy Faith. Now go with a good will."

Quash had understood the words, having been born to a father from the land of Luanda, but the meaning behind those words eluded him.

"Beware of foreign men of foreign brow," the elders of the village had said.

The road of the foreign men was a path straight to hell.

Juba, his woman now heavy with his unborn son, was both his salvation and his anguish. That he hadn't lost her, that he could touch her, hold her, was a gift of the gods. And that he actually found some comfort that she was here with him was wrong.

White men worked the nearest ship at the docks below. Here in this land of the Spaniards, they'd been bought by a man nearly as dark as himself, bartered in the same way ivory was bartered in Luanda. Now another sea voyage awaited them. So many of their number had died on the crossing, and many more were still sick from it. He wondered how many would live to walk on this final land. A place called Saint-Domingue.

Another Spanish holy man trudged up the hill. Instead of salt he carried bread, which he shared among them. Quash snagged a piece and insisted Juba eat it, guarding her lest one of the others try to steal it.

The holy man also carried water, but instead of tossing it over them, they were allowed to drink. Juba gratefully sipped her portion, staring at him when he'd refuse his own. He didn't want to take anything from these demons, but at her mute appeal, he did accept a mouthful. Because, he acknowledged, he wanted to live.

"They say he is a true saint of their God," Juba whispered as the holy man passed.

His robes were ragged and dirty, unlike the wealthy garb of the man in Luanda.

And this white man has touched each of our number, Quash realized. The other had carefully held his clothes away from contact, as if they were a muddy water hole.

The holy man gazed at them all, a sort of glowing light in his eyes. He laid a hand on Juba, and her shivering ceased. Then he moved on.

Juba clutched at his passing robe, and a piece came off in her hand. Quash prepared to shield her, expecting retribution, but the holy man did not notice or did not mind.

"This is sacred," his wife told him, clutching the scrap of cloth. The heavy weave seemed to glow. "It has power. It will save us."

Quash clasped her hand, lifting her palm to his cheek. Ever since they'd been taken, she did not touch him. But when he touched her, raising her skin to his face, she would look at him and smile. The love was still there, shining in her eyes.

As long as there was that, he could survive whatever the gods flung at him.

Cries of fear rose. Quash looked up to see a small white man—this one's skin so pale you could see the blood veins beneath—striding through their midst.

The holy man had moved on to another huddling mass of slaves.

Juba hid her relic within her palm.

∞

In the late afternoon, Gerard received his first task—fetch a slave that had been sold.

His fear that he might not be able to handle them eased, as they seemed pretty docile. Besides, this one was a mere female.

He accompanied one of his fellow sailors to the Africans resting in the dirt beneath the sun's heat. They were looking for a pregnant girl—the only pregnant girl they had—but with them all slumping like cowering dogs, she was difficult to spot.

It was feeding time. He watched for a moment as bowls were set on the ground beside them. Most pounced on the offering just like his hounds at home, making him smile.

"There," the sailor beside him nodded toward a very tall, very scrawny African. Gerard realized the little thing next to him was indeed a pregnant female. The tall one handed a bowl to her.

Gerard froze.

She accepted it, even smiling as she tilted the contents down her throat. When she was done, the African exchanged her empty bowl with his own still full of food. She refused, uttering in some strange language. The African silenced her with a single finger pressed to her lips.

The gesture was so—intimate. So human.

The sailor stepped in to get the girl, plucking her up like a kitten and swinging her toward Gerard. Immediately she screamed, grabbing on to her companion, who tried to hug her to him.

The sailor kicked him aside and marched off.

After a second, Gerard followed.

But heading back to town, he couldn't forget the look on the African's face. Despair. Horror.

What if these Africans really were more human than animal? What if this girl was his mate? That the babe she carried in her belly was his child was possible, but what if they both actually knew it?

It was not a comfortable thought.

The girl's sobs ceased, and she hung limp in defeat.

Gerard would go on this voyage, as he'd given his word, but it would be both the first and the last time he ever ventured near such a ship.

∞

Juba's sobs subsided, but not because she feared punishment. In truth, they had done the worse they could do. She simply ran out of strength.

She hung now, carried over this white man's shoulder the same way they carried sacks of grain. That's what she was to these devils—so much grain.

Opening her hand, she realized it was empty. She'd lost the holy cloth.

They were doomed.

Man Down

WITH THE ROAR OF Matilda filling tanks, Mike could hear nothing else, so he was startled when he switched off the compressor to see the blonde posturing against the doorway.

"Want to come to my cabin?" She smiled.

"I'm wreck diving," he told her warily.

"Better off exploring this treasure." Melanie sashayed toward him. She had an enticing manner—a very enticing manner. He was pretty sure she hadn't moved quite that way in Delaware.

Her choice of outfits also appeared different, more revealing. Her hair swung at her shoulders, a sort of fresh-from-the-bed disheveled thing. Even her voice sounded throatier, sexier. He'd always liked women who aggressively pursued what they wanted.

So why was he suddenly repelled?

He detached hoses from air tanks. "Didn't you come here with Wall? In fact, didn't he pay for your trip?" He gave her a pointed look, expecting some embarrassment, a hasty justification.

Instead her smile intensified in a manner that made his flesh crawl. "Didn't Jon pay for yours? Doesn't the little black man always pay your way?"

Wrapping his hands around a silver cylinder—instead of her throat—Mike hoisted his tanks and strode off.

∞

Jon had waited for Jill.

He knew how upset she must be. He understood her mindset, her shock at the discovery. Her refusal to understand salvaging the wreck regardless. Talking to her was key.

Now that she sat alone in the cockpit, knees hugged tight to chest, her back against the cabin wall, the words he sought wouldn't come.

"Jill."

She jerked in surprise. Turning to him, she actually blushed.

"You okay?"

The blush deepened, and a soft smile curved her lips. "Fine."

Mike climbed out of the boat as Wall made his way from the bow. Something in the way the Brit glanced at Jill startled Jon, but Melanie emerged before he could probe it.

"I want to dive," the blonde announced.

Mike answered for them both. "You lost your dive privileges."

The blonde merely looked him up and down, as if amused. Her gaze slid smoothly over to Jill. "Well, you haven't. Surely you're not going to cower up here now? Not the mermaid—the 'best in dive class' girl?"

In the past, Jon had wished Mike could have been more diplomatic, but with Melanie, brutality would serve better. Or been at least more satisfying. "Jill can't wreck-dive either."

Wall set a hand on Jill's shoulder. "Would you dive with me? We'll remain outside the wreck, maybe scour the sand surrounding it. Who knows what treasure we'll find?"

Certain Jill would refuse, Jon stepped in to tell him so, but she was already nodding and smiling.

And blushing.

"I'll get your tank." Wall disappeared.

Mike dropped to the platform, setting his own tank among his gear. "Well, Sadicor? We diving or what?"

Suspicious of the soft look in Jill's eyes, Jon finally climbed down and froze.

Mike eyed him. "What?"

"Just for a moment, it looked odd the way the strap was wrapped about your wrist. Like you were missing a hand."

With a sharp snort, the big man screwed in his hoses.

∞

Forty minutes later—exactly twenty-five minutes behind Jon and Mike—Jill hit the water. Wall had first taken the time to remove a dive weight from her belt.

Hopefully she'd be able to hover a little better.

Bubbles percolating in her ears, she felt surprisingly calm. A little giddy, a blend of nerves and anticipation. *Don't anticipate,* she warned herself, watching Wall adjust his air valve. *Just take it as it comes.*

Sunlight streamed from the surface, bathing the sandy floor that rose to meet them. It seemed brighter than usual, but that was probably more her mood than weather. Her breath rasped in her ears as the wreck slowly rose into the frame of her mask.

Jill gasped.

The galleon's short stub of a bowsprit was now completely free of coral. So free, in fact, that she could honestly see a rope wrapped round it. For an instant she even saw sails fluttering above.

When she blinked, the sails were gone.

Even without the extra weight, her fins sank inexorably amongst some broken shells on the sea bed. With the wreck stretched out before them, it felt more like a Disneyland adventure ride than an actual dive. All that was missing were the fish.

Even the manta ray was absent.

Wall turned her attention to several mounds in the sand, just a short distance from the galleon. For a moment she panicked, as they reminded her of the other mounds. But these were small and outside the ship in sparkling blue water, so she dug.

Digging with their backs to the galleon, her eyes slid to study Wall. Was it a coincidence that they faced away from the wreck—or deliberate? The man could do odd things in the name of safety, and if he believed...

Abruptly she stopped that line of thought because he was a decent man.

She ought to feel shame for what had happened between them on the beach. Instead, a sort of tightness gripped her stomach—a happy tightness, as if her body knew something her mind hadn't yet puzzled out.

The Brit looked at her over a large pile of sand, shoveling enthusiastically, more for her entertainment than any expectation of discovery. Grinning around her mouthpiece, Jill shifted closer, matching his pace and his mood.

Her fingers found something. Wall noticed her reaction and helped her dig.

Together they unearthed a metallic lump twice the size of her fist, heavy and obscure. It looked fused, more like what she'd expect to find in an old wreck. A genuine artifact, as Jon would say.

As she tried to decipher its true shape, Wall nodded to the wreck.

Jill was reluctant to look. In fact, she suddenly dreaded it. But before she could find a way to let him know, Wall pushed off the sand, swimming for the bow.

She had to follow.

Jon popped out of the hole beneath the bowsprit. Freeing his line, reeling the last bit in, he gave her a nod brimming with excitement.

The ropes. The ropes weren't remnants from the wreck at all, but the tied-off lines of the divers. Really, this stupid ship was getting to her.

She tried to ask what they'd seen inside, what treasure they'd found, but of course it was a waste of air.

Amused, Jon gave her a double 'okay' signal, dropping to hover beside her.

Excited indeed, she saw in his eyes. They must have found something good.

Over their heads, Mike popped through the hole, turning to free his line. Something glittered from his dive bag, and Jill nudged Wall and pointed.

Still struggling with his rope, Mike drew his machete. The long blade caught on the wreck, and he lost his grip.

The knife drifted slowly to the sand.

Mike also dropped to follow and jerked to a halt, as if the bowsprit had grabbed his tanks. He dangled like a prize marlin on a fisherman's hook.

Jon doubled over with laughter. When even Wall chuckled, she giggled into her regulator.

Mike strained to reach back behind his tanks but couldn't do anything. His arms folded in front of him, the picture of patience in the face of his friend's amusement.

Wall floated higher, latching onto the sprit and leaning close to peer at the problem. After a minute, Mike gestured in mock annoyance.

The Brit slid his dive knife from an ankle sheath.

Jill saw it in her peripheral vision, soaring down like an eagle attacking its prey. So the manta hadn't vanished after all. Watching in wonder, mesmerized by its grace, she was glad it hadn't vanished with the rest of the fish. Her wonder died in a wave of fear as the thing seemed to aim for her head.

It flew past, in a beeline for Mike.

∞

For a split second, Mike froze.

He'd killed it, felt it die. In the instant before it passed, he glimpsed traces of white cartilage where the skin had begun to decompose.

The very violence of his scream ought to have shaken him loose, but the surrounding sea muffled the energy as it muffled the noise.

Images more than thought raced through his mind. Of Jon, of the Crusty Porthole. Of Nita, smiling provocatively beneath him, naked in her bed. He knew he could lose all those things.

The warrior within him rose and fought.

∞

Whirling, Jill saw the ray skim over Mike's head, clang-ing into the top of his tanks. Wall jerked back, losing his knife as the manta streaked past. The creature never even slowed as it vanished in the distance.

The blue handle of Wall's knife slowly buried in the sand; tiny air bubbles boiled around the top of Mike's trapped tank.

The ray must have damaged the air hose.

All the men hung frozen in the sea.

Until Mike erupted.

He thrashed violently, as if to yank himself free, but the bowsprit held fast. Bare chest heaving as he flailed, his powerful legs kicked furiously. Utter panic—from the man who'd lectured the class that the vast majority of diver deaths stemmed from panic alone.

He had to know there was air. They had spare regulators, sharp knives. They had procedures, skills, knowledge. He had to know they'd rescue him.

Even now, as Wall dove down to recover his knife, Jon shot up to Mike's mask level. He tried to get close, to grab Mike's mask, but the frenzied writhing held him at bay.

Wall bolted back to position, hands working furiously to free the man. Jon waved his spare regulator. Offering it, but the muscle man seemed oblivious. His wild twists made an impenetrable barrier.

She could see Wall's head shaking even as his fingers pried, twisted, and pummeled. He couldn't free the tanks.

Jon hovered a second more before diving in between Mike's arms, grabbing his head to force eye contact—an instant before a clawing arm struck, knocking the slight figure backward, flipping fins over head. Jon's mask and regulator fell away, and his hands clutched his face.

To Jill's horror, a dark trickle slipped up from between his fingers. She'd kept out of reach of Mike's wild thrashing, but Jon was still—and damned if she'd let him drown.

Wall was there before her, snagging Jon's bubbling mouthpiece. Gently he pushed it back in place.

Jon had air, at least, while Mike's struggles grew feeble. Her hands unhooked her octopus rig before her mind had made the decision. But with Wall tending to a stunned Jon, she was the trapped man's only hope.

Flexing her knees, she pushed off the bottom.

She rose up to see his eyes, wide and frozen within the black frame, almost as if he'd seen a ghost. Squelching that image, she finned closer.

He didn't move.

Cautiously she tugged his mouthpiece free and slipped her spare in its place. Just as slowly, his hands lifted and touched her shoulders. Relief swamped her. It was going to be okay.

And then he grabbed her throat.

Hatred burned from his eyes as he choked her. His strength had returned in full. Struggling as best she could, she felt like a tiny mouse in the big cat's teeth.

She felt—rather than saw—Wall at her side, grabbing Mike's muscular arm and yanking, in no way lessening the grip on her neck.

She doubted Mike even felt it.

Her knees had drawn up to her body protectively. Instinctively she kicked out, wedging her feet against his chest. One fin popped off, making it easier to plant and push. His clawing fingers scraped down to her shoulders, allowing precious air to flow, filling her lungs.

Jill breathed and pushed harder, levering her throat out of range. Hands skidded down her wetsuit.

She sprang free.

Hovering, gasping, she noticed something large beside her and whirled to see Jon, still and drifting. She kicked toward him, grabbing hold and shaking him. No reaction.

When her spare regulator floated between them, she impatiently swept it clear. In doing so, she saw Wall, holding his own regulator at Mike's mouth, who also hung limp.

In a moment of clarity, she knew—she knew—they could only save one man.

Jon.

She gestured frantically at Wall.

He hesitated, and she felt his indecision. Relief over-whelmed her when he swam to them.

Checking her cousin's face, Wall linked their B.C.s and pointed up, waiting.

Realizing what he waited for, Jill quickly nodded.

Holding the small man, Wall ascended.

The bowsprit lay so close, Mike dangling in the current like a macabre rag doll.

If I leave now, he's dead.

But if she stayed, Wall would be forced to return, and that might kill Jon. Even if she stayed, how could she free him now when Jon and Wall could not?

Her hand clasped her valve. Jill slowly ascended.

∞

Gleefully it swooped. It spun. The spin was frenzied, whirling so fast the carcass exploded. Bits of dead manta scattered to oblivion.

He was stronger now. Fear had fed him, though less nourishing than pure hatred. He thirsted for more.

Revenge on the warrior had satisfied his spirit on a deep level. But it hadn't sated him. In no way was he done. And he'd seen the traitor's anguish.

He thirsted for more.

The Vortex swelled at an idea, and then ebbed to gather its strength.

Trapped

Jon hunched on the dive platform, legs dangling in the water. His gear was off, but he couldn't remember removing it.

Mike's dead.

Wall had kept his tanks on, only removing his mask when Jill surfaced. Now he remained at the platform edge, tank on his back, waving her out of the sea.

"But he's still—" she began.

"Let's get Jon below," Wall cut her off. He seemed to think Jon incapable of moving.

Am I capable? Jon mused, and found he didn't care. His best friend was fifty feet below the *Sadicor*, stuck on a stupid piece of wood like a bug in a spiderweb.

Mike's dead.

Jon said the words aloud, trying to make them mean something. They were just echoes bouncing through his brain.

He saw Wall take Jill's fins and mask. Reluctantly, she climbed up the ladder, bursting with the need to voice her thoughts.

Shock, Jon realized. *Jill is in shock.*

"We can't just leave him," she whispered urgently, talking to the Brit and ignoring Jon completely.

He'd take her to task for that, if he could find the energy.

"I'll do it," Wall murmured.

"Not alone! I'm your buddy—"

The tall man touched a finger to her lips, silencing her completely.

Something about that gesture seemed familiar. Déjà vu, goose-over-the-grave familiar. His spine actually tingled and his heart ached. Overwhelmingly so.

To his horror, Jon realized he was openly weeping.

∞

It was midnight.

Wall woke with a start. He must have dozed off, lying on a cockpit bench propped against the cabin. Sprawled as he was on the seat beneath the moon, he'd earned a crick in his neck. He stood and stretched long and full, needing to release the tension.

It didn't release.

Mike lay in the compressor room, wrapped in an old tarp. Oddly, Wall had had no difficulty lifting him. His tanks had been caught in a notch under the bowsprit, not tangled in any rope. All he'd had to do was push down, and the body was free.

Strange that all his struggles hadn't dislodged him.

Everyone else—everyone alive—was sleeping. Or they had been sleeping—he should probably check in on them, then he'd make a bed for the night in the galley table again. Melanie had locked the cabin door, but she needn't have bothered. He was done with that.

Wall climbed down the ladder.

A single light cast weird shadows. Glistening teak stood out between black flickering lines near the compressor room door. Surreal.

Jon hunched in the booth, an open book before him, a bottle of Jack Daniels on the table and a glass in his hand. Wall thought him comatose until the man spoke.

"Thank you," he rasped. "For...getting Mikey. Bringing him home."

Wall nodded. "I'm guessing we head to Antigua tomorrow."

"Best friend and partner. And I let him down. I let him drown." Jon emptied the contents of his glass in a single gulp.

The title of the book loomed large, easy to read despite being upside down. *Revisits: Theory of Soul Returns to the Earth Plane.*

"You really subscribe to the theory of reincarnation?"

Pushing against the table top, Jon straightened his back. "We sail at first light."

Wall sat opposite him, tugging the book across the table and spinning it round. Chapter 7's title was "Karmic Debt." A tiny chill pierced the spot between his shoulder blades.

"Jon, do you think this is true? That we get trapped in old patterns...repeat our mistakes?"

Slowly Jon squeezed out of the booth and staggered off.

The words of the text seemed to dance before his eyes.

The true flames of hell lie here on earth.

"Wall?" Jon's voice drifted from the compressor room alcove.

Sighing deeply, Wall toyed with the whiskey bottle.

"Hey, Wall?"

He rose to his feet, suddenly feeling the need for a glass. He glanced at Jon, wobbling before the open doorway of the compressor room. Bathed in that peculiar, flickering light.

Shielding his eyes, the small man edged closer.

Wall sprinted for him.

A muted roar filled his ears before he saw the actual fire. Flames raced along the far wall, seeping across the floor. For precious seconds, he could only stare.

Sweet Jesus. "Extinguisher? Jon, where is it?"

But Jon merely stood, gazing at the inferno. And anyway, it was too far gone. Bloody hell. Fire and machinery rarely went well together. Whatever fuel there was...

"*Jon!* Go wake Melanie," Wall commanded, banging on the wall by Jill's curtained cubby hole. "*Now!*"

If Jill responded, he couldn't hear it. Jon remained beside him, frowning as if trying to decipher a puzzle.

"Bugger this for a game of soldiers." Wall shoved Jon toward the ladder as he yanked the curtain aside.

Jon staggered back, and the curtain came off in his hands.

Moonlight through the porthole revealed Jill sitting up, loosely holding a sheet to her body. She wore some sort of T-shirt, and he vaguely thought how fortunate that was.

Jon staggered against him. "Can't...go. Can't abandon the *Sadicor*. Dad'll kill me."

"Get Melanie."

Whirling, Jon bounced off the door frame before vanishing in the smoke.

"Wall?" Rubbing her eyes, Jill resembled a sleepy toddler. She made no move to rise.

Scorching heat flicked his back, spurring him on. He snatched her up, sheet and all, spinning as he tossed her over his shoulder and sprinted for the ladder.

Either she weighed next to nothing or adrenalin pumped his strength. Wall flew up the steps, feeling her head bounce off his back.

Stumbling out into the night air, he saw the inflatable already in the water. Melanie perched in the front seat, calmly munching an apple. The blonde actually smiled at him.

Jill wiggled. "Put me down! Wall! Put me down and go get Jon!"

He dropped her, rather abruptly, and dove back down the ladder. Below deck, he found the man standing in the middle of the cabin.

"Not here," he frowned, eyes fogged from smoke and alcohol.

Wall yanked him out, shoving him at the ladder. When Jon made no move to climb, he hoisted him over his shoulder and sprinted up out of the boat, chased by heat and smoke and the rising roar of flame.

Staggering onto the deck, Wall nearly tumbled them both into the sea. He dropped Jon hard, seeing the unholy glow from the compressor room porthole. "Jon!"

Jon leapt, landing awkwardly in the launch.

Wall jumped for the stern seat in the now wildly rocking inflatable.

"*Go! Go!*" Jon cried.

It took two nerve-racking tries before the motor roared to life. Leaping across the waves, the boat veered madly before taking aim at the island. Over his shoulder, Wall saw the painted '*SADICO*' blazing out at them.

They were halfway to the beach when the night exploded.

Flaming debris flew overhead, fiery threads outlining their path. He could feel the heat, bracing for a more fiery impact that somehow—by the grace of God—never came.

In the bright flash, his companions' faces were etched forever in his brain. Jill horrified, Jon in shock. Melanie smiling like a child at a fireworks festival. And he suddenly thought of one item he shouldn't have left behind.

The radio.

∞

The swirling mist receded.

Standing before Nita with a warm smile curving his mouth, Mike drew her close in a gentle embrace. The kind of embrace she'd always known he was capable of.

"I love you, my witch woman," he murmured against her temple.

His skin gleamed dark in the first light of dawn, eclipsing the Mike she knew. The redneck Mike, as her aunts labeled him. His muscles stood out, different somehow. Muscles garnered through genuine work, she thought. Not artificially cultivated.

Here was a true warrior.

"I wanted to bear your children," Nita whispered. "I wanted..."

At the touch of his hand against her head, her words died.

"Heaven makes room for every dream," he told her. "Some just take longer than others."

She relaxed, sinking into his warmth. Bathing in his love.

When her eyes fluttered open to the reality of a pale blue ceiling, she was still smiling.

Even as the sobs racked her body.

∞

Something was different.

As Jill slowly rose from a deep sleep, she felt the stillness. No gentle rocking of the sea, no sloshing of waves against the sailboat hull. Because, she realized, she was lying on cool sand.

The fire.

She sat up, blinking away the film in her eyes.

Before her stretched the calm Caribbean, tickling the edge of the launch. They ought to drag that higher, before the tide could steal it away. The sun had already risen, but lingering dawn colors painted the sky.

Red skies in the morning, she recalled the words. *Red skies in the morning, sailors take warning.*

They should have checked the sky yesterday.

Judging by the croak of Jon's snoring, he slept nearby. A long, blanket-wrapped figure lay off to her right, near enough to make her feel safe, far enough away to observe the proprieties. Wall had said that hours earlier. She smiled at the memory.

Missing a third blanket with a muscular form, Jill felt tears well even before her mind remembered.

There was no Mike this morning.

Waves lapped the beach, and her cousin's fitful sleep disturbed the rhythm. The *Sadicor* had burned last night, and her prized T-shirt sported a hole in the sleeve. At least the garment was big enough to cover her ugly red underpants. With little camels, no less.

She didn't realize a tear trailed down her cheek until Melanie touched it. "For the hero?"

Jill recoiled and scraped the moisture off her face. *Scraping the sorrow away,* she realized. Like she was seven again and her mother had just abandoned them.

The green eyes narrowed, reflecting pity and amusement and something else. "We're well and truly stuck here now. I wonder what will happen next?"

Jill shrugged, staving off conversation while she cleared her throat. "Uncle Ray will find us. He's smart. He'll know where to look."

"But not for weeks, right? Not today...not tomorrow."

"They have to figure out we're missing first."

Melanie shook her head. "That'll be too late."

"What is with you?" Jill burst out. "You've gotten down right...strange. Cruel."

The green eyes turned inward, as if actually pondering the question.

"It's sort of like an amusement park ride. A roller coaster, maybe. Once you get in the cart, it goes where it goes. All you can do is hang on."

"Where is it going?" Jill heard herself whisper.

The woman stilled beside her.

"It's arcing over the apex at the highest point. About to rocket down." Melanie walked away.

When Wall touched her arm, she barely contained a shriek. "Wall," she hissed.

She saw the gentle concern on his face. It wasn't nervousness, no matter what Mike said.

Had said.

"All right?" he asked.

She nodded, forcing a smile that faded too quickly. "Wall, what happened? I mean, how did the fire..."

"I have no idea." He sat, sharing her blanket. His warm presence felt good beside her, making Jill feel guilty. It wasn't right to feel good.

"Short circuit, faulty something. I know it started in the compressor room."

"Mike..." she choked on his name. "He took good care of it. Couldn't have just flamed out."

His arm went around her, pulling her head against his shoulder. Or maybe she did that all on her own.

It was wrong to take comfort in anything this morning. But she couldn't find the strength to move.

∞

Wall relaxed when Jon returned from his walk.

"I sorted through the supplies as you asked," he said, waving at the provisions scattered on the blanket. "Ten gallons of water, a few tins of beans, tuna fish. One unopened bottle of good tequila. A cylinder of potato chips, of all things, and dozens of tins labeled Spam."

Jon lips formed the ghost of a smile. "Mike loved Spam."

"I only knew of it from an old Monty Python song." Wall found he couldn't quite manage a grin himself. "Some of the expiration dates have passed."

"We used to diligently keep up the emergency rations. Even kept a bag of Oreos. But after a few years, it just slipped in priority."

"Also a mask, snorkel, and one dive light."

Jon nodded. He looked ten years older this morning.

"There was an EPIRB on the boat, right? Will the Coastguard look this far from the equator?"

Wavering on his feet, Jon shrugged. "We did buy one, years ago. And yes, those are monitored worldwide."

Wall relaxed.

"Pretty sure it was on board."

So much for relaxing, Wall sighed. "And if not?"

"We usually tell the dive shop in Antigua where we're going and when we'd be back. Hopefully Mike did that this last time. And if not, Dad should be looking for us within a week or two. This is the first place he'll check."

He could understand Jon's distraction and hated to badger the man, but the difference of a week was critical.

Even with careful rationing, the water would be gone after ten days. The inflatable wasn't exactly suitable for long distance on the ocean, but if some inhabited island lay close—or even one with nothing but fresh water—it might improve their odds over simply waiting for rescue.

Jill strode up the beach to join them. She'd gone to find Melanie, but apparently had failed.

"Shouldn't we move up to the cave?" she touched Jon's arm.

He looked as surprised as Wall felt.

"Why? The beach is pleasant, and we've got sand for a mattress instead of granite."

"No animals to worry about," Wall tacked on.

"But the weather." Jill nodded toward the heavens. "Red sky in the morning?"

Jon shook his head. "Forecast was clear. It's June. We're not in hurricane season."

She looked unconvinced.

Jon moved on to inspect supplies.

Wall grasped her hands. "I think we'll be fine." He smiled.

∞

Hours later, he wasn't so sure.

The soft breeze had morphed into a gusting wind, forcing them to secure the blankets under water containers. The clear sky suddenly wasn't. Dark clouds swelled over their heads, appearing out of nowhere.

Close clouds, as if they hung mere meters above the trees. And the rain was not far behind.

As the first splatters drummed the sand, Jon shot a look to Wall before hoisting one of the two water jugs and heading for the cave. Wall yanked his shirt over his head and stooped to gather loose food cans into the material, creating a makeshift sling. Even so, he couldn't quite manage it all.

"Jill, if you can carry this—and Melanie, take as much as you can—I'll get the water and return for any leftovers."

Standing, Melanie unbuttoned her shirt. He hoped she was wearing a bra.

Apparently she gathered the gist of his thoughts. "Would you rather Jill remove hers?"

Wall knew Jill's clothing situation—or lack of it—far too well.

"I'll get the water." Cheeks tinged red, the brunette bent over the remaining water jug.

"It's heavy," he warned, stepping to her with his makeshift carrier. Jill-like, she grabbed the handle with one hand and yanked, her eyes widening as it remained in the sand.

He set his burden in her hands. "It's a five-gallon container, over forty pounds. Best let me carry it."

"I can manage forty pounds."

Wall thought of the distance, the rocky path and narrow ledge. Lifting the jug, he simply grinned. "But then I'd feel inadequate." When he got his answering smile from her, he gestured the women ahead.

Melanie had managed to gather the remaining supplies. Thankful there was no need to return—and that her bra was less revealing than her bikinis—he followed them up the trail.

The upper ledge grew slick with wet. He learned this on his first step, dropping the carrier before recovering his balance. The plastic dented but kept the water safe.

Fortunately.

If Jill or Melanie lost the food they carried they'd all still live, though less comfortably. To lose half their water would cut their survival time in half.

Wall treaded more carefully.

Foam specked his bare legs. Glancing down, he saw a churning sea pounding against the stone wall supporting him. The white caps rose higher as he watched.

Dizzying fear rose apace with the ocean, a primal terror which threatened to swamp reason and drown him.

Wavering on his feet, Wall realized how close he was to drowning literally. He tore his gaze away and forced himself on.

When he knelt at last before the cave entrance, he gulped a calming breath of air before sliding the water container ahead and crawling through the short tunnel.

Jon bore the water to the far side of the cavern, where Jill stacked food tins. Melanie donned her shirt clinically, no trace of taunt.

Jon marched back to the tunnel, ducking down.

"We got everything," Wall told him.

"I'm getting driftwood. For a fire."

The polite thing to do was help, so Wall followed, being very careful not to look down a second time.

∞

Melanie knelt in the rain mist, plucking twigs and tree bark from wet sand. Dry leaves worked best, but there were none here.

She might not know much about diving, but she knew how to build a fire.

Fuel, kindling, and tinder, she recalled the words from her Girl Scout summer.

Once upon a time she'd been a Girl Scout. So long, long ago.

The men collected hefty driftwood specimens, as men were wont to do, and she'd set Jill to finding kindling. The brunette had eyed her suspiciously—exactly what the hell was suspicious in smaller sized wood?—but obeyed. Jill liked to think herself a rebel, but she was very obedient just the same. Easy to picture the girl scurrying on all sorts of foolish errands, trying to please.

Anyway, Melanie had assumed the more difficult task herself. While kindling littered the island, actual tinder was scarce.

Wall labored nearby, trying to yank free a large log from a bramble bush. Typical male, applying brute force to the problem.

The Brit ceased, studying the tangle, before he circled round to lift it out easily. So he had noticed it hooked on the plant trunk. Mike would have braced his feet and muscled it free.

Wall is, she reminded herself, *different from most males.* Very different from Mike.

"Well spotted," she told him, using his own vernacular.

Already walking away, he gave her a quick nod.

"You don't have to run off. I know about Jill."

That made him pause.

"You did nothing wrong. I sort of pushed you away first."

He turned, looking her in the eye.

First time someone has looked directly at me in days, she realized.

"I figured you were more attracted to Mike."

Melanie pondered this. The muscle man had been more...masculine. Less cerebral. Cerebral tended to make more money, so her mother always said.

Realizing he expected an answer, she shrugged. "It's a moot point now." To her own ears, she sounded callous, but the tall man returned to stoop beside her.

"I'm sorry, Melanie. Sorry for your loss, for anything I did wrong. For—"

She stopped him with a gesture.

After a moment, he rose again and turned away.

"Wall."

He hesitated.

"We need to shelter in the lower cave. It's safer."

He stared as if she'd truly lost her mind.

She wasn't altogether sure she hadn't. "I'm serious. It's more protected. All we have to do is push firewood and supplies through that chimney hole on the ledge. Nothing can reach us there."

"And just how do we get ourselves inside? All the dive gear sank with the *Sadicor*."

She looked at him, willing him to see, to understand. The upper cave was far too exposed. They had to go underground.

But whatever that switch was, it flipped again. Wall smiled, but a fake smile meant to reassure. "We'll be fine." He marched away with his ridiculously large log.

Well, at least now she could stop scouring for tinder. Tonight's fire would be the last.

∞

By nightfall—judged by Wall's watch, as it was already pitch black outside—they huddled in the upper cavern, around a tiny fire Jon swore would not smoke them out. It hadn't, but that was the only bit of good news. The pounding rain and gusting winds battered their shelter, leaving them all clustered, scared and miserable, around a small flame gallantly trying to survive.

"This isn't possible," Jon insisted for the fifth time. "Storms of this magnitude can't just spring up out of nowhere. This thing feels like a full-on tropical storm."

"Perhaps you lost track? With the wreck, blowing the cargo hold?" Wall tried to make it sound a minor thing, easily excused, but no one sailing his own boat, let alone deliberately isolated in foreign waters, could risk ignorance of weather conditions.

Not and live long.

"Mike says the sea's like a sexy woman," Jon spoke softly. "She'll sooth your senses, tempt and tease. And destroy you for the merest perceived slight."

Jill clutched the lone flashlight. Shut off as it was to save battery power, it was just cold metal, but still she held it like a lonely child with a stuffed toy. Maybe her claustrophobia, or whatever it was, was flaring up. She'd moved away when Wall tried to comfort her.

Wall checked the blankets, which were stretched out on a rock near the fire in a futile attempt to dry them. One was still sopping, but at least it was semi-warm instead of the chilling cold.

He distributed them.

Melanie gave him an odd look as he held out the faded yellow material. "For me?"

Wall nodded.

She took it, shaking her head. "You cannot like me anymore." She watched him wistfully, as if regretting past actions.

He compromised with a smile before tossing the soggy blanket aside and settling on a spot close to the fire.

There were no good nights, no well-wishes. Instead the conversation died with the flame.

And the wind howled.

∞

She watched Wall hauled away, forced up a gangplank of another ship. Light rain trickled down her face, or maybe she was crying.

Jill woke from her bad dream to the roar of the storm. She shot upright, shrouded in pitch black.

The cave, she realized.

Outside the storm's fury ranted like a living thing, a hideous beast pounding on their door.

Intent on their destruction.

She forced herself to breathe, calming slightly as her vision returned. Dwindling embers bathed the cavern in a flickering red, offering the tiny comfort of seeing she wasn't alone. Wall's tall form was near enough she could touch him, and she had to stop herself from doing so. Jon lay closest to the entrance, as if guarding the tunnel passage.

She couldn't see Melanie.

The blonde, she remembered, had chosen a spot against the back wall. As far from the rest of them as possible. Squinting, Jill tried to pierce the shadow, searching for some sign of the woman.

No lump presented itself—no slumbering form and no glimpse of blonde hair—but something did gleam oddly, sort of flickering. Fluttering as the manta had fluttered within the wreck, just before it attacked.

Her cry seeped out, and instantly, Wall jerked upright.

"Melanie," she told him.

He didn't ask questions. Grabbing the flashlight, he swept the beam along the back wall as Jon rose on elbow.

The fluttering was a discarded blanket. And the gleaming...

"Wait a minute." Jon crawled to it, extracting a large metallic thing from the cloth. He checked, fumbling it. The long blade clattered against the rock floor, twinkling in the pale ember light. "What the hell is she doing with this?"

Mike's machete.

The word 'keepsake' floated through Jill's brain, but she didn't believe it. A girl might snatch an old T-shirt, or a photo or a piece of jewelry, but this blade spoke more of macabre than romance.

Wall swung the light wider, scouring the stone floor, the entrance, the sides. "Bloody hell. She's out there. In this storm."

Staring at the gleaming blade—the edge looked unusually sharp—Jill's peripheral vision caught Wall wrapping a tarp about his shoulders. "What are you doing?"

"She said something earlier about feeling safer in the lower cave. Maybe she attempted it. Might be in trouble on the beach or on the path."

The last of his words drowned in a shriek of storm.

Jon barred his way. "Wall...that's bad out there."

"We can't just leave her to die. I'll take it slow. "

"You could die if you go after her." Jill rose up on her knees, clutching his arm. Looking pathetically desperate, she knew, but she couldn't make herself let go.

"That ledge is slick right now," Jon corroborated. "Wind gusts...blinding rain. A sudden blast could whip you straight into the sea."

A tiny, gallant smile curved his mouth. She stared back hopelessly, knowing nothing would dissuade him.

Wall cupped her cheek. "I'll crawl if need be. If it's too dangerous, I'll come back."

Her fingers wrapped around his hand, trying to hold him there. "Wall, please. Don't risk your life to save another."

His palm slipped down to her chin. "That is the sensible thing." His lips twitched in a fleeting smile. "But maybe it's not the right thing." He kissed her, long and lingering, proving his reluctance to go. "No unnecessary risks. I promise, sweetheart."

He snagged the flashlight, crouching down by the opening. The man actually winked at her before vanishing into the tunnel.

Still holding the machete, Jon glared at her. "What's going on between you and the Brit?"

∞

The wind wailed louder, the cold deepening as he crawled away from a fire he thought useless before Wall reached the outside.

Suddenly wind slammed him, blasting water up his nose. Gasping, choking, he banged his skull against the stone behind him. He braced there, snorting, until he could breathe.

That jest about crawling might be his only option.

The image of returning to the cave tempted him. Wherever Melanie was, whatever trouble she might be in, she'd brought it on herself. No one had pushed her outside.

But if it were Jill, he'd knew he'd go. Or Jon, for that matter. Crawling was a relatively safe option, and once off the rock, his only real danger was getting wet. He could turn around if it got too difficult.

Dislike should never factor into the equation.

"Melanie!"

An oily slick coated the ledge, keeping him on hands and knees. His right shoulder scraped along the granite beside him as he pressed away from the sheer drop to his left. One glance at the raging ocean below was enough.

Afterward he kept his eyes pinned on the bushes ahead. It had to be a full force gale now, and for the first time he wondered just how strong this tempest could grow.

Was it possible for a force five hurricane to spring out of nowhere?

At last he reached the path. Wall kept low until trees surrounded him. The wind still buffeted, but now surrounding branches helped anchor his body. Or perhaps their safety was just illusion.

Glimpsing the ocean through the vegetation, he couldn't believe Melanie had gotten anywhere near it. Ten foot seas pummeled the island, wave after wave after wave. Impossible to swim through those.

"*Melanie!*" He could barely hear his own cry. A yearning to return to the cave flashed, but he pressed on.

It was hard going reaching the beach, and scarier when he got there. The flat sand strip was gone, consumed by surging seas now threatening the line of palm trees. Wind and salt water stung his eyes, cutting visibility even further.

"*Melanie!*"

Spotting the launch, poised just feet away from the greedy surf, he struggled to it, dragging it higher, tying the boat's line to the thickest tree. Even so he doubted it would survive.

He refused to dwell on their own survival.

"*Melanie!*"

Despite mounting fear, Wall went as far as he could, pushing through thick brush around the crescent-shaped lagoon. Pushing past the 'unless it's too dangerous' promise he'd made Jill, but he felt better for doing it. Even though he found no sign of the blonde.

Which wasn't really surprising. The storm seemed intent on cleansing the entire island.

∞

"Jill."

Hugging her knees beside a woeful fire—Jon had done his best with what driftwood remained—Jill heard Melanie's voice. At least, it sounded like Melanie's voice.

"Ji-ill."

She glanced at Jon, blowing at a promising ember. "Do you hear that?"

Crouching low to a promising smolder, he didn't even hear her.

"Jilly Jill!" It came from the tunnel.

Well, she wouldn't leave the shelter, but she could take a peek. Shifting close to the opening, she strained her ears listening for anything above the storm. She heard nothing.

Peering through the tunnel's dark void, she saw nothing.

"Jill...please..."

Reluctantly she crawled inside.

Sound echoed oddly within the stone tube, almost as if someone was sobbing. Or laughing? But when Jill paused, the noise turned out to be just the wind.

Vaguely reminding her of old horror movies.

Jill poked her head out. The storm's fury smacked her face, blinding her with water and grit, deafening her with its inhuman wails. Instinctively she turned her head sideways.

In a flash of lightning she saw Melanie, huddled on the ledge. Arms crossed to protect herself, eyes riveted downward at the violent surf.

The beautiful blonde now looked like a drowned rat.

"Melanie! Are you okay?"

The woman seemed petrified.

Jill reached out, barely able to touch her. Melanie shuddered violently.

Jill inched onto the ledge, keeping low as Wall had said. Wind buffeted her body, but she was safe enough with the solid rock at her back. "Melanie?"

Gaze fixed on the water below, Melanie shook her head.

Jill inched close enough to wrap an arm about her shoulders. "Come on. Let's get you inside."

At last Melanie looked up. And grinned.

She shoved Jill off the ledge.

∞

For an eternal instant, there was nothing.

Jill tumbled through void, a roaring silence shrouding her. If there was a passage way to hell, this must surely be it.

Then she hit the sea.

Instantly a wave engulfed her. Feet thrashed, hands clawed her way back to the surface. Her head popped through the water, lungs sucking in air. A clap of lightning revealed the rock cliff looming close, far larger than she remembered. She could still feel its threat when darkness swallowed her sight.

Her whole body slapped against granite. Flesh raked across it, cutting her forearm and shoulder. It unnerved her that she felt no pain.

"JON! HELP!" Seawater choked her, even as she braced for striking the cliff again.

Now it gashed her back, her calf. Peering frantically up at the ledge, she glimpsed the empty footpath. Even if Jon stood directly above her, he wouldn't hear a thing.

A surging wave broke over her, driving her deep. She barely gulped oxygen before hurtling to the bottom, smacking the sand before clawing her way back to the surface.

Gasping air, she knew she had to get away from the rock cliff. Her chances of making the beach in this violent sea were not good, but she'd be battered to death here.

Jill turned, striking out for open water. Putting her head down, she swam with all her might. She was carried a mere few feet before the ocean body-slammed her against the cliff again.

It drove her under with enough force to embed her feet in the sea floor. The current yanked her out again, tossing her at the rock while still beneath the waves. Cheek scraped stone, fingertips shredding as she braced against it. Only her feet were spared, finding a hole in the cliff wall.

A hole. The underwater cave.

Rolling, tumbling. Jill realized she was on the surface. Gasping, she heard her own hysterical whimpers. She was running out of options.

Running out of time.

The underground cave had that chimney opening on the top ledge. She might even yell loud enough to be heard. Maybe Wall could get down to her, so she wasn't alone in the dark.

If I stay here, I'll die.

Another wave pile-drove her down, slamming her sideways into the cliff. This time her hands searched frantically and found the opening. She grabbed the edge.

Launching herself through, Jill prayed that she'd reach the pool surface before her lungs gave out.

The Climb Back

IT TOOK FOREVER to get back to the others. Wall had searched, had shouted. There'd been no trace of Melanie. Nor, as far as he could figure, any reason for her leaving the shelter. If she had tried for the lower cave, she'd most likely been blown out to sea.

He ought to feel more remorse. Probably would, later. Now he only felt...exasperation.

The storm grew stronger. The wind's howl rose to a shrill pitch, the brush around him flattening against the earth. Without the flashlight, he never would have found the path back.

The storm itself fought him, a living thing determined to sweep him away. He'd begun grasping branches to stop them slapping his face, and now held on to anchor against forceful blasts.

At last he crawled onto the ledge. Below the sea raged, waves smashing chaotically against each other. A boiling white frenzy. The stuff of nightmares.

Dizziness engulfed him.

For an instant, watching the fury below, he lost balance and his grip. An image of tumbling into the torrent overwhelmed him.

He snapped off the flashlight, turning his face to the granite wall. And took deep breaths.

And crawled.

Light flickered ahead, marking the tunnel entrance. Relief spurred him on, knees banging against rock, eyes clenched to mere slits against the storm's fury. He intended to dive inside the tunnel.

Something stopped him. It might have been the length of ledge, longer than he remembered. As he ducked to enter, a turtle-shaped knob caught his eye. Recognition stopped him, allowing memory to catch up at last.

The lower cave. The turtle knob marked the lower cave chimney. Crawl through that and he'd never crawl again.

Slowly he inched backward until he found the entrance hidden beneath a palm frond. Wall peeled it back. The wind ripped it away.

The change in pressure on his ear drums deafened him, unnerving until he emerged into the cavern glowing with the ghost of a fire. The silence now struck him as unnatural.

Wall switched on the torch.

Jon lay face down on the stone, a thick dark cloth trailing across his forehead. No, not a cloth. Blood.

Sweeping the beam around the cave, he saw no sign of Jill.

"Jon." Dropping to his knee, Wall felt for a pulse.

"Wall?"

Jon coughed, rolling up on his elbow. "What happened?"

"I was going to ask you."

Blinking, Jon suddenly moved, feeling the area around him. "The machete. It's gone."

"So is Jill."

∞

Roiling waters pummeled her ears, spinning her dizzily. For a few precious seconds, Jill wasn't sure which way was up.

Her lungs screamed for oxygen.

Then her bare foot scraped the rock bottom. Gathering knees to chest, Jill thrust against it, shooting for the surface. Swimming, kicking. Praying.

She broke through.

Gasping air, she sputtered, coughing up seawater she hadn't known she'd swallowed. Her body shook violently. She had no idea how much was owing to cold and how much to fear. Thank God the pool surface was relatively calm. Fleetingly, she wondered how that could be with the water raging just outside.

I can see, she realized.

There was light shining from the second chamber. The one with the hole in the ceiling, where her shouts just might be heard.

Chills poured down her spine.

How can there be light?

There was nothing else to do but swim across the pool and climb out.

∞

Wall sat back on his heels. "She's in the bloody cave."

Jon slowly lifted his gaze to stare at him.

"The lower cave. The one underwater."

"How the hell would she get there? Why the hell would she go?"

Wall leapt to his feet, sprinting for the pile of supplies. Tossing cans of food aside, he unearthed the mask, a snorkel, and a length of line. He used the latter to tie the dive light to his belt loop and prayed it would hold.

"Jill's not stupid." Jon tried to sit up but winced instead.

Something was snared in the mask strap. Jill's cloth. Her lucky artifact. Impulsively he shoved it deep in a pocket before tugging the mask on, pushing it up his forehead.

"You're insane. Wall, she can't possibly be down there."

"I saw a light through the chimney. She's down there." He moved to the tunnel, dropping on his hands and knees.

Jon grabbed his ankle. "This is lunacy."

Wall almost smiled. "A good old British tradition."

"I don't want to be the only idiot left when my father gets here."

Wall sped through the tunnel.

∞

Cartagena
Wednesday, October 14, 1648

Gerard trod the boards of the dock past all the ships, past all the men hauling cargo, replacing rope, and swabbing decks. So many working bare-chested in the heat. That they were Spanish did not scare him. On this side of the world, a man willing to work was valuable no matter his country of birth.

He had left England the day after his father's death—his father, the Earl of Staffordshire. Gerard's mother was not the countess, and the countess herself had never agreed with her husband's recognition of his birth. Thus he became persona non grata.

He'd pursued his thirst for adventure and set sail to see this new world with his own eyes. Now, with the flurry of men surrounding him and the sun blazing overhead, he thought he'd made a good choice.

A better one, his new friend Tomas told him, was the island of Santo Domingo. "Cartagena is Spanish, thoroughly Spanish. But the islands—they are still developing. No one would frown on an Englishman there. You might even claim land, try your hand at a plantation. All of Europe wants sugar, and Brazil cannot keep up."

"I have no money for passage, my friend."

Tomas grinned. "But you have a strong back. Ships do not seek passengers these days, but they always need good men. That one"—he pointed to a four-masted galleon bustling with activity—"is the *Catalan*. She leaves within the week."

Gerard nodded toward a smaller ship at the end of the wharf. "She looks ready to sail now."

"The *Caridad*. Captain Sadico's craft. Avoid that one. You do not have the stomach for his methods."

"I have a strong stomach," Gerard said.

"Not so much, my friend. They call his ship el Viento del Diablo. The Wind of the Devil."

Another herd was being driven to the smaller ship. Twenty of the creatures. Gerard stared, unable to credit his eyes with what he saw.

Hairless apes, Tomas called them.

"Come." The Spaniard smiled, leading him to the herd.

One of the sailors recognized Tomas and beckoned.

Tomas strode up to the tallest ape, grabbing its arm and offering it to Gerard. "Satisfy your curiosity," he told him.

Gerard touched the peculiar skin. The creatures were very similar to men, but their skin was ebony black, as if they'd been cooked in coal. It was astonishing to behold.

"In Africa, these things run wild. They are a step above the other animals. Strong, yes, but they can also learn. These, my friend, are the secret to the sugar plantations."

Gerard rubbed his own skin for comparison. "They don't seem that different from us."

"Across the ocean," Tomas explained, "they prey on each other. Wild and dangerous, until we tame them. We give them a purpose under God."

"Can they talk?"

"They bark, like dogs, but they cannot understand us."

Gerard nodded. "Santo Domingo," he said aloud. "Sounds very exotic."

"It is."

Glancing over his shoulder, Gerard noticed the glaring eyes of the creature he'd touched. Almost a look of...hatred. "You are sure they are animals? With no intelligence—no understanding?"

Tomas nodded reassuringly. "They are like dogs, but not as friendly," he said.

So Gerard sought out the *Caridad*'s first mate.

∞

The ship was leaving on tomorrow's tide, and Gerard was granted free passage in exchange for serving as second mate. He spent his last day taking leave of those who had helped him.

Tomas had merely shaken his head.

Father Miguel, the priest who had first befriended him, smiled warmly. "I have been to several of the islands. They are God's best creation."

Overhearing them, Father Peter paused. "Do not travel on a ship of evil."

Father Miguel sent Gerard an apologetic look. "Father, this young man wishes to see an island or two. God has provided passage for him."

"Choose a vessel laden with sugar. One of the Dutch ships, perhaps."

Gerard didn't understand. "Is it Captain Sadico? I should not travel with him?"

"The trading of men is evil. It taints everything around it. And that captain is worse than most."

Father Miguel disagreed. "Gerard works for his passage, Father. He does no harm. None of this 'karma.'"

"What is karma?" Gerard asked.

"It is a silly word from the India spice traders. They see everything in terms of debt, including bad deeds. Only a trader could believe such a concept."

"It comes not from the traders, but the teachings of India," Father Peter said. "We Spanish are not the only spiritual men. Some of us lack the spirit of God altogether."

"Only a merchant could talk of a 'soul's indebtedness.'"

Later Father Miguel would assure him there was no harm done, and Tomas insisted the Africans were nowhere near human.

"Just like dogs," Tomas insisted. "We train them."

Still, Gerard could never dismiss Father Peter's words. Especially that foreign word 'karma.'

∞

If the wind on the ledge had buffeted him before, it now pounded with such force Wall doubted he could even crawl. Instead he sat, legs dangling over the edge, gasping in his first deep breath.

Lightning revealed the seething waters below. For an instant, he saw the seas rushing up dizzyingly. Wall shook his head and blew the air from his lungs. The ocean returned to its proper distance.

Setting his mask in place, he drew his second breath.

Another flash—memory from an old nightmare. Clinging desperately to a ship's mast, his fingers clawing at the ropes.

He expelled all the oxygen in a single huff.

Drawing in his third breath, the image in his mind added sound. Male laughter as he hovered above his doom.

His lungs could hold no more. Wall jumped.

For seconds he fell through the storm before his body sliced through the waves, aiming for the sand floor. The raging currents stopped him, flinging him like jetsam away from the cliff face. Away from the cave.

Out toward the open ocean.

He swam for the surface, breaking through as a monster wave lifted him high, then crashed, hurling him backward and ripping his mask off. His body smacked granite, scraping down the cliff face, flesh tearing from his back. Wall gasped another mouth of air before rocketing under to smash the bottom. Feet and hands became embedded in the sand, holding him in place as the current tried to suck him away.

Lightning momentarily lit the undersea, and he glimpsed the cave entrance meters to his left. It reminded him of a sketch in an old book of the gates of hell.

His lungs reminded him he needed air.

Clenching his jaw, he waited for the strong current to ebb. There should be a tiny pause before the waves surged again. Hopefully.

The pulling ceased. He yanked his hands free, launching himself toward the opening. His feet remained stuck.

Wall kicked, thrashing with strength born of panic. One foot tore free, and the other stayed. The sea gathered itself, preparing for the next surge.

Lungs screaming, he kicked his free foot down, yanking his other clear. Immediately he swam for the cave. The current drove him at an up angle, aiming for the solid stone above the entrance. Grimly he dove lower.

His cheek smashed rock, but his fingers gripped the tunnel edge. He pulled himself down, down, and in.

He shot straight up for the cave pool surface. Wall broke through just as his lungs overrode his brain, sucking in a spray of water along with the cold air.

His choking gasps rang out through the cavern.

As his coughing subsided, Wall felt the unnatural stillness of the cavern. Like a tomb, he thought, and instantly regretted the image.

His fingers found the rope on his belt loop, and somehow the light was still attached. Gratefully he clicked the switch, sweeping the beam across the flickering pool surface and the large dome overhead. The beam refused to penetrate the more distant shadows.

"Jill?"

A slow drip of water echoed. Reluctantly he swam to the ledge and hoisted himself out.

He realized, as he watched the ledge more carefully, that the pool water was rising. In fact, rising fast.

"Melanie? *Are you here?*"

No answer.

Wall strode to the second chamber.

On the hard stone floor, a softer lump appeared in the flashlight. Somehow he knew before his mind puzzled out the contours. "Jill!"

He sprinted, knelt. Rolling her over, he saw the gaping wound in her abdomen, harsh and uneven. Deep. With his own pulse pounding in his ears, it took precious seconds to establish she was still alive, if barely.

"There was an accident," Melanie said behind him.

He turned to find her watching him calmly, as if they were discussing dinner menus.

"She fell."

The ruby necklace he thought she'd lost glittered on her throat, and Mike's machete glittered in her hand.

Observing the direction of Wall's gaze, she tossed the latter aside.

The blade never touched the ground.

It flew backward, sucked into some sort of...disturbance. A whirlwind of debris—a sort of hurricane microburst—hummed as it swelled and then shrank, as if breathing.

Noting his interest, Melanie smiled, and he had the bizarre impression the dust devil stood at her command. Or she at its.

Yanking his shirt off, Wall turned his back on both. "Why are you doing this?"

"He commanded it." She sighed. "He's furious at all of you. Especially you."

His shirt was soaked. Not the best of bandages.

"Here."

Cloth appeared over his shoulder, perfectly dry. Her shirt. Wall suppressed an impulse to ask how she'd gotten here, but he honestly didn't care anymore.

"Mike led that rebellion, and Jon betrayed him. And you—eternally useless. You failed to help Mike. You failed to help him. Always the best intentions. Always falling short."

Seawater trickled through the chamber opening.

"And then you all abandoned him here."

He ripped the shirt, making a thick pad bandage and a strip long enough to tie around Jill's body. "And what did Jill do?"

"She's nothing. Just a lever."

Ahead of him a flash of light lit the area, bright, flickering, then vanished. Lightning from the top hole.

Jon's hatchway. The dangerous rock climb beneath the ledge opening. The last ten feet sloped backward, requiring an arm strength Wall lacked, requiring bouldering techniques he didn't know. Jon swore he'd never attempt it again, but then Jon didn't have this motivation. Already, Jill lay in six inches of water.

"I wonder what happened to my bra." Amusement laced the blonde's purr. If she'd expected him to turn around to see, she'd be disappointed.

Impulsively he fished in his pocket, finding Jill's treasured cloth and placing it against her wound. He then tied the wadded shirt over it, sacrificing gentleness for security.

"It'll bleed through," Melanie said.

Ignoring her, Wall studied the climb out of the cave. There was no question of trying to swim. Even if he somehow got Jill through without drowning, they'd never make it to the beach.

The water rose to Jill's ears. He pulled her up before it could reach her nose. Thinking rapidly, he grabbed the line he'd used for the flashlight and looped it round her leg and his shoulder. Without more rope, it was the best idea he had: an improvised sling.

"You'll never make it, you know." Melanie slid around him, half-naked, fingers spreading out against his chest. "Better leave her here. You might make it without extra weight. She's dead either way."

Wall stepped through the loop, pulling the unconscious girl against his back. He moved his shoulders, testing its security, and then strode through the rising water for the hatchway.

Melanie followed at his side, a fingernail digging a circle on his shoulder. "Don't risk one to save another. Remember?"

Water at his knees, he studied the climb. Marking his first handholds, he balanced the flashlight atop a rough stalagmite.

"You'll fall again," the blonde cooed.

"If you try to climb out of here, it'd be best to wait till I've gone, one way or the other," Wall tossed over his shoulder. "Or stay here and drown. I don't give a damn."

Feeling his first handhold, he climbed.

∞

Jill must be drifting in a small boat.

Rocking motion, staccato movements, and her head smacking against the side. Smacking against something. She pried her eyelids open.

Dreams, she thought hazily, *should disappear when you open your eyes*.

This one did not, for she saw below—far below—Melanie watching her, laughing. The blonde stood naked in water up to her waist.

And behind her was a...dust devil. Whirling debris.

The Whirl advanced.

Still grinning, Melanie was pulled backward toward it. Blonde hair lifted, sucked in before her head rolled back. Her body followed.

The Vortex swelled to double its size. Jill clearly saw a dive light flying around within. And a T-shirt.

And human feet.

"Oh dear God."

"Jill?" it was Wall's voice.

She was somehow on his back, and he was climbing.

"Don't move," he grunted.

Having engulfed Melanie, the Vortex glided closer.

Within the debris, twin lights flickered. Eyes—not Melanie's green, but blue. Pale, icy blue.

"Hurry," Jill croaked. "Wall, hurry."

A rumble shook the cavern and the rock face they climbed. Jill shut her own eyes, but it didn't matter. She saw the Monster either way.

∞

500 Miles Southeast of Santo Domingo
Monday, October 19, 1648

A bowl set beside him slid away even as the sailor let it go. The ship's roll was wilder than any time during the first crossing. Whimpers of fear filled the vessel's belly, and Quash was glad Juba was safe on land.

As the sailor set bowls in the next row, the one-handed African fell against the man's leg. The sailor kicked him, chains clanking over the sounds of the sea, yelling something in his foul language. He moved on without giving that one food.

The one-handed African watched him walk away, catching Quash's sliding bowl with a subtle gesture. Raising it to his lips, he stopped when he saw Quash watching him.

He offered Quash his bowl back. "You should eat."

Quash made no response. Waiting a second more, the man downed the contents in a single motion.

Other sailors gathered the empties, disappearing up the ladder and taking the light with them.

"Do not give in so easily," the one-handed African said. "They've chained your body, not your spirit."

Quash closed his eyes, leaning against the rough wood side of the ship. "They have taken my heart," he heard himself whisper.

He felt the chains moving, the iron anklet on his foot suddenly lighter of weight. Startled, his fingers explored the circlet and found himself free.

"I took the key while he was busy kicking me," the one-handed man said.

"I cannot swim," Quash worried.

"Let us see if the white devils can."

∞

It took time to free them all. But once the chains fell away their energy returned. Men who had sleepwalked through the last few months suddenly sprang to their feet. Backs straightened, chins lifted with purpose.

With determination.

The evil vessel heaved side to side, rolling as the waves slapped the wood. Unused to walking on heaving decks in the dark, the Africans made their way slowly up the ladder to the hated door.

It was not locked.

The one-handed man beckoned them through as the wind and rippling canvas muffled their sounds. The Africans rushed out, shoving Quash aside. Anxious to flee the black hell they'd occupied for days.

When the last man passed—the last that would leave, for many still cowered below—Quash approached the open doorway. The moon peeped through the clouds, reflecting off the rolling sea, the wood deck. There was no place to go, he saw. They merely exchanged one hell for another.

The moonlight flickered and died as clouds boiled through the sky.

"Now," the one-handed warrior shouted. The Africans raced to attack the surprised sailors.

The ship heaved, throwing Quash back inside. When he emerged again, the sailors were gone. Tossed over the side, he realized.

But more whites swarmed, these armed with cudgels, with blades. With bodies strong from doing men's work instead of wasted away by starvation.

The vessel rolled, as if the sea herself joined the battle. And the one-handed African fought like the strongest tribal chief, screaming his defiance, felling three more whites before a blade sliced open his shoulder.

For an instant he saw Quash, still on the threshold.

"Fight!" he shouted. Their eyes locked.

Quash hesitated no more than an instant—but the battle turned just as fast. The warrior fell to his knees as an arcing blade sliced through the night, through his neck.

His head bounced across the deck, landing by Quash's foot. The eyes gazed upward, accusing.

∞

Lowering his blade, Gerard stared at the slave he'd just killed. The creature had no hand and no way to defend himself, yet he'd fought like a devil.

Dogs do not fight for freedom from the leash. These were men, no matter what the Spaniards claimed. Desperate men, aware of their fate. Willing to die rather than accept it.

"Fetch me that head," Captain Sadico growled.

Gerard tossed his blade at the captain's feet and walked away.

There'd be consequences, he knew. But he'd suffer them rather than take further part in this evil.

∞

Watching the Englishman stride away, Sadico roared in anger. Slave bodies now littered the ship around him, each one representing lost coin. He strode to the head himself and spied one alive and uninjured.

For some reason, its name came to mind. Quash. The one with the pregnant female. Or without now, as Isabelle had claimed her.

"Sir." Duerte, his first mate, pointed to the darkening night above. "The mainsail rope has torn apart. We need a new rope and quickly, or we'll find ourselves beam on."

"Then do it, fool."

"Leon, go!"

"I cannot! Not in this sea," an old seaman piped up.

They all ceased their motions, watching the captain fearfully.

Sadico whirled and glared, and then he slowly turned back, pointing. "Send him."

∞

His unnatural blue eyes burned through Quash's skull. "Send him," said the evil captain.

The smaller white shook his head. "There's no time for this. Someone skilled, who knows what to do, and has strength to climb."

The great ship itself was spinning, Quash realized. Lightning split the heavens, revealing the whirling tall tree with canvas sheets attached. Always, always these sailors had controlled the ships, making them do their bidding just as they made the Africans do.

Not now, he saw. Now the ship rebelled, just as they had rebelled. The sea and the sky sought to punish the whites as they liked to punish the Africans.

"Climb," shouted the one called Leon, shoving a rope in Quash's hands.

When Quash didn't move, Leon dug a blade point in his gut.

Backing away, Quash found himself against the largest tree growing from the low deck.

"Climb!"

Spinning, Quash did.

There were man-made handholds, he discovered, slick and cold. He sprinted upward, out of the blade's reach.

"Throw it over the arm!" the man below shouted, pointing.

Quash scurried higher, finding it easier not to look down. Not to look anywhere but straight in front of his nose. Maybe if he did this, they would not hurt him. Even let him go back to Juba.

"There! Go there!" Hearing the urgency—the panic—he glanced down.

Already dizzy from the heaving ship, Quash now saw raging sea water churning furiously, as the tree he clung to rolled toward it. For an instant, he hovered so near the great ocean he could touch it.

Then he catapulted skyward, high above the boiling seas, only to roll back the other way. Foaming crests and deepening troughs filled his vision. The whole world was caving in around him. Punishment for failing Juba and his unborn son. For not following the one-handed warrior when he'd had a chance to fight.

A tiny chance, he now realized, was so much better than accepting defeat.

His fingers slipped from the nail-hold as the sea rose up to greet him.

He crashed into the water and was swallowed by the dark.

Wall's hand slipped, and for an instant, he dangled over the swelling waters below.

In that instant, he clung to wood, not rock. Lightning flashed above him, revealing waves in the cavern beneath. A whole raging sea reaching wildly up to him.

He was clinging to the mast of a ship, and that mast dove toward the ocean. His hand slipped from the iron nail.

"No!"

Falling—he was falling, he realized.

∞

Flesh tore from his fingers as he clawed at the rocks, but he barely registered the pain. No matter what happened, he had to get Jill out. Saving her would mean something. A single gain yanked defiantly from disaster.

As that thought rose in his mind, he knew it for truth. Better to fight a losing battle, try to rescue some good from it, than bow to defeat. Win or lose, at least he'd made a choice.

It wasn't a rock but a gap that saved them both. His hand dove in, fingers spreading instinctively to hold him there. Only for a second, but in that second, he found purchase for his toes. Flattening against the wall, they were momentarily safe.

"Wall," Jill's broken sob was in his ear.

If nothing else, she lived.

She lived.

Silencing his protesting muscles, he climbed. He countered the slickness by testing each grip, moving only one hand or foot at a time. Slow going when icy water pummeled the face.

His hand stabbed through the ledge opening. Pelted with rain, his fingers found an outside grip. Wall stepped up, looking out at the storm.

He'd never witnessed a hurricane until now.

The opening was too narrow to pass with Jill on his back. There was so little time, with the spurt of adrenal strength fast waning.

Shrugging the cloth-sling off his shoulder, Wall caught the loop in one hand. Then, before he could think, he thrust his head outside. The howling gale nearly pushed him back.

A shout erupted from his gut as he fought through the opening, falling forward across the outside ledge, hugging it with the length of his torso as he rotated on his belly. Face down on the icy rock, storm slamming his back, he swung his legs out.

Pulling Jill through took his last ounce of energy.

First her head, dark hair drenched and clinging to her face. Then her shivering body. Somehow she seemed lighter, and he realized she was helping him.

Dear God, she was helping him.

Her face rolled toward him as she lay on stone, blinking to clear her vision. "Wall?"

He'd been certain he'd only imagined her voice. That wound...

"Run. Wall, run now."

Shoving rainwater out of his face, he saw her staring beyond him. He glanced over his shoulder.

The Vortex from his nightmare was solid and very real. It rose up the chimney toward them.

Scrambling to her feet, Jill dove into the upper cave.

Wall was right behind.

∞

Jon had managed to rekindle the fire somewhat, enough to stare into its depths while clutching the bottle of tequila. Now, surely he was the lone survivor. Beyond that, he didn't want to think.

So Jill shooting through the tunnel caught him off guard. She scrambled in the ashes, trying to right herself.

"Jill—"

Wall dove in behind her, landing awkwardly, sprawling next to Jill.

"What the hell—" Jon couldn't finish his question, which was just as well, as neither paid him the slightest attention.

Wall actually pushed Jill over, lifting her shirt off her stomach. No, not her shirt. A bandage.

Still unable to form a coherent sentence, Jon leaned closer.

The makeshift bandage on her abdomen scared the hell out of him until the Brit pried it up, ripping off the cloth none-too-gently.

"Nothing," Wall said, feeling the area. "Barely a scratch."

Jill seemed more interested in the bandage. When she clutched it protectively, Jon realized it was that stupid rag she'd found.

"I was injured," she whispered. "She stabbed me...deep. So much blood. I blacked out."

Wall shook his head. "That blood couldn't have come from you. Was Melanie hurt?"

Jill stared at her cloth. "This! You put this on my wound, Wall! It healed me!"

Tired of waiting for answers, Jon leaned close to Jill's injury. A tiny scratch marred the skin, tinged in red. "Just a graze," he told them, glad to get a full sentence out. He must have drunk more than he realized.

"It was a gaping hole. Lots of blood," the Brit insisted, touching her stomach again.

Jon yanked her shirt back in place. "Hey! Watch where you put your hands."

The wind howled, drowning any further words. To Jon's amazement, both Wall and Jill both scrambled back, away from the tunnel opening. They dove behind the natural half-wall of the cave.

"Jon!" the Brit shouted. And then the world exploded.

The tunnel—the entire wall around it—vanished. In its place, a whirling Vortex hovered, a dark tornado of...rage. Inside the black smoke spun glimpses of cloth, of machete. A hand with pink fingernails.

Jon backed away, dropping his bottle. It flew straight into the Vortex. "What—the hell—is that?"

∞

From deep within, two lights flickered, eyes blazing from the Thing. Ice cold blue eyes.

They focused on Wall. "Quash," it rumbled.

Wall's blood chilled.

Memory hit him—an image so strong Wall couldn't fathom it. Alone in a raging sea, fighting to stay afloat. Dark sky, high waves, horrible storm. And a giant ship beside him, teetering. Sinking.

A man stood at the rails, glaring. He couldn't see them, but Wall knew his eyes were ice cold blue. That man never stopped glaring hatred, even as the ocean swallowed them both.

Wall shook himself back to the present.

The Vortex swelled, howling with laughter.

"Jesus!" Jon's feet slid toward it. He threw himself backward, diving behind the half-wall ridge.

Wall braced himself with his heels, looking to join Jon. Then Jill's body slid toward it. He grabbed her, holding her tight.

She was staring at the thing with a peculiar frown. Had she also heard it speak?

"Give her to me," the Vortex purred.

His arms tightened around her.

"Give her to me and I'll let you live," it rumbled, sounding more like thunder than human. "You know I'll take her anyway."

Jill turned to him, her eyes swimming in tears. Those soft brown eyes. She could hear it. She knew what it wanted.

Her lips parted, and he placed a finger there to silence her. "I won't let you go."

"Then die and remain here with me forever," the Vortex roared, in fury and laughter and something more. Hate. Its hate filled what was left of the cavern.

Hate is the essence of evil, Wall recalled from some-where.

The Vortex swelled. Pebbles and dirt and embers of the dying fire flew into it, firefly specks prickling the black whirl.

Wall's feet slid toward it, and Jill buried her head in his shoulder.

"You're crazy to try to save me," she cried.

He wanted to set her straight—make her understand. His need was to defy this monster, to stand up to it. He must, more than anything, fight back.

But when he glanced at her—at those soft brown eyes and at the light reflected there in the midst of this hell—it hit him that he did need to save her. Not as a symbol of defiance, but for the girl herself.

Jon had said the only thing real in life was people. Not places, not things. People. For the first time, Wall felt the truth in that.

This was what life was about. This was worth fighting for.

Jill still stared at him. Jill, who'd gallantly fought her own dragons, with no doubts nor hesitation.

He kissed the tip of her nose.

The Vortex swelled furiously as she reached up, stroked his face. The bit of cloth flew from her hand.

Straight into the Vortex.

And the pitch changed. The cloth settled in the center, floating calmly among frantically whirling obstacles. Hovering for precious seconds before slowly turning in the opposite direction.

The Monster howled.

Gray cloth spun faster, countering the Whirlwind and reversing its direction. Unraveling its coil. A dive light flew out, smacking the cave just above their heads. Wind whistled shrilly as pebbles pummeled them.

The whistle reached a pitch beyond human ears. Wall winced away, chin in Jill's hair. And then silence.

He turned back.

Where the Vortex had raged, a man now stood with a dark beard and watery blue eyes. Gazing at Wall, the man smiled and saluted. And vanished.

"Did you see...?" Wall croaked.

But Jill's head was buried in his shoulder, so of course she hadn't seen.

Jon crawled past to something glittering in the now bright moonlight. The storm itself had vanished with the Vortex.

Lifting the glittering thing—the half-empty bottle of tequila—Jon drank.

Aftermath

THE RESCUE BOAT arrived before they'd eaten a dozen cans of Spam.

Ray Sadicor, it turned out, was more aware of Jon's activities then Jon knew. Being distracted, neither he nor Mike had checked in with the Antigua dive shop in the days before the fire. Such lapses were not uncommon, but what Jon never realized was his father not only checked in with the shop, he pushed the shop to check in with the boat.

Jon had always assumed the Antiguans were just overly curious about his whereabouts.

Ray had flown down the second day, later riding to the rescue on a sixty-foot Predator, a yacht complete with three cabins and two heads. For once, instead of disparaging his father's extravagance, Jon savored the luxury of hot water.

Now, sitting alone in the stern, clutching a coffee for the sheer warmth, Jon stared at the sea.

His father had quietly asked Wall about bodies, and the Brit had shook his head.

Neither man knew what Jon had seen, walking the island at dawn because he couldn't sit still. Neither man had tramped past the hibiscus bush, blooming with the white flowers, to see the still whiter hand on the beach. Such a cold, unnatural white.

Melanie, tangled in storm debris. That stupid necklace beside her, the gemstone shattered. Her treasured ruby must have been fake after all.

Jon could have told them where to find her body, but he had not.

If Mikey don't go home...

"Jon." Wall appeared, carrying his own mug and smiling a little too broadly for Jon's taste. The Brit stretched out on the nearby lounge. "Ray said there's no sign of the wreck, because of the storm?"

Jon grimaced at hearing Wall say his father's name. "He didn't say no sign of the wreck. He said there was no wreck. As if we all suffered a mass mirage."

"I don't think he meant it that way."

"You don't know my father." Jon lifted his cup to his mouth but didn't drink. He didn't want coffee, he realized. He wanted tea. Proper good tea, like Earl Grey. "That grandfather of a storm destroyed the bottom. Wreck's buried in a ton of sand. Or pummeled into oblivion. Either way, it's gone."

"Apparently they were unaware of a storm."

"My father," Jon stated firmly, "is frequently unaware of anything."

Hearing his own words and the tone in his voice startled him. Here he was still at it—his personal rebellion against his dad. Maybe, just maybe, it was time to give the old man a break.

"Your dad offered to look, you know. Pay for equipment, expert—"

Jon tossed the contents of his mug overboard. "I know. And...and I appreciate it. I just doubt we'd find anything. Even if we did, I don't have the stomach for it."

Jill burst from the cabin, arms wrapped around an old book with fancy binding. "Saint Peter Claver!" Heaving the volume over, Jon saw the title: *A Collection of Catholic Saints.*

"He ministered to the slaves until 1654. The Spanish Slave Trade!"

"Until 1654? Isn't that early for slaves?" Wall frowned.

Her eyes sparkled. "Apparently not! Saint Peter was in Cartagena, the hub of the trade. The Spanish used them to work sugarcane. He—the saint—would throw his cloak over them"—she hastily found the passage—"over the worst of the lot, despite open sores, vermin, disease."

Jon plucked the book from her hands. "Pillow for the sick, pall for the dead, shield for the leprous."

She was so excited she almost tripped over Wall's long legs. "His cloak was old and ragged. Pieces of it were holy relics. They say the cloth's very touch could cure! And you"—she turned to the Brit—"put it over my stomach."

"You weren't injured." Jon shut the book.

"It cured that—that thing. It...unraveled the evil within it."

Shoving the tome at her, Jon jumped to his feet. "That was a storm phenomenon. The Caribbean version of a desert dust devil."

"A dust devil with eyes? C'mon. You're the one with the karmic vortexes."

"Theories, Jill. Theories of subtle energies. They don't spin flashlights."

∞

Jill retreated a step from her cousin's derision, this time tripping over Wall's legs and landing in his lap.

She shifted to stand up, but the man held her still.

"Storm-caused microburst," Jon told her. "And the rapid dissolving proves it." With that parting shot, he disappeared into the cabin.

"Dust devil my ass," Jill called after him, springing up to follow.

Wall snagged her wrist. "Let him go, Jill."

She wavered, wanting to hash it out now—needing to hash it out once and for all—but perhaps Wall was right.

"What, exactly, did you see?" he asked.

Her mind, she realized, had been shying away from that question because she'd seen flickers of her own nightmares—old scary images merging with new ones.

Dear God, what had I seen?

"I saw Melanie...possessed by something left over from that galleon." She heard the tremor in her voice. She sat down again, somehow ending up too close to Wall.

But he didn't seem to mind.

Grabbing the book, she opened it haphazardly, finger stabbing a passage.

"Truth is not absolute; it differs by point of view."

Now that made no sense. "Jon's random opening of books doesn't always work." She sighed.

Wall's arm went around her comfortingly.

Too comforting. They were very different people with very different backgrounds. He'd even come here with a tall blonde.

A tall dead blonde.

Jill shifted to stand up, to get away from him before it was too late. His arm merely tightened.

"Wall, you don't have to do this."

"Do what?"

"It was just...events. We were thrown together. Heat of the moment. I understand."

He grasped her chin, turning her so he could study her eyes. "Just sex?"

Her nod of agreement died because a different answer shone in his eyes.

He kissed her, probably to shut her up. Her lips parted to tell him so, which he took as an invitation. And everything shifted.

They clung to each other, two souls having weathered a storm, having found safe harbor. Jill's mind still roiled with doubt, with fears of her world changing.

But her body simply surrendered.

∞

She was too young, too foolish. Too bloody American. Yet somehow, kissing her, he felt better.

Much better.

Love, so he'd heard, wasn't anything like the stories promised. It was far messier, complicated, inexplicable. It defied logic. It thrived in family bonds, friendship ties. It lived in shared moments, however brief, with fellow human beings. And was reborn in the recognition for a woman, a fellow traveler, who somehow filled the gaps in your soul.

Best not to overthink it.

Thank You

To Janet Tapper, an editor and a friend.

To Matt Davies, for a beautiful cover.

To Tracy Peterson, for her sharp proof editing.

To Sarah Levison, for her diving expertise.

To Reilly Levison, for his stories.

To Ian & Steve & Ian, for a glimpse of all things British.

To my Ian, for making me love of all things British.

And to you – for reading this book. May all your endings be happy.

About the Author

A well-known Century City producer once said Jo Sparkes "writes some of the best dialogue I've read."

Jo graduated from Washington College, a small liberal arts college famous for its creative writing program, and went on to study with Robert Powell: a student of renowned teachers Lew Hunter and Richard Walter, head of UCLA's Screenwriting Program.

She's won a Kay Snow for her comedy script, 'Frank Retrieval,' a Silver IPPY for 'The Birr Elixir,' and BRAG Medallions for multiple books. A member of the Pro Football Writers Association, she was (unofficially) the first to interview Emmitt Smith when he came to the Arizona Cardinals.

Jo served as an adjunct teacher at the Film School at Scottsdale Community College and even made a video of her most beloved lecture.

Her book for writers and artists, *Feedback How to Give It How to Get It* has garnered strong praise.

When not diligently perfecting her craft, Jo can be found exploring her new home of Portland, Oregon with her husband Ian and their dog Oscar.